REACTIONARY BEWITCHMENT

DETECTIVE DUARTE MYSTERIES

JAMIE SANDS

ROOKERY

ROOKERY PUBLISHING

First edition 2023

978-1-99-117867-1(Paperback, New Zealand)

978-1-99-117868-8 (EPUB)

978-1-99-117869-5 (Kindle)

978-1-7386183-0-9 (Amazon Print-on-Demand Paperback)

978-1-7386183-1-6 (Print-on-Demand via Draft2Digital)

978-1-7386183-2-3 (PDF)

To everyone who has been told that they/them pronouns are too confusing to remember.

ACKNOWLEDGEMENTS

Sometimes it takes a village to raise a book. Long Covid and a distractable author certainly don't help. Thanks to Rookery publishing for all the direction, feedback and encouragement. Thanks to Gillian St Kevern for cheerleading, productivity sprints and editorial feedback. Thanks also to everyone who loved the first book and who have asked for the next installment, you've given me motivation I couldn't have manufactured. Thanks also to everyone in my ersatz writing club, and to my delightful spouse for always being on my side.

No thanks at all to Pokki and Care Bear who upturned my life and demanded pats, cat food and playtime while I was trying to edit.

PROLOGUE

Days like this Constable Teuila Gilchrist really disliked her job. She didn't have to deal with murder-suicides too often, thankfully, but it was always very wearying when she did. Auckland had more crime than was reported on the national news, but a scene like the one in front of her still wasn't common.

They'd been called to the little two-bedroom central city apartment at three a.m. on Tuesday after the neighbours had heard shouting and thumps.

Teuila and her partner Enid had been closest when the call came in. Met at the apartment entrance by the neighbour, a young student with purple hair and several piercings, whose name was Bri, they made their way up to the sixth floor.

"I actually have a spare key," Bri said. "But after those noises, I didn't want to go in alone."

"That's the right call," Enid said. "Let us in and we'll see what's happening."

Bri unlocked the apartment. When Teuila pushed the door open, the smell of blood and death was unmistakable.

"Stay in the hall, Bri," Enid said.

"Fuck..." Bri said, their voice faint.

There was a noise within the apartment, a muttering. Teuila went on full alert, pulling her taser from her belt. She signalled to Enid to stay silent.

"Get that fucking monster!" a man's voice said.

"It's quicker than it looks." Another man, younger than the first.

Teuila's heart was racing now. She stepped closer to the source of the noise. If whoever was in there was armed, it was important to be quiet and move slowly so as not to startle them.

"It's not quicker than you, just corner it!"

Enid stepped on a floorboard that creaked horribly. Teuila's eyes went wide and she pushed through the door to the room where the two men were. They were both dressed for stealth in black matte skintight gear with Kevlar vests and hoods covering their eyes. They were clearly muscular. Teuila's brain said "ninjas" or "Mission Impossible."

"Leave it," the older of the two men said. He turned, impossibly fast, towards the window.

"Freeze, hands in the air!" Teuila shouted.

The men slipped out the window and onto the fire escape too quickly to see. Teuila would later attribute this to her own adrenaline, they couldn't have possibly moved that fast. Enid was at the window in a second, looking down and then up, then radioing to alert any units close by to the fleeing men.

In the corner of the room, a small black rabbit with wide, terrified eyes watched the police officers.

Teuila located a hutch and opened the door for it, crouching down to coax the rabbit in. After a long half a minute, the rabbit relaxed, and hopped obediently into its enclosure.

Enid set down the radio and breathed out heavily. "Let's check out the rest of the place."

Teuila nodded, got to her feet and braced herself.

The bodies were in the bathroom, a young man slumped in the shower, blood pooling in the tray. He had cuts over his chest, through his shirt, and his throat was slit. It seemed like he'd been slashed several times before the killing blow.

Another man, older, grey about the temples, was crumpled between the toilet and the shower stall, as if he'd killed himself seated on the toilet and fallen sideways. His blood was everywhere. Teuila's heart went out to the clean-up service who'd have to make the bathroom spotless again.

Enid immediately called the station with a report and put up police tape. She then ducked out to talk to the neighbours and record what she could of their initial reports. Teuila remained on scene, made some notes. Both men were dressed, track pants and T-shirts. Perhaps that's what they slept in?

The man in the shower's eyes were wide, bulging and his mouth hung open in a perpetual scream for his life. The older man looked more serene, the long blade he'd used to cut his wrists still partially in his fingers. He had tattoos over his arms and hands, but they were hard to make out with the blood covering them.

Sighing, Teuila checked her gloves were on securely and then went into the main apartment. Although it appeared to be a pretty clear-cut situation, you never knew what you could find if you looked.

The apartment was one in a block of three nearly identical buildings. Thrown up fast to deal with the housing crisis. No doubt corners had been cut but the apartment itself was nice enough, if on the small side. The view was largely of the next building over, although Teuila could see the sky beginning to lighten with the first of the summer dawn.

The kitchen was tidy, a row of potted herbs lining the benchtop. The first bedroom was cosy, with a soft looking bed and a bookcase stuffed with books the first two things to catch Teuila's eye. The sheets and handmade looking quilt had been tossed off the bed, as if the owner had got up very fast. There was some art on the walls, abstract drawings which evoked symbols of some kind.

She moved into the next bedroom. This one was a lot fuller, packed with belongings. A number of guitars were in racks up the wall. The bed was relatively small, although this was clearly the bigger bedroom. Next to the guitars, a bookshelf stuffed with sheet music and music theory books.

A rustling noise put Teuila instantly on edge. When she looked for the source, she found a lop eared brown rabbit in a large hutch. She was surprised that she hadn't smelled the rabbit or the straw it was bedding down in. Perhaps she was catching a cold? Or the blood was just an overwhelming smell.

The rabbit seemed perfectly happy, so she went back to looking around the room. Looking closer at the books her hackles went up - some strange titles there. *New Book of Magick, The Green Witch's Guide to the City, Simple Charms and Rituals...* Was this guy a pagan of some kind?

While not immediately cause for suspicion, it could put a weird spin on the crime scene, and the reason for the crime. She went back into the first bedroom and examined the books there - more of the same, and more alarming. *Speaking with Spirits, Secrets of the Dead, Advanced Necromancy in the Modern Age.*

Teuila battled a rising feeling of unease. She headed back to the bathroom to check the bodies.

Enid intercepted her. "Did you notice the symbols carved into the door?" she asked, her voice thin and strained.

"No, I didn't." She made the sign of the cross over her body, more out of muscle memory than intention. "They have some weird books on the shelves, I think maybe they were pagan or something. The bodies look like a murder suicide but maybe it had some occult purpose?"

Enid exhaled hard through her nose. "We ought to call in that Detective, you know? The spooky one."

Teuila nodded. "Jack Duarte and her partner. I'll call the station and get them to put her name on it. Maybe it's nothing, but if it's not at least she'll know."

CHAPTER 1

"You really ought to name this cat," Emmaline said.

Jack looked over at her with surprise and shook her head. "No, he's not my cat, I can't name him." She spooned out a couple of sardines into a bowl, mashed them with the back of the spoon and set them in front of said cat.

It was early morning, just past seven. Jack had already showered and dressed for work. She'd put on some toast and opened the window to let in the cranky orange tom who had adopted her and her sardines.

Emmaline, who had been staying about a month now in Jack's spare room, laughed, a musical, tinkling sound. "You feed him every day, you let him sleep on the couch, and he clearly has adopted you."

Jack scrunched up her nose and scratched the cat between his ears. He made a rumbling noise which may or may not have been a purr. "I don't know what you're talking about. He just comes round sometimes, isn't that right?" She addressed the last part to the cat.

"Ridiculous," Emmaline said. But her voice had a warm fondness in it which sent warm flutters through Jack's chest, although she ignored those as best she could. "I'll name him then. How about Bartholomew?"

Jack glanced at Emmaline and then back at the cat, tilting her head. "That's a bit of a grand name for him, don't you think?"

"But it has 'mew' in it, it's cute."

Jack's phone buzzed and she grabbed it, relieved to be rescued from the intimacy of naming a cat with her flatmate, who was also a potential girlfriend. "Duarte."

"Jack, this is Constable Suzan Lee at the station. There's a new case for you, rung in overnight, apparent murder suicide, but the reporting officers think there might be some kind of occult link. Apanui's looked over the pictures and agrees you should head down."

"Right, thanks." Jack looked around for a notebook and pen, finding one on the bench by the fridge. "What's the address?"

Suzan rattled off a central city address and Jack copied it down.

"Tell them we're on our way, I'll pick up Piper and go straight there."

"Will do, good luck." Suzan cut the call.

"Something came up, huh?" Emmaline said.

Jack frowned and fired off a quick message to Piper, telling them to get ready. "Mm-hm, possible occult killing, Suzan said." Jack pursed her lips. "I'd like you to come and see if there's anything actually magical going on or if it's just heavy metal fans or something. Are you free to come now?"

Saying the words 'actually magical' left a strange taste on Jack's tongue. Only a handful of weeks ago she'd learned that yes, magic was real, and there were alternative worlds that housed things like fairies. That Emmaline wasn't really a psychic so much as a real, practicing necromantic mage. Jack's mind had adjusted to the new information, but talking about it in such a conversational manner was still surreal.

Emmaline was already on her feet, cup of tea forgotten on the table. "Yeah, just let me change into going out pants." She hurried into her room, already pulling off her pyjama pants as she closed the door.

Jack got ready to go, checking her phone to see a thumbs up response from Piper.

Emmaline reappeared in tight grey jeans, her hands working to quickly plait her long blonde hair into a braid. She was lovely as ever, but Jack tried not to linger on that thought.

Jack's phone buzzed again. Piper had sent a selfie, their face bright with a wide smile and a reusable coffee cup in hand.

Piper: Ready to go, Detective bossy pants!

She thought back to her life two months or even six weeks ago. There'd been no junior partner, no mage living in her house with her, no complications. Well, aside from her ex-girlfriend and absolutely everything about being the police detective assigned the 'odd' unsolvable cases.

Jack wasn't sure if her life now was better than it had been, but it was certainly more interesting.

CHAPTER 2

T he drive into the central city was slow, the morning traffic reduced to a crawl as the commuters of the outer suburbs made their way into the CBD.

"Couldn't you put on the siren?" Piper asked from the back seat. Growing up in Christchurch Piper had, of course, got caught in traffic, but it was nowhere near as bad as Auckland had it.

"It's not an emergency," Jack said from the driver's seat. "The victims are already dead."

Piper sighed and considered kicking the back of Jack's seat, but such an action would be childish. "Right," they said instead.

Emmaline glanced back and gave Piper a warm smile. "Feeling antsy?"

"A bit." Piper swallowed the last of their coffee and tipped their head back against the car seat.

"I think that's the building," Jack said. "Just need to find a park..."

A few minutes later, Piper flashed their badge to the constable minding the crime scene. They put on masks and gloves and went in with strict instructions not to move or touch anything unless absolutely necessary. Emmaline trailed in after them. She had an official police ID as well, now, since Apanui had agreed to keep her on as a contracted assistant to Jack and Piper. She hesitated at the door, looking around, but Piper found they couldn't ask what the hold-up was.

"Victims' names are Matthew O'Brian and Robert Clark," the Constable said. "Been living here a couple of years, not sure if they're flatmates or dating. Matthew's the younger one."

Jack had briefed Piper that it was a murder suicide scene, but the smell still hit Piper hard. Their stomach turned over in a particularly threatening way. They had to swallow the urge to vomit three times.

"Here, this helps." Jack gave them a breath mint.

Piper slipped it under their mask and relaxed as the mint flooded their senses, masking the smell enough to keep their breakfast down.

Emmaline didn't seem bothered by the smell.

They examined the scene. The bathroom was the worst, blood all over the floor, and two bodies slumped. Piper swallowed again, breathing through their mouth so they could avoid the worst of the iron smell.

"This isn't right," Emmaline murmured, joining them at the bathroom door. "The front door is covered in sigils for protection, but they've been corrupted somehow, twisted to allow people with bad intention in..." She exhaled heavily and approached the bodies.

"So, these guys, the victims, are magic users? Er, mages?" Piper asked. When they'd visited mages before their doors had sigils, some visible and some not.

"Looks like it, which means these two might have been killed by..." Emmaline crouched beside the guy who was beside the toilet, careful not to step in any of the dried blood. "These slashes...it's hunters, I'm sure of it."

"The mage hunters? The ones who went after you?" Jack asked.

"Most likely," Emmaline said. "There are hardly enough magicians in New Zealand to encourage a whole troop of hunters, but... I guess it doesn't matter how many, if there are any they'll keep on coming."

Piper swallowed. "How do we report this? We can't just tell Apanui that there's magic and these guys hate it can we?"

Jack tilted her head to one side, moving closer to Emmaline to examine the cuts on the man's chest. "No, but we can maybe frame it like an anti-Wiccan hate crime. Radicalised conservatives and bigots can get pretty violent about things they don't like."

"Their spirits are close still," Emmaline said. Piper shivered, still not quite used to Emmaline's particular brand of magic. "I can talk to them."

"Does it have to be right here?" Jack asked. She looked at the man in the shower. "We don't want to have to explain spirits to forensics and the uniformed officers."

Piper, feeling a bit useless and awkward by the door, pulled out their notebook and wrote down some bullet points noting what had been said.

"No, I'll just need a couple of things of theirs." Emmaline's voice had gone thin and reedy, strained perhaps.

"I can find something in the bedrooms," Piper said, glad for a reason to leave the bathroom. They knew this sort of thing would happen on the job as a detective, they did. And they'd been prepared, in all the ways you could prepare before actually seeing the aftermath of a killing, but nothing was quite like seeing it in real life.

Piper was never part of any murder investigations in Christchurch. Their assignments had been almost entirely the dull stuff no one else wanted to do. Being here in the room with the murder victims was both exhilarating and terrifying. Exhilarating because they were finally here, working the big cases. They'd been let into the big kid's club, or behind the velvet rope and into the VIP section.

But they hated it.

Being happy about something like that was terrifying. Besides that they didn't want to have to deal with the dead bodies.

They took a deep, steadying breath. This was their job. They wanted to prove themself, so they would.

With a grind of the teeth and a powerful force of will, they set aside their discomfort and retrieved items from each bedroom as quickly as they could, slipping each into forensic bags with careful fingers.

Knowing the two were mages, the symbols on the walls and the titles on the books had obvious magical meaning. Not that Piper knew what those magical meanings were, but hanging out with Emmaline and sometimes her brother, Piper had picked some things up about what magic looked like.

As they were about to leave the bedroom, Piper paused and looked back at the room. Something had twigged their interest, stuck them as interesting for some reason. They frowned, slowly scanning the room for what it was.

There, on the ground by the mat, a smudge in the carpet. Mud, with a few grass clippings on it. Piper took a photo and marked the area for the forensics team. The apartment wasn't close to any green spaces and there hadn't been mud anywhere else... perhaps the killer had knelt here, and something had smudged off their shoe?

Piper knelt alongside it, looking closer and caught sight of something under the rumpled bed... A stray air pod. There was every possibility it belonged to the occupant of the room, so Piper took a photo and then looked around carefully, moving things only with gloved hands, but couldn't find the ear pod's mate. They marked it for forensics and went back out, feeling pleased with themself.

Emmaline had moved from the bathroom to the main room. Piper handed her the victim's objects - a bracelet with a rune inscribed metal plate from one bedside table, a well-thumbed hardback book from the other. "Will these do?"

"Yeah, these look perfect," Emmaline stashed them into her shoulder bag. She looked rattled. Piper glanced towards the bathroom, but Jack didn't appear to be coming out any time soon. She might not have even noticed that Emmaline needed comfort.

"Do you need a hug?" Piper asked, moving closer. "Let's go out into the hall."

"Yeah," Emmaline said. They moved out into the hallway, out of hearing of the forensic team. Piper hugged her and the blonde woman slumped against them, holding on tight. "Thanks."

"It's... you know this isn't your fault, right?" Piper whispered. They felt relieved to be needed in this way, it meant they could properly set aside their own fears and emotions about the crime scene, focus on Emmaline instead.

"Yeah, well, I knew the mage hunters were around. I knew they were, because they came after me," Emmaline said. "And I hid, instead of doing something about it." Her back shuddered with a heavy breath, and she pulled back, swiping a hand over her eyes.

"That's still not your fault," Piper said. They rubbed a hand up Emmaline's back. "We had no idea what they would do."

"We did know." Jack stepped out of the apartment and approached the two of them. "They're hunters. We knew they'd target mages and that they were in Auckland." Her voice was cold, deadpan.

"Um, maybe not really helping," Piper said.

"It's *my* fault," Jack said. "I should have looked into it right away, we had them breaking into Emmaline's and with all the... everything else that was going on, I just let it slide. It's no one's fault but mine."

"No, but-" Emmaline started.

Piper cleared their throat. "Blaming anyone won't help." Their voice came out satisfyingly forceful. "Just, stop both of you. We have the case now, and we can pursue it."

They looked at Jack, who had screwed her mouth to one side. But she nodded, then raised a hand to push her hair back off her forehead. "Yeah. This looks like a murder suicide but we know it's a murder, and we know the motive. We just need to know who did it and track them down." She pulled out her notebook and started making notes.

Emmaline looked at the apartment door, her arms wrapped around herself. "I'd like to get back home as soon as possible so I can contact their spirits, I'm sure they'll be able to tell us something more."

"We should warn the local magic community too," Piper said. "Get the word to Valerie so she can tell her customers."

"Yeah, good idea." Jack chewed her lower lip. "How about you two do that and I'll get in touch with Apanui, get her on board with giving us this case to work on exclusively. It shouldn't be too much convincing, but she might need to come down here."

Piper nodded. "Good idea, we'll take the car. Call if you have any news, okay?"

"Yeah." Jack, stony faced, turned back to the bathroom and pulled out her phone.

"Come on." Piper took Emmaline's elbow. "Let's get out into the fresh air. That'll make you feel better. And hey, maybe Valerie will let you use her back room for your ritual?"

"Yeah." Emmaline leaned into Piper's hand. "Sounds good."

CHAPTER 3

Apanui had been driving to the station when Jack called. She changed routes and was in the apartment within ten minutes. Jack was constantly in awe of how Apanui filled a room with her calm and commanding presence, and it was no different when she strode in, scattering forensics workers before her. "All right, Duarte. What have you got?"

One day Jack would confess to her Sargent that magic was real and there was more to the universe than had been covered in police training college, but today wasn't that day.

Maybe Jack was just being a coward, but yeah, today wasn't that day.

"A double homicide made to look like a murder suicide," Jack said. "I think it might be the work of someone who's killed before, maybe a couple of people."

"A gang hit?" Apanui went to the door of the bathroom and looked inside.

"Maybe, but also maybe a terrorist cell, targeting people like... more like hate crimes," Jack said. "These two are both Wiccan, going from the books on their shelves."

"Why do you think this is an organised group?" Apanui's gaze landed on Jack.

She resisted the urge to squirm. "Emmaline, the psychic I've been working with, had a run in with some people who were targeting Wiccans, last month. They broke into her place with weapons, but she got away. I should have investigated back then but I was still wrapped up in the Armstrong case. I think the constables shelved it as a break and enter. Emmaline's heard rumours about other pagans being threatened, but we couldn't find any actionable leads."

Apanui nodded, expression unreadable. "Fine. What else were you working on?"

Jack shook her head. "Nothing that can't wait."

"All right, I'll give you and Gage some time on this. Report back in forty-eight hours and take some constables if you need them. Perrone's contract is open as well so make sure she bills for time. But Detective, I can't be clear enough on this point."

"Yes, Sargent?"

"None of this gets into the news media, is that clear?" Apanui shook her head slightly. "Officially I'll only tell them the facts. The coroner can deal with the cause of death. If the media get wind of anything like what you just said, terrorists, serial killers, people targeting a minority group, people will panic and it'll make my job a million times harder. We don't want either of those things."

"Yes, Sargent. I agree."

"Good. So, be careful who you talk to and how much you let slip. I'm sure you know this anyway, but I have to emphasise it." Apanui clapped Jack on the shoulder then turned to leave. "And stay safe."

"Yes, Sargent."

Apanui swept out.

Jack exhaled, letting her shoulders slump. Forty-eight hours wasn't long, but if they had something to show for themselves in that time then they'd get longer. It was a matter of finding a first lead. Hopefully Emmaline could provide that.

Emmaline. Jack's heart thudded dully. These killers would execute Emmaline if they found her. And here Jack was involving her in the investigation.

It felt all kinds of wrong. Her instincts were to protect Emmaline at all costs. Even though Emmaline was a formidable mage, some part of Jack thought of her as a delicate flower, or a small fluffy bunny needing to be hidden from the world. The rational part of her never expressed it, of course, but her heart was soft for Emmaline, and it made her cautious.

But none of that mattered. She knew it wouldn't go well if she told Emmaline she was off the case... and her magic would certainly make it easier for Jack and Piper to solve it.

Jack would just have to be extra vigilant and protect Emmaline in any way she could.

CHAPTER 4

The warm scent of lemongrass enveloped Emmaline as Valerie pulled her in for a hug. Emmaline squeezed her and inhaled, letting some of her tension go. Valerie apparently had read Emmaline's emotional state all over her face, and Emmaline was glad for it.

Valerie ran the magic shop, The Full Moon, on Karangahape Road where Jack had gone to ask about 'psychics.' It was how Emmaline had first met Jack and Piper.

"I'll put some tea on. Come on through to the back, Em. You too, Piper." She gestured for them both to go through then turned to the goth teenager who was stocking shelves. "You're in charge for a bit, Amber."

"Sure."

Emmaline pushed through the beaded curtain and flopped down on the ancient sofa. Piper followed her in and sat next to her, a steady, comforting presence.

"I'm all right," Emmaline said. "I just... it was a shock is all. I need some time to do a ritual. Do you mind if I use your space, Valerie?"

"As long as you don't damage any of my stock." Valerie handed Emmaline a delicate teacup full of an infusion of lemon and chamomile.

"I won't, thank you."

"But get yourself together first." Valerie's eyes searched Emmaline's face, her expression concerned. "You can't focus if you're all a flutter."

"No, of course not," Emmaline wrapped her hand around the cup and inhaled.

"Valerie," Piper said, their voice a little softer than normal. "We think there's mage hunters in town, they uh, yeah, there are two dead. I don't know if you can increase the protections on this place or whatever, but you might want to. And let your customers know as well."

Emmaline watched Valerie's face go from warm and serene to serious and steely. "Right." She gave a sharp nod, her lips turning to a thin line. "Thanks for letting me know."

Piper's phone beeped. They pulled it out, quickly reading what was on the screen. "We've got the go ahead to investigate, so that's... Hopefully we can get to the culprits before they kill anyone else."

Emmaline sipped her tea, gathered herself up and then set the cup down. She concentrated on taking a deep breath, feeling the golden well of magic inside her and releasing the tension she had been feeling. She could do this. Years of practise had provided her with self-control for just this kind of situation.

"Okay, I think I'm good to do the ritual now."

Valerie hovered in the doorway, clearly torn between the shop and Emmaline. "Do you want help, hon?"

"No, it's something I do pretty frequently, really," Emmaline said. "You can go back out the front. It might be noisy just at first, but I can usually get spirits calm fast." She smoothed her hair back from her forehead, cursing the wispy strands that always came free of her braid.

"Can... I help?" Piper's voice wavered slightly.

Emmaline had never forgotten the panic attack Piper had experienced; the first time they'd seen dangerous magic performed. They'd both already had a rough day as well, what with the bodies and blood and blame.

Was the panic something Piper's body did as a reaction to their own latent power? As far as Emmaline could tell, Piper didn't have any natural magic talent, but it wasn't always obvious. With some careful nurturing, people sometimes manifested power... But today wasn't the day to test anything like that. Perhaps a panic attack was just a panic attack.

Emmaline shook her head, trying again to focus. "Uh, not exactly, Piper. You could light a candle at the North point of a circle to help, but I'll do the magic myself."

"Oh, that sounds really good," Piper said, visibly relieved.

Emmaline smiled at them and set the book and the bracelet down on the floor. Just one candle at the North point would be enough, Emmaline didn't believe there was any threat from the recently deceased mages. They'd understand what she was doing. Her protection was in her own jewellery if it came to that, and only a word away.

She knelt on the floor, waited until the candle was lit, and cast a quick spell circle. When that was done, she hummed, letting her mind provide her with the best song for what she was about to do.

It came to her almost instantly: a lullaby her mother had sung to her as a child, a French folk song. Relaxing into the memories it triggered, she began to hum.

Piper sat on the sofa, leaning their elbows on their knees and watching.

The song drew her magic out of her, slowly and surely, lighting her fingers with gentle golden light.

She raised her voice as the magic swelled, and traced her fingers over the items, feeling the vibrational energy of their previous owners. She let the song die on her tongue and called them by name.

"Matthew O'Brian, Robert Clark, I can sense you. My name's Emmaline Perrone, I want to talk. Please show yourselves and converse with us."

The air above her shimmered like a heat mirage and she sat back on her heels, one hand raised over the books, channelling her power into them to sustain the appearance of the spirits.

Slowly heat shimmer began to look like steam, and then like smoke. The billows of energy formed into the faces and shoulders of two men. New spirits often couldn't make up their entire bodies.

Emmaline smiled as brightly as she could manage, projecting a friendly, safe presence. "Hi there, Matthew, Robert. Do you know where you are?"

The first sound came through clear and not too loud. "Lucifer, please tell me someone's looking after Lucifer." Matthew's tone was distressed.

"Lucifer?" Emmaline set her hands on her lap and tilted her head to one side. "Please explain further."

"My rabbit, my familiar, Lucifer, please tell me she's safe."

"Oh, the rabbit!" Piper spoke up, startling Emmaline, who had all but forgotten they were there. "One of the constables said something about getting an SPCA rep around to take it."

Emmaline spared a glance at Robert, but he was fading away, the concentration Matthew demanded sucking the power away from him.

"No, she can't go to the SPCA." In mid-air the spectral form of Matthew whirled, looking panicked. "Please, you have to rescue her, she won't know what to do with other, regular rabbits, she's important."

"That's fine," Emmaline said. "I can totally make sure she gets a good home. I love animals." She added the last bit like it was a job interview and she needed to prove herself.

Matthew fixed his eyes on her, and his expression softened. "Thank you..." He regarded her for a while longer and then nodded. "You're a mage, too. That's how we're talking, isn't it?"

Matthew was demanding a large chunk of attention from Emmaline, which made it harder to maintain the spell tethering him to the Earth. "That's right, my gift is for necromancy, so I do things like this. I'm really sorry that you died. And Robert, too, is there anything you can tell us about who did it?"

Robert was little more than a wisp of protoplasmic mist at this point. Emmaline felt a twinge of guilt that she hadn't anchored him better. But she had Matthew at least, and he was talkative. She had her limits, after all, and it wouldn't do to wear herself out so early in the investigation.

Robert spoke but his voice was more of a distant mumble than clear words. Emmaline closed her eyes and intentionally sent more of her power towards Robert.

"... two men...they said..." His voice faded out again.

"What did they say?" Emmaline asked.

"That we deserved to die," Matthew said. "I tried to force them back with magic, but they... It was like they could push it aside." He sighed and shook his head.

Emmaline's throat threatened to close up around the lump that formed there. Across from her Piper's eyes widened and tears leaked out.

"I'm so sorry," Emmaline said, her voice hoarse now, barely over a whisper. "You didn't deserve any of that. I'm so, so sorry."

"The men, one was tall, but... It was hard to see much, it all happened so fast. There were tattoos on his arms, they were magic, I think... I couldn't understand why he hated magic so much if he was using it."

"Hunters," Piper said. "For sure, then."

"Did you hear them use any names for each other?" Emmaline asked. It was a faint hope, if these men had been professionals they wouldn't have, but it was still worth asking.

"No names. One was American though, he had one of those California type accents..." There was a long pause. Matthew seemed to forget for a moment, what they were doing.

"One from the USA and the other, was he another foreigner, like me?" Emmaline prompted, her voice gentle.

"Local," Matthew said. "The other was a Kiwi."

"*Bon.* Thank you," Emmaline said. "Is there anything else you think might be useful?"

Matthew had tipped his head and was looking up, his expression one of gentle wonder. Emmaline recognised he was ready to move on.

"I'm so sorry," she said. "No one should have to die like that."

Matthew nodded, his eyes sad. He started to fade from sight again. This time, Emmaline let them go. They'd got enough information and these two men deserved to rest now, or move on to whatever was next. She reached up and wiped her own damp cheek. Swallowed the lump in her throat, she met Matthew's translucent eyes.

"We're going to stop them doing it to anyone else," Emmaline said. "We're going to do everything we can, and you've helped us with that."

Piper made a choked hiccup noise and Emmaline gave them a watery smile, trying to convey 'it will be all right.' To her relief Piper didn't look at all in danger of panicking. They were sad, for sure, but they didn't seem upset by the use of magic.

When she looked back up, all traces of the men's spirits were gone.

CHAPTER 5

Jack sat at her desk at the station. A fresh made coffee steamed beside her, tantalising her nose, and making her mouth water. She opened some databases and a Google search tab and then had a total mind blank on what to search for.

"What is the next best step?" Jack muttered. Her training hadn't covered terrorist cells or crime organised to this degree. Besides that, it was hard to concentrate entirely on the problem because the fact that Emmaline was in mortal danger, and had been in mortal danger for weeks, kept occurring to her.

She should have already been on this case, not waiting for the hunters to strike again. She dug her fingers into the paper blotter the desks all came with and reprimanded herself for being slack. If her father ever heard that she'd ignored a lead like that, he'd be so disappointed. Jack bit her lip and decided never to tell him.

All this time, Emmaline had been in potential danger and Jack had done *nothing* about it. Aside from giving her the spare room, of course. So far, that had been enough to keep her safe, but Jack didn't think she'd be particularly effective if Hunters came to break down the door and take Emmaline. She could fight, and she had a nightstick and pepper spray, a gun in a safe in her car that she needed verbal permission to draw... but these were supernatural super soldiers.

And they were supernatural super soldiers driven by an intense hatred and an organised terror cell.

She hated the thought of anyone being hunted for who they are, but the fact that it was Emmaline, her friend, her assistant in these weird cases, gorgeous, clever, funny Emmaline... It was just so much worse.

Jack took a deep breath and scrubbed her hand over her forehead.

"Morning, Jack. Looks like you're making some great progress there."

Jack cringed as a familiar, and unwelcome voice sounded from directly behind her. She spun her chair around to settle a withering look on Detective Coleson, the office annoyance and the subject of a complaint Jack and Piper had filed for inappropriate behaviour. He hadn't seemed particularly cowed by the complaint. "Coleson. What do you want?"

"Nothing, just checking in on our resident ghost hunter," Coleson said. "Heard you got a murder suicide, can't be too much to research around that?"

Jack frowned. "You'd be surprised. Since when do you check in on me, anyway?"

"I don't know," Coleson said, airily. "Since I've been reprimanded for inappropriate behaviour to my delightful co-workers. I'm being more friendly, aren't I?"

"So, what're you going for now, Coleson? The two for one special? Do you get a special asshole plaque if you get three reprimands in a row?" Jack leaned back, folding her arms. She raised an eyebrow and hoped he got the hint that she wasn't kidding around.

His lips went thin and his forehead wrinkled. "Whatever." He spun on his heel and stalked out of the office.

Piper left Emmaline at the Full Moon talking to Valerie in a more depth about what it meant that Hunters were in Auckland. They stepped out into the sunshine and took a deep breath, trying to centre themself and set aside the horrible sadness of the ritual.

They were pleased that despite their initial worry about being there with Emmaline, they'd kept their panic at bay. Focusing on the emotion of the ghosts had distracted from their own fear. That was growth! And now?

They had a job to do.

Piper drove back to the station to ask about what had happened to the rabbit, Lucifer.

"Oh, SPCA is coming to pick up the bunny." Constable Harris hooked his thumb towards the evidence room. "It's chilling in there for now. Weird thing, the intruders were apparently trying to kill it too, like it was a witness or something." Harris snorted, shaking his head.

"I want to take it home," Piper said. "Is that okay?"

Harris shrugged. "Doesn't matter at all to me. Just call the SPCA and tell them they don't need to collect it and note down your details in case it comes up in the investigation. The SPCA might want your details for adoption, I guess."

"Cool." Piper went in back and found the carry cage with the small brown rabbit in it. They crouched down to look at it. "Hey, Lucifer. You want to come home with me? Jack sort of has a cat and I don't think she'd make a great bunny mum, anyway."

The rabbit twitched its nose back at them. Piper smiled, picked up the cage and took it to their desk.

Piper saw that Jack was in deep thinking mode, so they left the rabbit with a fresh bowl of water, took their laptop into the quiet break room and went straight to Google. They started entering every keyword they could think of into the search bar, opening tabs for each term which occurred to them until their browser was a sea of tiny tabs.

"Hunter, hunted, magic, mages, cleansing of magic..." they whispered as they clicked into each one. The results were of varied use. Magic was far too broad a term, and they closed the tab instead of pursuing it. Hunter, likewise, brought up a lot of farming supplies stores so they added the modifier 'mages' and 'mission' to the search results to try and narrow it down.

Twenty minutes of intuitive browsing later, Piper got to a bookmarking site with long screeds of discussion which felt relevant. People talking obliquely about the 'scourge on Mother Earth' and the 'unnatural freaks' and so on. It looked to be mostly vague on the public chat. Piper made a burner account and applied to join to get into the inner workings of it all.

More promising still was a web series. It was a local ghost hunting show, mostly one guy walking around supposedly haunted buildings in New Zealand, but his more recent work seemed to involve a real honest to goodness magic user. That or there was a spectacular and sudden increase in his budget and special effects and the channel owner had decided to go a different direction with the show.

Piper noted down the names mentioned: Sebastian Black and Basil at the Mt Eden library and clicked through related links. Experience on the video platform had taught Piper that the longer you clicked through related content, the quicker you found the weirdest parts of humanity.

Sure enough, it didn't take long before they were seeing videos with titles like "the REAL TRUTH that the government DOESN'T WANT YOUT TO KNOW" and "Truth drops, wach all the way to the end for a surprise! #3924" caps lock and typos and all.

Sighing, Piper adjusted their headphones and started to watch the first one. It was on a channel named MindCraft22, which seemed innocent enough. Piper guessed that if they scrolled back through their channel's history, there would be video game play through videos before they'd got into conspiracy theories. The host was a white man, his dark hair hanging long and shaggy and unshaven, with pink framed signature glasses. He was normal looking except for the overzealous excitement in his eyes.

A lot of it was painfully familiar, run of the mill conspiracy theories linking billionaires with the puppet masters of the world governments. Social media moguls were involved as well.

Piper skipped thirty seconds forward and did it again a few times, until something caught their attention.

"These witches, they're not like the nice, Earth Mother, working with nature idea like you'll see on Pinterest. No, these are people who can actually twist reality to their whim, and if that doesn't scare you... well." The man shook his head at the camera. He raised an eyebrow. "Now, I'll get into some more detail, but I just wanted to take a minute to talk about this episode's sponsor..."

About to skip past the advertorial, Piper paused, curiosity piqued. What kind of company would pay to advertise on this particular channel?

It was some kind of meal replacement powder mix. Piper frowned, disappointed. Maybe it was just a lingering sponsorship from when MindCraft22 was still playing video games?

Maybe they had no idea what the video they were advertising in was about.

Piper made notes once the man got back into his rant. He described magic users using only the term 'witches', and detailed various stories he'd heard, citing them as incontrovertible evidence. He interspersed his talking to camera with clips from horror movies featuring witches. Poorly restored clips from seventies horror where the women all had twisted features and evil red glowing eyes.

For a moment, Piper considered commenting, just to ask him for more credible sources, but it hardly seemed professional for a police detective to do such a thing. After several of these stories, the tone shifted a little.

"I know what you're thinking, and I know how this sounds, but hey, you don't have to listen to just me. There's a whole group of us who have seen the truth, and if you're strong enough, maybe you could join us. Go to my channel, and look up the curated playlist I have in there called The Real Truth, educate yourself. I'll see you on the flipside."

"Huh." Piper hit pause on the video before it auto-played something else and sat back in their chair. They looked at the notes they'd scribbled down and leaned in, adding a few more observations, before clicking on the curated playlist as instructed.

No point going to Jack with this unless they were really sure that this was relevant, and that meant going further down the rabbit hole.

CHAPTER 6

J ack picked up her phone again, checking for messages. For the last hour, most of what Jack had been doing was texting Emmaline. It hadn't been terribly fulfilling as Emmaline didn't text back with the speed Piper did. Jack looked listlessly at the documents she had from the crime report of the murders and from the break in at Emmaline's rented place before she'd moved in with Jack.

Her nose twitched. The rabbit that Piper had put on the desk had buried itself in the straw and gone to sleep, but it did have a certain smell.

She sighed.

How do you find a secret organization that has generations of experience at avoiding notice? And on top of that, it's hunting an even larger community of people who have passed unnoticed in society since... well, forever, more or less? If you didn't count things like fantasy novels and Halloween, of course, but everyone knew that was all make-believe so. It didn't count.

Jack sighed and got up to make herself another coffee in case the extra caffeine spurred something in the problem-solving part of her brain.

Piper was in the break room, massaging their forehead with thumb and forefinger.

"Are you all right?" Jack didn't want to intrude but didn't want Piper to feel like they were all alone.

"Oh, yeah, just. The doublethink these guys employ to make their conclusions work is really wrinkling my brain."

"Doublethink?" Jack wrinkled her nose. "What guys are you talking about?"

"Good question, I think I have enough to show you." Piper tapped on the keyboard a couple of times and looked over their notes.

"Want a drink?" Jack poured a coffee. Piper shook their head. Jack brought her coffee over to the table Piper was seated at, feeling a mixture of curiosity and dread. If Piper had a lead that was good news though, it was a relief. Jack flopped on the chair opposite to Piper.

"Okay, so." Piper flipped through the notes they'd made on an A4 pad of lined paper and scanned them for a moment before turning more fully to Jack. "The thing is, I think the mage hunters are recruiting online using viral videos."

Whatever Jack had been expecting, it definitely hadn't been that. "Recruiting via what?"

"Viral videos. You know how there are like, Nazis recruiting young boys online, preying on the weak, targeting kids and stuff like that?"

"Uh." Jack cleared her throat. "I might've read an article on that, but I haven't like, gone deep with it."

"Right, so basically, some background. Online videos and social media, there's a way people use the video algorithm. If you get your tags and things right, your video comes up on related searches. I found this guy called MindCraft22, and he's like, deep in it." Piper took a sip out of their water bottle and caught their breath. "He linked to a bunch of other creators, and they're all saying that witches are evil, that witches are secretly destroying the world, and that righteous people who know the truth can stop them."

Blood drained from Jack's face. She pushed her hair back from her forehead. "Sounds like the cult that Edith Armstrong was caught up in."

"Exactly what I thought," Piper said. "I think the same cult is recruiting this way, spreading the propaganda and then getting kids to sign up. I think when you get deep enough in they invite you to in person meetings."

Jack put her elbow on the table and propped her chin on her hand. "Well, fuck."

Piper frowned and nodded. "Yeah, it seems really widespread. It's getting to people in New Zealand but it's worldwide, well. English speaking worldwide. The YouTubers are based all over the place, and they've definitely talked about meetups in lots of different countries."

Jack closed her eyes and tried to imagine how they could even begin to shut down a recruitment drive that was happening online. It was too much, she couldn't do it alone. It was mind boggling, but they had to do something. Just...take the first step.

That was the key. One step at a time, small manageable steps. She opened her eyes.

Piper was watching her, concern written all over their face. "Sorry, is this... Am I losing you?"

"No, I followed, it's just a lot," Jack said. "But we knew going in that this wouldn't be an easy job, I guess. So, we need to find the first step. If these people are preying on teenagers..."

"Teenagers, people who are shut in or online a lot for whatever reason, but in particular people who are vulnerable, feel misunderstood or attacked."

Preying on the vulnerable.

"I really hate these people." Jack let all the annoyance she felt colour her voice. "But we need to find the locals. You said there's meetings somewhere. If we could get to one of those, that'd be the key."

Piper pushed their pad of notes towards Jack. "Yeah, I think you're right. It should be easy enough to get an invite, although it'll take a few days. It's just a matter of not spooking them."

"Deep into the basements, sheds and Reddit threads of Auckland's counterculture." Jack's shoulders slumped. She felt tired already and they'd barely started on the case. It was as if she stood at the foot of the Southern Alps and she had to climb it without a guide. Piper was eyeing her so she forced a smile. "Can't wait!"

"How are you such a terrible liar?" Piper asked, laughing.

That prompted a genuine smile out of Jack. "No idea."

Her phone buzzed with a message alert and she grabbed it eagerly.

Emmaline: hey, I think I have us a pretty cool lead, someone to meet. Can we drive North for a couple of hours tomorrow?

Jack read it aloud for Piper and then replied.

Jack: sure can if it's for the case

Emmaline: It is! Excellente, I'll tell Richie

"Guess we're driving North and meeting someone called Richie tomorrow," Jack said.

Piper raised their eyebrows. "Cool. I'll go deeper into these videos and see if I can't find some people to talk to in real life."

"Don't get sucked into the propaganda, rookie." Jack felt slightly embarrassed by how affectionate her nickname for Piper sounded.

"Oh, I won't." Piper nudged Jack as she stood up. "The last person these types want to recruit is a non-binary asexual panromantic with brown skin."

Jack winced but was reassured all the same. "Still, take care, okay?"

"I will."

CHAPTER 7

Piper went home on the bus that Tuesday with the rabbit in a cage on their lap. Although they could have ridden with Jack, they wanted more time alone with their thoughts and the things they'd found on the web.

The bus ride gave them time to listen to a podcast they'd found recommended on MindCraft22's channel, which apparently went deeper into the world of witches, Satan and real magic.

It wasn't pleasant listening. The podcast hosts were enthusiastic Australians with very little concern about how offensive their word choice was and an apparent tendency to believe anyone who called themselves an expert. But there was enough content that got close enough to true to be engrossing. Piper made notes in their notebook about the things which felt real to them, and the things which were absolutely out of the ballpark in a concerning way.

"The thing is, these people, they can work alone just fine. Some of them choose to be in covens or groups to work their magic, but they don't have to," podcast host Joey said.

"Yeah, that's kind of... like you'd think they'd all be in these covens of thirteen having black mass naked under the full moon," the other host, Becky, added. "And if it's like, restricted to the full moon and groups, you don't feel quite as unsafe."

"But it turns out it could just be anyone, sitting alone in their house and summoning the spirits of the dead to do their bidding," Joey said.

"Do they really summon the dead?" Becky's delivery felt fake on that line, a feeder line, Piper thought, so Joey could really bring the shock value.

"Oh yeah, and not just spirits of the human dead, but like animals and stuff as well."

"And stuff?" Piper rolled their eyes.

"Ew, I hate that, it's so scary." Becky brought a horror movie heroine's tremor into her voice. "I saw *Pet Cemetery* and it scared me so bad, I never want that to happen in real life."

Piper's stop was coming up, so they pocketed their notebook and pressed the stop button. They'd listen to the podcast until they got home, then turn it off, maybe call their brother for some rational conversation.

"And these spirits, you know what they're doing with them?" Joey's voice was a blend of revolted and excited.

"I dunno," Becky said, her voice quavering. "This is way scarier than the ghost hunter we had on last week."

"They send them out to corrupt people into their way of life. Converting people with weak minds to do their dark work."

"They control them with the spirits?" The quaver was gone out of Becky's voice now.

Piper had to admire the way she changed tone to make the podcast dramatic and engrossing. This was after all, the crux of their argument, that witches were bad and evil and wanted to ensnare your mind and eat your children.

"Yes, the spirits turn people into little more than zombies, bound to the will of the witches and without free will."

"Terrifying," Becky said. "So, this is all just out there happening? What can people like us to do stop them?"

Ah, there it was. Piper nodded, pleased that they'd been able to see where the argument of the show was going.

"Well, you can't just call the police, obviously," Joey said. "I mean, if you call the cops on your neighbour because of some chanting or whatever, you can't exactly expect to be taken seriously. But there are options." He paused, possibly to take a breath, but Piper thought it was probably for dramatic emphasis. "There's some really great websites and stuff, places where concerned people are gathering and sharing information."

He read off some sites. Piper paused in front of the building next to hers to set the rabbit cage down and make some notes.

"That's great," Becky said. "I can't wait to log in and meet some people who get it, you know?"

"Yeah and of course, we'll be going deeper into this in an upcoming episode. In fact..." Joey paused again and there was a rustling like of papers being moved around. "Next week we've got an interview booked with someone who used to be involved in all this witch stuff, but has reformed. I reckon we can get some really in-depth info from them on what to look out for and what can be done."

"Oh yeah, I can't wait for that one," Becky said.

The podcast hosts went into the familiar end-of-podcast reel of social media links, places to send money and so on. Piper flicked it off and let themself into their building, removing their headphones as they took the stairs to their apartment, lugging Lucifer in their cage.

Piper felt tense and annoyed, pissed off that there were people out there preaching information, misinformation to make people fear witches. Especially witches who could summon the dead like Emmaline. There was no way Emmaline would use her spirits to control anyone, Piper was sure the idea would be abhorrent to her. And sure, there were bad witches out there, of course there were, just like there were bad people of any kind.

Frustrated, Piper kicked the door of their apartment.

The door to the next apartment opened. Piper's neighbour Beau Kaminski popped his head out. "What's the noise? Wait, is that a rabbit?"

"Uh, yeah, this is Lucifer." Piper held the cage up so Lucifer could see Beau and vice versa. "I uh, inherited her today."

"Keep it hidden at property inspection time." Beau came out, shrugging on a jacket. "We're not meant to have pets anywhere in the building."

"Got it." Piper nodded. "You going out somewhere fun?"

"None of your business, but yes. I'm attending a meeting of like-minded individuals," Beau said. He walked towards the stairs.

"Have a nice time!" Piper waved at his back. He didn't respond. They frowned, then dug out their key. Juggling Lucifer's cage, they unlocked their door and went inside, setting the rabbit down.

They looked briefly at the kitchen and then decided tonight was a food delivery night. But first they pulled out a carrot and some lettuce to give to Lucifer and filled up the water bottle fixed to the side of her cage. "This is your new home," Piper said. "Once you've eaten, I'll look up how to properly look after you and see if you want to hop around outside the cage, okay?"

Lucifer looked up at them with shiny eyes.

How much did she understand? Matthew had said she wasn't an ordinary rabbit, right? If she was a familiar, that had to make her more intelligent, or more in tune or something. Piper should text Emmaline and ask.

Besides that, the hunters had been trying to kill her. It was possible, Piper realised, far too late, that they'd just brought home with them something that made them a target. Lucifer was definitely on the hunters list. Would they still be looking for her?

They'd have to ask Emmaline that as well.

But first, they collapsed onto the couch and ordered from the nearby Thai food place, then flicked a message through to their brother, Ben.

Piper: hey Benny, what you up to?

He replied within seconds.

Ben: watching that new game show, it's a delightful train wreck

Grinning, Piper hit the call button and grabbed their remote. Ben picked up.

"Hey Pipes, you'd better not be interrupting my viewing of Five Gold Rings."

"No, I'm calling to watch it with you, which channel is it on?"

With the phone on speaker, and Ben's familiar husky and kind voice telling them how the game show worked, it almost felt like Piper had their brother in the room with them. They laughed together and it felt like old times. Their food arrived and they had to dash to the door to get it, but then they were back on the couch, eating Massaman curry and roti and laughing with Ben at the ridiculous puzzles and the way the pairs of contestants bickered. Lucifer happily munched on her carrot and greens dinner nearby.

For a few hours, Piper could forget about the hidden Hunters and the conspiracy theorists, and just relax.

CHAPTER 8

On Wednesday, Emmaline was awake before Jack, clattering around in the kitchen making herself breakfast. It was unusual for her to be the first person up as Jack kept weirdly early hours, but she'd been excited about what the day held.

Talking with Valerie the day before had turned up a lot of concerns about the local magical community, how vulnerable it was in the face of an attack from the mage hunters. Valerie was at the centre of the magical community in the city. She'd assured Emmaline that she'd get the word out, encourage everyone to strengthen their protections and so on, but that was only within the circle of the central city. She had given Emmaline the name and number of Richie, centre of the more rural magical community to the North. And even more exciting, he was the centre of it because he ran what was essentially a habitat for displaced magical creatures.

Emmaline couldn't wait to see what he had out there, and she was equally excited to see Jack and Piper's faces when they realised what the place was.

She made coffee for Jack, tea for herself, and toast and porridge for the both of them. Jack would need her strength, if things went the way Emmaline guessed they might. She was envisioning not just meeting weird people and animals but hiking through the farmlands and bush that housed it all. She was happily daydreaming when Jack's bedroom door opened, startling.

"Good morning!" she said, her voice strained from the surprise. Her heart fluttering at the sight of Jack's hair, all mussed and rumpled from sleep. "I made you toast and coffee and porridge."

"You're energetic this morning," Jack said. "Thanks."

Emmaline had the sudden, wild urge to slip an arm around Jack and kiss her good morning, but she resisted it. They had made an agreement that if anything were to happen between them it would be later. They were to be friends first and then if anything happened, well, it would be up to Jack to initiate it.

Although she had traded her love for her ex to the fae, and she no longer actively loved Marlo, the trauma remained. Jack couldn't just forget all the things which had happened in the relationship, even if the main emotion had been removed.

Emmaline liked Jack and didn't want to push anything she wasn't comfortable with. So she patted her shoulder and handed her a cup of steaming coffee.

"You're welcome. What do you like on porridge?"

"I usually have brown sugar and slices of banana," Jack said. "But I can do it."

"Nope, it's on me this morning." Emmaline waved a hand dismissively. "Sit, I'll bring it over to you."

"All right, if you insist."

"I'm just really excited about today." Emmaline set the food down in front of Jack a few minutes later. "It's going to blow your mind. In a good way, I mean."

Jack chuckled. "Are you going to give me more information than that or...?"

"In the car, with Piper." Emmaline bounced in her seat and suppressed the urge to clap her hands together. "I promise."

Jack tapped Emmaline's leg, startling her.

"Well, we're in the car, and Piper's here now."

Piper had taken the back seat even though Emmaline had offered to move out of the front passenger one. The drive North of the city was a long one for Auckland, two and a half hours, perhaps more if they hit traffic.

"I am, and I had no idea how to dress for today," Piper grumbled. "All you said was sensible footwear. Are we going on a bushwalk? Out in the sun? Because I would have worn less good jeans if that's the case."

"I don't know, maybe." Emmaline turned to look at Piper's outfit — black skinny jeans, a loose-fitting grey tank top with a flowered bomber jacket over the top. "You look great, it'll be fine. This place, well, I'm not exactly sure what it will be like, it might be like a farm or it might be like a park or it might be like a retirement village, but whatever it is, it's going to be incredible."

"I don't mean to sound overly sarcastic," Jack said, slowly. "But retirement village doesn't sound incredible at all to me."

"Just tell us?" Piper added.

"Okay, yeah." Emmaline fiddled with a piece of her blonde hair which had come free from its braid with one hand. "It's a magical reserve, for like, magical creatures and people who don't want to live in the city. Run by local mages."

"You mean it's like a magic farm?" Piper's voice barely contained their excitement. "For real? Oh man, I should have brought Lucifer, I didn't want to put her in danger but she'd love that."

"I think so!" Emmaline turned briefly to grin at them. "Cool, huh?"

Piper shook their head, their smile wide. "I had no idea there'd be something like that in Auckland. Wow."

"I mean they're probably all over the country, but this is the closest, obviously." Emmaline switched her gaze to Jack, who was staring at the road with a certain intensity. "What do you think, Jack?"

"When we talk about magical creatures, like they're real, because... Yeah, okay, they're real, we saw some stuff in Faerie, but what are we talking about here?" Jack spared a quick glance at Emmaline and then back at the road. Emmaline thought she saw a flash of fear in Jack's eyes. "Like, is there a lake with a giant Loch Ness monster in it? Are dragons real? What should I be preparing myself for here?"

"Oh," Emmaline bit her lower lip. She wanted to lay their fears to rest but she couldn't. "I guess I don't exactly know what kind of thing we'll see. But no dragons, they're... I mean I'm sure they exist deep in Faerie but they wouldn't be on this side of the mirror. And really big stuff like Nessie, they'd never be able to hide in a small country like New Zealand."

"We have taniwha, though," Piper said. "I assume, I mean. I've never seen one."

"Maybe, but at the reserve, most likely it'll be humanoid things, or things which can shapeshift to human, smaller than a big cat if they can't. I mean, I don't really know. I guess I should have asked Valerie for a bit more detail, *désolé*."

Jack flashed Emmaline a quick smile. "You don't have to apologise, it's fine, I just kinda need to steel myself for whatever we're gonna see. If I can."

Emmaline checked her phone, scrolling through the directions. "We want the next turn off after this one, on the right."

"Gotcha."

"It'll be fine, Jack, they're not gonna be dangerous or Richie wouldn't have said it was okay to drop in."

Jack nodded slowly and put the indicator on as they approached the turn off. As they turned off the main highway, the road wound up over a hill.

"This doesn't feel right," Jack said. "I think we should go back."

Emmaline blinked at her, then realised she'd felt a frisson of magic. It must be a deterrent charm, plant the idea that people thought they were coming the wrong way. "No, this is fine. Stay on this road."

"It really doesn't feel right, but okay." Jack gripped the wheel a little tighter.

Emmaline looked out with window, spotting more charms here and there, attached to the markers at the side of the road or embedded in the road itself. If she hadn't been in the car, Jack and Piper almost certainly would have turned back, but she was able to dispel the worst effects of the charm.

The landscape wasn't farmland like most of the landscape outside Auckland city, but forest. Emmaline saw the odd pine tree here and there, but it looked like it was mostly native bush, thick, deep green and lush. The native forests were made up almost entirely evergreen varieties, rainforests full of tree ferns. Emmaline never ceased finding it beautiful. She felt excited all over again at the thought of walking among the New Zealand trees.

The road mounted a handful of small hills, and the forest got thicker, pressing closer to the sides of the road. Making the lanes feel narrower than they were with overhanging fronds. Then they started to see signs.

'Department of Conservation reserve ahead - strictly no access to public'

'Turning bay ahead'

'No access past this point.' This last one was mounted on a lowered barrier arm, which spanned the road. Jack brought the car to a stop and looked at Emmaline. "What now? Because I have to tell you, every cell in my body is telling me to turn back. I should turn back."

"There's an intercom, I'll give it a go. Just, don't drive off, okay? No matter how bad the urge is." Emmaline hopped out of the car and went to the stout box with the wide plastic weather shield over it. She tapped a few buttons. Static crackled.

"This is private DOC land," a gruff male voice said. "Please turn around and head back to the main highway."

"Hi, my name's Emmaline Perrone, I'm a friend of Valerie's. Valerie at the Full Moon shop on K Road." Emmaline's mind raced, trying to think of the quickest and easiest way to establish that she was a friend. "I saw what you did with the ward on the turnoff, really good work. I liked your use of the road itself to compel people to turn back."

There was a pause, and then a staticky chuckle. "All right, Emmaline. And who are those two with you?"

"My friends, I'm helping them with an investigation. They're cops, but they're cool, they know about this stuff. There were some people like us killed, so..."

"Arm's coming up, follow the road to the hut. I'm the one in the hat."

Emmaline went back into the car as a faint alarm sounded and the barrier arm started to raise. 'The one in the hat' wasn't much to go on, but she got the joke ten minutes later when they pulled up at the end of the road. There was no one around but one man in a hat.

He was a tall man, with broad shoulders and bright brown eyes under hazelnut coloured hair. He waved them into a car park in front of a small wooden hut, which had official looking Department of Conservation signage up.

"Richie?" Emmaline asked. She got out of the car, Jack and Piper followed.

"That's right, nice to meet you, Emmaline." They shook hands. Emmaline instantly liked him. He had a warm aura and looked as if he'd give great hugs.

"You too. This is Detective Jack Duarte and her partner Piper Gage."

"Pleased to meet you," Richie said.

"Are you really with the Department of Conservation?" Piper asked.

"Yeah, I am. A few of us with the gift work for various government departments," Richie said. "Just so we can continue to hide the stuff the general public doesn't need to know about."

"Huh," Jack said. "I could've used a little help with a case last month. It's a bit hard to prosecute crimes involving magic. Most judges and juries would laugh it out of court."

Richie's smile faded and shrugged his shoulders. "Yeah, police is kind of a whole other thing, I guess. But...uh, what did you say about people being killed?"

"Two murders," Jack said. "We believe it was Mage Hunters. They're in Auckland."

Emmaline chimed in. "They struck in the Central city and they busted into my North Shore place as well. You'll want to spread the news around to everyone you know."

"But that's part of why we're here," Piper said, quickly. "We want to shut them down. They killed some people so it's an official police investigation."

Richie nodded slowly, his expression turning grim.

"This is my card." Emmaline produced one from her pocket and pressed it into his hand.

He turned it over a couple of times and slipped it into his pocket. "Never had Hunters around here, before. That's some bad news."

"Yeah." Emmaline felt awful for ruining his morning all of a sudden. "Sorry to be the bearer of bad news. But Valerie said you have some cool stuff out here and that you might be able to help a bit?"

Richie rubbed his hands together and smiled again. "She's not wrong, it's a very unique place. You all want a look around?"

"Absolutely we do," Emmaline said.

"As long as it's not dangerous," Jack added.

"Well then, I'll just get you to sign in. You can grab water bottles inside, then we can set out," Richie replied.

CHAPTER 9

Piper wasn't sure if they should be afraid or ecstatic. They had a million questions about what it took to run this place, or even get it established in the first place. But Richie and Emmaline were talking protection spells, and they didn't want to interrupt.

"There's a glade just in here." Richie stopped on the path. He gestured with his head into the bush. "Usually got some little bird things hanging around there. You want to have a look?"

"Sure," Jack said. "Little bird things sounds vague but manageable."

Richie laughed, an easy-going chuckle. "Very true, they're pretty harmless these guys. I think they might have manifested from dreams... We get a few new ones every year or so."

He turned off the path. Piper had a sudden horror, like they were leaving the path in Faerie and opening themselves up to harm. But this was the real world, their world, and there was no reason to fear stepping into the bush.

Well, there was.

Piper flashed back to all the bush safety videos they'd watched in high school that warned of exposure and the risks of hypothermia if you got lost in the bush. But this was different. It was the middle of the day and they had a DOC worker with them, an expert in bush safety.

They hesitated as Emmaline and Richie led the way, Jack close behind them. They took a deep breath and followed, half expecting some sort of attack.

Their fears took a backseat when they heard Emmaline's delighted exclamations.

"Oh, they're so sweet!"

Piper caught up and looked over Emmaline's shoulder to the cluster of tall trees. Richie had been rather generous to call this a glade. In Piper's mind, a glade was full of sunshine with long, green grass and wildflowers. This was just a bit of a larger gap between trees. But that wasn't the point. The point was the small, fluffy looking, brightly coloured flying things which perched in the tree's branches, and swooped around, making various noises.

They were bird... like. But not exactly birds. Some of them looked more like a child's drawing of a bird, long thin black legs with three toes, oversized beaks and rough edges to them. Some looked more like puppet birds, made of fur instead of feathers, and making noises like a dog's squeaky toy. One in particular caught Piper's eye. It was of the palest lime green, its feathers apparently made out of silk or satin, smooth and shiny. Its tail hung down, long and elegant as it sat looking at the group of humans with a wary black eye.

Why did it seem familiar? Maybe it looked like a soft toy their brother Ben had made back in sewing class at their primary school.

"Ohhhh..." Piper sighed and smiled, feeling all their anxiety melt away. "Look at them. They're amazing. Can I take a photo?"

Richie nodded and Piper whipped their phone out to get a picture. Not that they could show it to Ben, but...

"Is that a lemonwood tree?" Jack asked.

Piper realised they hadn't even noticed the type of tree the birds were living in. It had a lot of long thin leaves, of a bright apple green.

"Yeah. Pittosporum eugenioides, or as we call them Tarata. Most of the forest is natives. A bit further up the hill it's mostly ponga."

"Ponga is tree ferns right?" Emmaline asked. "I love those."

"Uh huh. These little guys like it a bit warmer, which is why they're here in the tarata, but the native magical beasties tend to hang around the ponga."

"How do you stop the birds flying away, like, out of the reserve?" Jack asked.

"Well, there are charms to keep them contained in the fences," Richie said. "But many of them can't fly for long periods anyway. Here we make sure they have plenty to eat, have a place to bed down and keep them safe from predators."

Jack eyed the surrounding bush. "Are there a lot of predators here?"

Emmaline moved towards the tree of mystical birds, lifting her hand out and making a soft cooing noise. The birds watched her distrustfully and the few which had been flying alighted further up the tree.

"A few," Richie said.

Piper eyed his expression. Being circumspect out of some kind of fear? Maybe he thought they'd try and shut the reserve down. Or that Jack would insist on putting down anything too dangerous. They cleared their throat, eager to head off that line of thought. "Our interest in being here is that we don't want to interfere in any way. We're really here to warn you about the hunters, and to understand a bit more. Nothing more than that."

Richie looked into their eyes and held their gaze for a moment.

Piper looked right back at him, willing him to see how honest they were being.

Finally, he nodded, his mouth curling up on one side. "Good to know. We haven't had a lot of good run ins with the police."

Emmaline had failed at getting any of the birds to trust her. They'd all retreated further up the tree and were twittering at her, clearly uncomfortable. Sighing, she turned back and re-joined Richie and the others.

"I guess I really am only good with animal spirits, not animals which are alive," she said, with an air of extreme disappointment. Piper patted her shoulder.

"I wouldn't take it personally," Richie said. "They barely trust me, and I bring them breakfast almost every day."

"What do they eat?" Jack cocked her head to the side as if she were a bird herself.

"Caramel popcorn is a popular choice, but we usually bring them bird seed and chopped up fruit." Richie nodded once and turned back to the path. "Come on, I'll introduce you to Kier, that will really show you what we're trying to do out here."

"Kier?" Piper repeated. "Is that a kind of creature?"

"I think it's someone's name," Emmaline said.

Piper tore their eyes off the tree of dream birds and followed Jack and Piper as they set off after Richie. The four of them soon regained the path and headed downhill.

"You're both right." Richie's walkie talkie crackled. He plucked it off his belt and spoke into it rapidly. "I'm here, go ahead, Colin."

"Yeah, just checking in. Found a tear in the fence out on the Southern side, so I'm gonna fix it."

"Sounds good. How big a tear?" Richie frowned.

"Not big, nothing more than a rabbit could have got in. Or a cat, I guess." Colin sounded unconcerned. "Could be something came in, but there's no trace of anything with bad intention. Nothing to worry about, probably just tore in the storm."

"Hmm. Well, I'm headed down to see Kier with some guests," Richie said. "Let me know if you see any more tears or anything weird."

"Good luck," Colin said. "Kier's in a mood today."

"In a mood," Jack said, deadpan.

"It'll be fine," Richie said. He slid his walkie talkie back into its holster. "I suppose the thing you need to know before you meet Kier is that he's a kelpie, and he's trying his best."

"A kelpie...? Isn't that like what Gerard's uh, friend, is?"

Emmaline nodded, turning back to flash Piper a bright smile. "That's right."

"And a kelpie is a person-eating horse that lives in water, isn't that right, too?" Jack's voice was still deadpan and getting colder by the moment.

"Yes," Richie said. "Traditionally, but they can shape change into humans, and Kier's very curious about our society. He wants to fit in, so he's learned not to eat people. He mostly sticks to fish now."

"Mostly," Jack repeated.

"Well, we bring him steaks every now and then."

Piper's heart fluttered and they licked their lips. It wasn't much different from meeting someone convicted of a murder, and they'd done that before. Maybe it was like meeting a murderer and a wild animal at the same time. It was frightening, but Richie's words had tempered their fear with curiosity as well. A monster who was curious and wanted to do better — they couldn't be that scary could they?

The path wound down through dense trees until the ground flattened out. The trees thinned and the ground became grassy underfoot. The lake opened up before them, larger than Piper had expected, nestled in between the hills as it was.

Further around the shore, maybe five hundred metres away was a human figure. Slight, and young looking, with thick dark hair.

Richie raised a hand. "Hey, Kier! These are humans come to meet you, how about you say hello?"

Jack had slowed, sticking close to Emmaline's side, but Piper felt suddenly impatient, and ducked around the two of them.

The figure had crouched to splash some water on their face, but now he stood up again and waved back, picking up a shirt from a nearby tree and pulling it on. Piper felt themself smiling even though they hadn't yet met.

"'Lo!" Kier closed the distance between them quickly.

Richie gestured for Piper to stop and leaned in closer to murmur to them. "Let him come to us, he'll be more comfortable that way."

Piper nodded and raised a hand to wave at the fae-looking boy. He looked about seventeen or eighteen, his skin pale and sallow, as if waterlogged. His hair was a thick, deep brown, but as he came closer Piper could see a strand of pondweed caught in it. His eyes were slightly too large, but his features were fine and delicate. He would grow to be very handsome but for now he was interesting and attractive.

"This is Piper, Jack and Emmaline," Richie said.

Jack blanched. "He's fae isn't he? Shouldn't we be hiding our names?"

"Ah, he's not that kind of fae," Richie said. "Perfectly safe with names and words. If he were going to kill you, you'd know about it."

Kier ducked his head as if Richie had praised him. He was close now, close enough that Piper could smell the peculiar horse-and-lake-water scent of him. He blinked at them and his mouth twitched up in a shy smile.

"Hey there," Piper said. "It's nice to meet you."

"You too," Kier said. He tossed his hair and Piper found themself distracted by the movement, drawn to watch his shiny locks.

"You want to tell our visitors a bit about the work we do here?" Richie asked, coaxing him.

"Oh uh." Kier looked at Richie. "They took me in about a year ago," Kier said. "Maybe a little longer. I'd come out of the river and gone into a town, I wanted to smell the people and see what they did all day."

With the redirection of his attention, Piper found themselves no longer distracted by his hair. Was that part of his fairy magic, to be extra charming? Piper supposed it made sense. If a kelpie wanted to lure someone into the water, they'd have to be alluring. But Piper didn't think there had been any malice or danger in Kier's actions. Was it was an unconscious thing? Or maybe there had been malice and they just didn't picked up on it yet?

"I found clothes and a place called a school and I tried to fit in..." Kier trailed off, eyeing Richie. "How much should I tell them?"

Richie shook his head. "Maybe skip to where you were rescued by Colin?"

Kier smiled, showing too many teeth. "There'd been some fighting. Colin found me in the road. I was trying to flood the town. It's not easy but I can raise the water up through the ground if I need to...but he shot me with a ..." he frowned. "The thing. It made me sleep."

"Tranquilliser?" Jack suggested.

"Yeah, a trank," Kier said, smiling easily. "And when I woke up I was here, and Colin and Richie explained about how in this world, we don't just eat and take and act on impulse. You have to think and consider others."

"And you're doing very well at that," Richie said. His expression was affectionate, watching Kier like he was a son or close friend. Piper sensed that whatever Kier had done on his own, he had been well looked after he arriving in the reserve.

"And what do you eat now?" Jack asked.

"Fish mostly." Kier nodded at the lake. "Unless one of the bigger things is hunting down there. Or I go into the bush for wild boar, they're delicious."

Piper smiled. "And are you getting any schooling?"

"Yeah, there's a great remote programme," Richie said. "A few times a week he uses the laptop and the dodgy Wi-Fi to get online and do some classes."

"I'm reading King Lear." Kier puffed up his chest. "It's delightfully bloody."

Emmaline giggled and Piper smiled as well.

"Of course, you'd love the tragedies," Jack mumbled.

CHAPTER 10

Jack couldn't deny that the young kelpie was charming, but her defences were up. She hadn't missed Richie had suggested Kier skip over some violence in his story. But it wasn't pertinent right now. In fact, as sweet as Kier seemed to be—Shakespearean tragedy affection aside —she wasn't sure why Richie had introduced them to him. She wanted to stay focused on the main problem.

"Kier, have you come across any mage hunters?" Jack asked.

Kier looked at Jack with confusion.

Richie cleared his throat. "Never up this way. Our 'turn back' charms on the road usually keep visitors well away."

"Hunters have a little magic of their own," Emmaline said. "They broke through some defences of mine, once..."

Richie folded his arms. "Well, if they did come out here, they'd have some trouble anyway. Between Kier, the larger inhabitants of the lake, and a few other things running round the bush here...they wouldn't stand much of a chance."

"How... How large are the large things in the lake?" Piper glanced back towards the lake.

"Er, quite large." Richie scratched the hair at the back of his neck and looked at the ground for a moment, contemplative. "I mean, you can come back at twilight when we feed them if you like?"

Piper folded their arms, suppressing a shiver. "I don't think so."

Emmaline shook her head. "You can't underestimate the hunters. They're enhanced, like super soldiers or something. There's a ceremony where they bind powers to them..."

Richie shook his head. "Never seen hide nor hair of any hunters out this way, and I've been working here for a while now."

"That's good," Jack said. "But we want to keep it that way as long as we can. The last thing we want is for them to come barrelling in and mess with what you have set up out here."

"And if there's one thing I know about hunters, it's that they don't want anything magical in the area, nothing magic left. If we can't stop them wiping out everyone in town, they'll head out this way." Emmaline wrapped her arms around herself.

Jack imagined the hunters breaking in and destroying the wildlife here and suppressed a shudder.

Despite her misgivings about past violence, and what Kier might do if he was left alone with say, Piper, Jack could see that he was better off here than out in the world. He ate fish and didn't attack people and had a huge lake and did home schooling. It was adorable really. Jack felt a growing need to protect this place and the folks who lived here. She turned to Richie.

He raised his eyebrows. "You want to know what's in the forest?"

Jack gave him a one-sided smile. "Obviously, my curiosity is piqued and I would love to know if there's werewolves, but that's not why we're here. Besides we don't want to treat your sanctuary as a zoo."

Rich grinned at her, apparently impressed by her answer. "Good. Come on back to the hut, then, and we can talk about defences and so on."

Jack nodded and turned to Emmaline. Kier and Piper were talking.

Piper handed Kier their business card. "Email me."

"Okay!"

"Makes friends everywhere they go, that one," Jack shrugged and followed Richie back to the hut.

Emmaline hurried to catch up with Jack, her expression troubled. "The problem is we don't know what we don't know. We don't know how many hunters we have to worry about, or where their targets are. For all we know they don't know a thing about this place."

"But on the other hand, they could be planning an attack here tonight." Jack frowned. "I'll see if we can get some constables out to watch the road, a kind of early warning system."

"I can maybe help Richie with the border charms as well," Emmaline said. "With your permission I could even bind a spirit or two at the four points..."

She skipped ahead to talk this through with Richie, leaving Jack to her own thoughts. She glanced behind to check Piper was following. They were with their phone raised, filming the trees.

If the hunters came out there, there were defences, like Richie had said. The charms would hold back some people, but Emmaline had walked through them without an issue. And if those came down, the workers, Colin and Richie would be around...somewhere. They hadn't seen Colin at all. Were there others working here as well? Then the things in the forest, Kier, whatever dangerous creatures were in the reserve, they could be anywhere. The reserve took up a huge space, encompassing hills and forest and lake... everything would be so spread out with no unified front to defend with.

But the solution... well, it was hardly to have constables stationed at the end of the road twenty-four seven from now until... the end of time? Until they could be sure there were no mage hunters coming? It wasn't reasonable. The police force was stretched tight as it was, and she couldn't exactly explain the need for assistance to Apanui.

Jack pushed her hair back from her forehead and clenched her jaw as they walked, her brain attacking the puzzle from multiple directions and coming up short each time. The goal was clear —protect the mages, the magical creatures and this whole place from harm. But the how, the solution, that eluded her.

The police force could do a lot, but Jack struggled to see how they could effectively help with this problem. Even managing the case with Edith Armstrong had been tricky at the end. Jack didn't like lying to her superior officer, but it had been the only way.

Jack chewed on her lip until they got to the hut. Richie invited them to sit on the folding chairs as he bustled around making tea and coffee. Jack leaned on the door frame and worried at the problem.

"What do you think the best thing we can do is?" Jack asked Richie. "We want to help, and we want to protect you and all the people... community... family?...you have up here. Make sure you spread the word to anyone else you know up here who's like you."

Richie spared her a glance over his shoulder and gave a tight smile. "I dunno, if they're determined to come here, they'll come here, I guess. But Colin and I will be ready for them."

Of course, both of them weren't just DOC workers. They were mages as well.

"What's your speciality?" Piper asked.

Jack blinked. She'd been so deep in her own head she'd barely remembered there were other people there. She took a seat and tried to focus on the room rather than her thoughts, curious to hear Richie's answer.

"Speciality?" He handed Piper a steaming cup of tea and then a coffee to Jack.

"Thanks. Yeah, like, Emmaline does things with spirits," Piper nodded at Emmaline. "And her brother does charms and things?"

"Oh, right, magic," Richie said. "Speaking with and understanding animals is my biggest one, some degree of communication with magical creatures as well. It's hard work, but this is the best place for me. And Colin's a plant witch, he loves to help the trees grow. Maybe..." He paused, his eyes unfocusing and his hand freezing halfway to handing Emmaline a mug of tea.

"Maybe?" Emmaline prompted.

"Maybe Colin could make the trees grow extra thick around the borders, put in some spikes and things..." Richie said.

"A good idea," Jack said. "Every extra bit of defence you can get."

Emmaline frowned. "I don't love the idea of twisting trees into weapons."

"It doesn't make a difference to the plants." Richie shrugged.

Jack's heart twisted but she shook her head. "We could be talking life or death here."

"Hopefully they don't find out about this place. We don't know how they're getting their intel." Piper breathed out heavily. "But I think they're recruiting online, through videos, so just... Be careful, I guess."

"Eh, I'm hardly ever online anyway." Richie chuckled, and patted the ancient looking laptop on his desk. "Just to file reports and read the emails from above. I don't even have a Facebook account."

"Probably for the best," Jack said.

CHAPTER 11

The drive back into Auckland was largely quiet, each of them lost in their thoughts. Jack and Piper planned to go back to the station. Emmaline asked to be dropped in town on the way. Jack pulled in on the crest of the hill, Victoria St West, where Emmaline could walk to any part of the inner city she wanted.

"Please be careful," Jack said without thinking as Emmaline got out of the car.

"I always am." Emmaline ducked back down to give Jack a warm smile before walking away.

Jack's cheeks heated, both from Emmaline's smile and for well, being so obvious about caring. Like she was Emmaline's girlfriend, and it was normal to be protective of her. They weren't together, and Emmaline was a grown woman, a mage with impressive magical powers, and she had travelled the world. It wasn't like she couldn't handle a walk through central Auckland.

But the mage hunters were out there somewhere, and they had surprised her before.

Piper nudged Jack in the elbow. "We should probably stop blocking the road and get to the station." They were suppressing a laugh, Jack could tell.

Feeling her cheeks burn even further she indicated and pulled back into traffic, relief flooding her when they got to the station.

"What are we going to do?" Piper asked, once they were out of the car and walking into the station.

"We're going to see if Apanui will spare some people to keep watch over the reserve," Jack said.

Sergeant Apanui was mercifully at her desk when Jack knocked on the door.

"Detectives," Apanui said. "Welcome. What can I do for you?"

Jack smiled, although she suspected it came off as a nervous grimace. She thought of the vulnerability of those in the reserve and used it to strengthen her resolve. "Sergeant, I want to request a police presence at a nature reserve up North. There's reason to believe they could be on the hit list of the terrorists we're trying to track."

Apanui frowned. "A nature reserve? These people are operating out of the city aren't they? We don't have any cases of them attacking wildlife."

Jack bit her lip. When Apanui put it that way it did sound kind of outrageous. She hesitated.

Piper took a half step forward. "I know how it sounds, Sergeant. But this isn't an ordinary reserve. The people who work there are Wiccan, like the victims of the murder. What's more, we've found out that there are people all over the country, people like them, who know about the place. If someone was to let the information slip, there's a chance the conspiracy theorists would target the reserve."

Apanui narrowed her eyes but didn't respond immediately.

Jack's heart leapt. That was a good sign. Piper glanced at her and she nodded, giving encouragement to continue.

"We're honestly not sure if such a thing would happen," Piper said. "But if it did, well, I can't imagine that we could keep the news media out of it. They'd be splashing stories about the endangerment of native animals, innocent DOC workers being harassed and they'd be asking us why it had happened."

"Hmm." Apanui folded her hands and inhaled. "I suppose a story like that would get a lot of attention."

"More than that." Piper's voice was tinged with passion now. Once again Jack was awed at the depth of feeling they could convey with just words. "We as police need to be protecting our most vulnerable, and that includes the non-humans. Even if it is a bit out of town."

"I suppose I could spare some constables. I'll talk to the stations on the North Shore and further up... Maybe between all the stations we could cover it for a few days."

Jack felt the tension in her chest release and suppressed a joyful smile.

"Thank you, Sergeant," Piper said. "We really appreciate that."

"But it's not something that can be done indefinitely," Apanui said. "So the pressure is on both of you to get this case sorted as soon as you can."

"Of course, Sergeant," Jack said. They had every intention of solving the case as soon as possible anyway. A little extra pressure wouldn't make a huge amount of difference—hopefully.

"I'll get on the phone to the other stations," Apanui said. "Give me the address of this reserve and I'll let you know how I get on in a couple of hours."

Piper wrote the address down on a piece of notepaper for Apanui and they left her to it.

"Nice work." Jack patted Piper's shoulder. "I don't think I could have got through to her in the same way."

"Thanks," Piper said. "But it's no big deal. You don't become a police officer unless you truly believe in doing the right thing."

They walked past Coleson on their way back out of the station. He was chewing on a pen and glaring at his computer screen as if it had personally offended him.

"I'm not so sure about that," Jack said. "But it's nice that you think so."

CHAPTER 12

Jack drove Piper home, then went to her own place. Now that things at the station were more or less sorted, Jack's mind was reeling over what they'd seen that morning at the magical reserve.

Fae kind living in the real world, well that wasn't exactly new. The Timaris opened doorways for a time, and the Wild Hunt travelled in and out at will. But fae creatures which didn't look entirely human, or not entirely, who wanted to live in this world was a surprise.

Kier's interest in human society, and in learning new things, trying to fit in, was a shock. Would it take? Was he even capable of making such a change? But watching Piper bond with him, Jack had felt a wave of affection, as though he was a teenager with a record of shoplifting who just needed some support and redirection to become a good kid again. Whatever good kid meant.

Jack sighed as she pulled her car into the park assigned to her townhouse and switched off the ignition. Part of her wished that she still lived alone, that she could go into an empty flat and find no one but her adopted stray cat. Then she could take her time and process things in peace.

At the same time she looked forward to seeing Emmaline. The conflict in her emotions was frustrating. Jack pushed her hair back from her face and groaned, annoyed with herself. If anyone could help with processing this, Emmaline was the best choice. She knew and understood magic. She could shed some light on the confusion Jack was feeling, maybe answer some of her questions, too.

Jack went inside.

Emmaline was in the kitchen, stirring something in a huge bowl she must have dug out of the very back of Jack's kitchen cupboard. She wore a cotton head scarf, keeping her long blonde hair off her face, and an apron, which she must have brought with her stuff. There was even an adorable smudge of flour on her cheek, completing the image of cottagecore domestic bliss. Jack's heart thumped uncomfortably, her stomach turning over with pleasant tingles and fluttering.

She wanted so much. Wanted Emmaline. But she was so afraid of diving into something without thinking. Before she was ready.

"Hey, Jacky, I'm making crêpes. I thought it might be comforting after the day you've had."

Jack swallowed hard. Emmaline had been worried about her, or at least, knew she'd be in need of comfort, and had done something about it. Emmaline was looking after her. Jack didn't know what to do with that.

"Oh. Crêpes? Sounds kind of perfect, to me." Jack fought the urge to slip her arm around Emmaline and kiss her cheek. They didn't have that kind of relationship. She smiled and nodded. "Thank you."

"You're welcome! Now, do you want sweet or savoury?"

"Uh...." Jack blinked. Had she ever had a savoury crêpe before?

"I'll just do both," Emmaline said, quickly. "Both are good, and then you can decide which you like best. Should be ready in, say, half an hour?"

"Thanks," Jack said. The relief of not having to make a decision, even one as simple as what to put on a crêpe, was incredible. Her shoulders loosened slightly. It's all taken care of. "I might have a quick shower then."

"Perfect." Emmaline turned back to the bowl and the curious domed pan on the stovetop. Another thing she must have brought to Jack's house.

Jack was deep in her thoughts as she washed off the day's grime. "How do I protect the innocent?" she mumbled into the stream of hot water. There were too many variables. Sure, they had the support of the police force for the moment, but that was a finite resource. As soon as a larger threat or headline worthy crime was committed, the force would be redeployed. They had to cut off this threat at the very root, which would be hard... all those videos. All those people making and sharing misinformation.

The people involved wouldn't divulge what they knew. They certainly wouldn't want to talk to the police.

Jack frowned as she massaged shampoo into her hair. Emmaline felt like another complication. That was an unfair conclusion, but that's how it felt. She had to, for now, ignore her feelings of attraction, instead focusing on the protectiveness Emmaline brought out of her. That would be motivation to solve the case fast. Once the threat was shut down, well, then she could examine what her feelings really were, what they meant and talk about them with Em.

She smiled, allowing herself an indulgent daydream of Emmaline as she rinsed her hair under the shower stream. Her long, soft blonde hair, her huge blue eyes, all doe-like and enticing... Her smile and the way she peppered French into her conversation when she forgot herself. That confusingly adorable accent which was a patchwork of British, some French and some Californian...

Jack shook her head and shut off the shower. Trains of thought like that wouldn't get her anywhere useful. She would focus on the protectiveness and get the damn case solved. After dinner she'd look up some of the videos Piper had sent her the links to and make notes. Tomorrow, they'd start knocking on doors.

CHAPTER 13

Piper got home on Wednesday to a messed up front door lock. It was scratched, tampered with. Someone had tried to get in—and failed. Piper silently thanked Emmaline for dropping by and putting a 'do not pass' spell on their door. They called it into the station, and sent photos of the damage to the building manager.

Their key still worked.

Piper hurried inside. "Lucifer?"

The rabbit didn't seem worried. She wiggled her nose up at Piper.

They changed her bedding, and gave her fresh water and new greens. This was a good physical task they could focus on to ease their nerves.

Once Lucifer was happily munching, Piper went into their bedroom and screamed. They did it into a thick cushion so as not to alarm their neighbours on any side, or the rabbit, but it was an urge they'd been fighting all day and had to give into.

Once they had got the scream out of their system, Piper sat down on the couch and did some deep breathing exercises. Their heart raced. Although they'd managed not to have a panic attack all day, something that needed to come out now that they were alone.

Process it all, but in a healthy way. That was the goal. They texted Jack about what had happened, asked if Emmaline could come over to put some more magic locks on the door, and thanked the building manager who had arranged for a change of locks the next day. For good measure, Piper set a chair under the doorhandle.

They made themself a soothing cup of chamomile tea and put it in their 'Just another day wishing I was at Disneyland' mug, before heading for the couch. A faux-leather bound journal lying on the side table caught their eye.

Piper had bought themself the journal over the weekend on impulse because it was so pretty. Now they thought of a good use for it—a record of all the weird and magical things they were learning about. A journal of the bizarre.

Next to the book was the paper bag it had come in, containing a hexagonal ballpoint pen with the inscription 'curiouser and curiouser.' Another impulse buy. The pens were right by the till and the inscription had made Piper smile. It all felt a bit too perfect, like the universe or some guiding hand had provided just the right tools when they hadn't even known they needed them.

If only they'd thought to do this weeks ago when they'd first discovered magic was real. Piper shook themself. There was always time to catch up.

Piper opened the journal, clicked the pen and swallowed. Should this have some kind of structure to it or should they just write down everything as they thought of it?

Structure, Piper decided. A double page spread for each subject they had encountered and what they knew about it, with space to add more information later if they learned more.

They got headed up pages with titles like 'Mages', 'Spirits of dead things' and 'Kelpies' and then got stuck into the work of remembering and writing down. An hour and a half later, their stomach rumbled. Piper realised that they hadn't had dinner and their tea had gone cold.

They turned to a blank spread and headed it up "Familiars", then looked at Lucifer doubtfully. They needed to know more.

They set the book down and got up to check the kitchen. They had a Cup Noodle that would be ready in three minutes, so they boiled the kettle and rummaged in the fridge for a drink.

Their phone buzzed in their pocket, and they took it out to see three messages from their brother, Ben.

They thumbed through them, just him checking in sort of messages. Piper hit the call button and set it on speaker. They were pouring water into the plastic noodle cup when Ben picked up.

"Hey Pipes," Ben said.

As always, his warm, cheerful voice soothed Piper. Something inside them which had been fluttering was at peace again. It wasn't gone perhaps, but it wasn't in distress anymore. "Hey bro, good to hear from you."

Ben's reply barely contained his laugh. "You called me."

Piper smiled. They clicked the camera on. "I know, but it's still good to hear your voice." Ben turned his camera on too, and they smiled at each other for a second before Ben yawned. "Oh god, how late is it? Am I keeping you up?"

Ben shook his head, shaggy hair flopping into his eyes. "Nah, I was thinking of going to bed soon but I hadn't done anything about it yet."

Piper checked the time—almost nine. It wasn't late for most people, but then, most people didn't get up at four in the morning to work on their sourdough and sugar cookies.

"I won't keep you long," they said. "Just had a bit of a weird day. A familiar voice is very welcome."

"I get that." Ben nodded. "You want to talk about it?"

"Do I want to talk about it? Yes. *Can* I talk about it? No." Piper was misusing the police confidentiality clause a little there. Hiding the existence of magic from her brother wasn't exactly the same as preserving the privacy of those affected by a crime, but it served the purpose. Piper looked down, stirring the water through the noodles. It still felt awful to lie to him. "Tell me about you, instead. How's the bakery?"

"So good. You know I told you that a food blogger who travelled through Christchurch did a review last week?"

"Mmhm?" Piper picked up the phone in one hand, the noodles in the other and went to their table, propping the phone up against a potted plant.

"Well, turns out they had a really huge following. Like, the review has been shared all over the place, I suddenly have a thousand more followers on my Instagram, well... More than that, and people messaging, asking me to do Tiktoks and start OnlyFans accounts on my selfies and all sorts of stuff."

Piper's eyes widened. "Really?"

"Yeah, and when I open in the morning there's always a queue outside. I'm trying to hire another kitchen hand and another front of house person just to keep up."

"That's awesome." Piper bounced in their seat and grinned. "No one deserves to go viral more than you do, Benny."

He smiled, and ducked his head to hide his smile, the slightest blush on his cheeks. "You're biased."

"You must be really making some money," Piper said, impressed.

"Yeah, it's kind of incredible." Ben grinned wider. "If this is going to continue, I might have to branch out..."

"Branch out how?" Was he hinting at moving up to Auckland to open another branch of his bakery? Piper swallowed their hope. Surely it was too soon?

"Well, we'll see. But I have been thinking you need someone to keep an eye on you."

"I'm the older sibling." Piper tried to sound outraged and incensed, but they were smiling too much. "I should be looking out for you."

"Well, maybe, but also you seem a little lonely and I miss you, so..."

"For your information I'm not lonely, I have a rabbit now."

"A rabbit? Show me."

"I'll send you a picture later."

"Okay, so, you think moving my business to Auckland is a good plan?"

Piper grinned so wide their cheeks hurt. "I'd love it if you could manage it."

"We'll see if this is a flash in the pan or if the customers keep on coming," Ben said. "That'll be the decider."

"Of course." Piper sat back and beamed at him. "I'm so proud of you."

Once they'd said goodbye, Piper felt a lot more relaxed. They played with Lucifer a bit, sent a picture to Ben. Finally, they opened up YouTube on their laptop, picking up where they left off on the conspiracy theory videos.

CHAPTER 14

Piper didn't need a pickup on Thursday so Jack went into the station alone. She sat at her desk with an extra strong coffee and a tension headache. This whole case was annoying her, because of the scope of it, and the unfairness of targeting the innocent, just because they happened to know about or use magic.

An hour later Piper emerged from deeper in the station. A black rabbit under one arm and several pieces of paper in the other hand.

"I got in touch with the techs at the station." Piper handed Jack a piece of paper as if Jack knew what this was about and had asked for it.

Jack blinked and cleared her throat. "Uh, can I have some context, please? And why have you got a rabbit under your arm?"

"Right, course you can." Piper shook their head once, as if laughing at themself. "First, this is Lucifer from the mages' apartment. Someone tried to break in and get to her I think, I'm getting new locks. Anyway, last night I was watching videos and found this one guy who seemed to really be trying to call people to action on his website. I checked it out and it was all 'sign in and use a VPN' and everything, and I didn't want to corrupt my hard drive or whatever." Piper paused to take a breath.

Jack smiled. It was good to see Piper so enthusiastic about a case.

"So I sent it all to the tech guys, and they sent back what they found on the sites, and tracked the IP addresses to real addresses in New Zealand and we finally have some people we can track down and interview."

Jack skimmed the piece of paper. "Good work, Piper. This is great stuff."

"Not just that." Piper suppressed a smile. "Sergeant Apanui has applied for search warrants. The judge must've been in a very good mood because they're through already. We can use them right away."

"Fantastic. Let's start with the closest one."

"That'll be Joseph Larson, online handle is AthensKnowledge221."

"You can't bring the rabbit with you."

"Um, I sort of have to." Piper had the decency to look sheepish. "She's in danger, she's like an animal mage. They could be searching for her right now."

"I can't believe this." Jack stared at the rabbit. "I didn't think anything could be more annoying than those damn fae."

Piper was eventually persuaded to leave Lucifer in the care of one of most trustworthy officers who was on phone duty and could keep an eye over her. But Jack felt like they wouldn't be able to avoid having the rabbit along next time.

They drove to the suspect's address; a fancy apartment building on the waterfront. Piper drove, because they'd said the week before that the inner city was intimidating to drive in, and Jack wanted them to get used to it.

Parking in that area was a pain, but eventually Piper found a spot and they made their way towards the huge building. A man in a red waistcoat and a superior expression greeted them at the door.

"Detective Duarte, and this is Detective Gage." Jack produced the warrant with the building's address on it. "We have a warrant, but we'd rather just door knock and be invited in. We're here to see Joseph Larson."

The man carefully looked over the paperwork and nodded. "Go ahead, Detectives. I'll unlock the lift for you. The Larsons are on the eighth floor."

"Thank you," Piper said, brightly.

He gestured for them to go to the lifts and leaned in to swipe a card over the security panel before pressing the eight button for them. "On the left, number 811."

"Thanks." Jack wondered just how often someone working his position would have been through this very procedure. People with this much money often worked slightly above or outside the law, in Jack's opinion. He hadn't seemed terribly surprised, but then perhaps that was part of his job, to just not react to events such as this. To just remain calm and professional whatever the circumstances.

Jack couldn't think of a worse job to have.

The lift was quick and silent, and opened onto a tastefully decorated corridor with plush grey carpet and potted plants with large leaves dotted here and there.

Jack led the way to the door marked 811 and knocked sharply. There was, of course, every chance that there was no one home. Would the doorman have mentioned if they were all out? Jack imagined he was paid to know things like that, so he could let in cleaning and service staff when they wouldn't disturb the residents.

The sound of footsteps approached the door and then it was opened. The man who stood on the other side looked just past his twentieth birthday. He was unshaven and half asleep, his eyes barely open. He wore what looked like expensive but well-worn work out gear.

"Yeah?" He looked between them and yawned.

"Joseph Larson?" He nodded. "I'm Detective Jack Duarte and this is my partner, Detective Piper Gage. We've got some questions for you."

"Oh?"

"May we come in?" Jack moved forward.

He pulled the door wider and took a step back in response. "Yeah, uh, sure. I don't know what this about though."

"Thanks." Jack and Piper walked into the apartment.

It was stunning. A huge black marble countertop dominated the kitchen area, which was immediately on the left. The kitchen overlooked a large living area with a neutral stone-grey carpet and white leather couches. The entire outer wall was glass, gigantic windows and ranch sliders with a generously sized tiled balcony outside. The view was stunning, all sparkling blue harbour and the white sails of yachts, the familiar shape of Rangitoto to the East.

Piper looked around, wide eyed.

Jack hardened her expression and pretended not to be impressed by the surroundings. Growing up as she had, moving place to place with her father every couple of years, she'd dreamed of having a permanent residence. Something like this was very appealing. Jack could see herself happily retiring to a fancy apartment like this someday, with no garden to tend. But she had to focus on the reason they were there, which had nothing to do with house hunting.

Joseph sat on one of three couches, arranged in a U shape. Jack sat on the one opposite his and pulled out her notebook and then her phone. "Do you mind if I record this conversation? It's mostly for me to refer back to."

Joseph eyed the phone with a certain level of suspicion but then nodded. "Sure. I have nothing to hide."

Jack set it to record sound and placed it on the glass top coffee table between them. "Thanks. So, Joseph, is your YouTube username AthensKnowledge221?"

Joseph's eyes widened. "Uh, yeah, it is."

Piper leaned forward, sitting on the couch in between Jack and Joseph. "You recently uploaded a video entitled '*the scourge on our innocent women*,' is that right?"

Joseph's cheeks went pink. He nodded. "Yeah."

"You're not in any trouble just yet," Piper said. "We need some information on who you've been talking to about this, and where you first heard about the existence of... how did you put it?" They checked their notes. "Uh, 'evil magical witches who want to turn men into mindless sex slaves.'"

Jack swallowed a sigh. She mustn't look like she was judging this man, no matter what tripe he published online. She schooled her face to be blank and unreadable.

Joseph hesitated. He looked between Jack and Piper, his face pale aside from the pink spots on his cheeks. Considering making a run for it? Some part of her wished he would so she had an excuse to tackle him. "Listen, you two are cops, I'm sure you're feminists, if what I said offended you, I'm really sorry but—"

Jack held up a hand and he went silent. "We're here because we're cops, not because we're feminists."

"Although we are," Piper added.

"We're here because two men were killed," Jack said. "And the reason they were killed appears to be because they were practising magic."

Joseph's eyes widened. For a moment there was a weird shiny quality to them. He frowned and shook his head. "I don't know anything about that."

Piper tilted their head to one side. "Joseph, we know you didn't have anything to do with the murders, but the community you're involved in online does. It's in your best interests right now to cooperate, to tell us whatever you know, so we can make sure you don't get into trouble for something which wasn't your fault."

Joseph's lip quivered. He swallowed again and stood up. "Okay, well, I guess you'll want to see the chat group I'm in, then..."

Jack grabbed her phone. "Yes, that would be incredible."

Joseph turned and then looked back sharply. "Wait, show me your IDs. And do you have a warrant?"

Jack produced the paperwork. They waited as he read it, his eyes checking her ID again and again. Jack's estimation of him went down a bit. For a conspiracy theorist it had taken him a long time to remember to ask to see their official IDs.

CHAPTER 15

Piper's heart went out to Joseph. He appeared a lonely young man who had found a community online who made him feel part of something. He had a beautiful and large place to live, but there was no sign of family at all. The house was decorated more like a showroom than a family home. Used cups of instant noodles stood on the bench and chip packets littered the part of the couch he obviously sat in. His room had an expensive looking laptop and three monitors attached to it, a chair which looked like the driver's seat of a race car and state of the art sound system, but the curtains were closed and the room smelled musty.

It would be easy, if you had no one else, to find a community online. Piper knew that from experience. When they'd been a teenager questioning their gender identity and trying to find a label which fit, they'd had an amazing community online. People who actually understood and gave them an outlet to try things out until they understood themself as well. Luckily for Piper, that community hadn't just been warm and welcoming, it had been kind as well. There had been no ulterior motive from the community's leaders.

The chat room that Joseph showed them had about fifty members. "This is just the New Zealand one." Joseph sounded defensive, as if he was pre-empting criticism. "There are a lot more worldwide, but they have their own groups of course."

"Of course." Jack scanned the member names and then clicked through some of the channels to read what people were saying.

To Piper's eyes, this was a front for something bigger. They wouldn't be planning murders and so on in such a forum. Although there did seem to be a lot of vitriol against a few different groups of people, it was mostly in the form of memes, doctored photos and jokes. Not pleasant, but not murder.

"These people, do you know them in real life?" Piper asked.

Joseph shrugged. "Some of them, yeah. A few of us meet up to shoot pool and have drinks every couple of weeks. There are some others, who take it a bit more seriously. They turn up sometimes, but just to meet and then they head out..."

Jack looked at him sharply. "Who are the ones who take it more seriously?"

"Uh." Joseph looked afraid again. "I don't want to go around pointing the finger and getting people in trouble."

"You'll just be helping us out," Piper said quickly. "You're not narking or whatever."

Joseph chewed his lip.

Jack straightened up and shot him what Piper recognised as Jack's *take no bullshit* face.

"It's up to you, Joseph," she said. "We're going to have to confiscate your laptop—there's information on here we need it for our investigation. But you can get it back, and you don't have to come down to the station with us right now, if you can answer our questions civilly and with as much information as you have."

"To the station?" Joseph's voice was losing volume. "You'd call my parents if that happened, wouldn't you?"

"Yes." Jack folded her arms. "What's it going to be, Joseph?"

Joseph wasn't the gambling type, and he should never try to be. His eyes bulged, sweat beaded on his forehead. Piper could see him weighing up the trouble he'd be in for talking to them versus the trouble he'd be in with his parents if they had to pick him up from the station.

He started to name names.

CHAPTER 16

The arrests were quick after that. They had five in the holding cell that same afternoon, all white men of varying ages.

Kevin Jones was one that Joseph had thought was quite high up. Unlike Joseph, he wasn't keen to talk to them.

Jack stalked up and down the room they were using to question him, tapping her fingers on the sleeve of her blazer.

Piper was sitting down, trying to appeal to him with their characteristic charm, but it didn't seem to be working. "We just want to get to the bottom of the whole thing. These two men are dead, and we want to make sure something like that doesn't happen again."

"I don't know anything about two dead men." Kevin sat idly, as if this kind of thing happened to him all the time. He was tall and muscular, spray tanned, with blond hair and cold blue eyes. He looked like he did CrossFit or long-distance running.

Jack was sure he was used to appearing intimidating to women of her stature, but she was so annoyed that nothing he said frightened her. "We think you do." She crossed the room and looked down at him. He gazed back at her steadily. "And I know you're used to getting whatever you want and there being no consequences, but this is different."

"You don't intimidate me," Kevin said.

"We have records of you saying some pretty hateful things online." Jack picked up the notes from beside Piper. "About how sometimes you like to follow women in the street, just to make them afraid. Just to see how they'll walk faster and start looking behind you. You know what behaviour like that sounds like to a cop?"

His eyes narrowed ever so slightly, and he grunted. Good. If he wasn't mouthing back at her, she had the upper hand.

Jack set the papers down. "So that's to start off with. There are plenty of security cameras around town we can use to find evidence of the times you've done that, which...Well, we know exactly when you've done that because you like to boast about it. But more than that, you've said some pretty inflammatory things to the other members of the chat. Fired them up. Told them to get out of their houses and have an effect on the real world. Do you deny that?"

Kevin's jaw worked and his eyebrows pulled forward, giving him the look of some kind of early evolution of homo sapiens. He didn't answer.

Jack let the silence stretch out, putting a hand on Piper's shoulder so that they didn't try and fill it.

"No," he said, finally. "I don't deny it. But so what? This country has free speech doesn't it? I wasn't telling anyone to go out and murder anyone."

"We don't have free speech in the way you're thinking of it," Jack said. "Yeah, you can say what you like, but if those things are classified as hate speech, or threatening violence, then you can be convicted for them."

Kevin's face pulled in on itself, he sucked his lips in and practically closed his eyes. "This is some bullshit."

"Our job is to protect people," Jack said. "And that includes from internet trolls who prey on lonely people and fire them up to a dangerous cause."

"Your job," Kevin said. "Is to serve the people, I'm one of the people, aren't I? What about my rights? You're just here for some agenda of your own, a snowflake agenda for the terminally offended."

Piper sighed. There was such sadness in it, Jack wished she'd sent them out of the room for this interview. Piper liked to believe the best of people, and Kevin was intent on showing them both the worst of himself.

"I'm sorry, who do you think is offended?" Jack asked politely.

"Snowflakes." Kevin leaned forward, bracing his elbows on his knees, his expression intense. "Bleeding heart professional victims who bring shit down on themselves for the attention and then pretend they didn't want it in the first place. If someone's hiding the truth about what they can do, and then getting upset when people punish them for it, it's their own fault. Stupid, pass themselves off as yoga instructors or psychics, mind readers. When really they have actual abilities to control minds and hurt people."

Piper inhaled and Jack squeezed their shoulder. She wasn't sure if she should urge Kevin on or if he'd remember they were in the room if she said anything. She bit her tongue.

Kevin barrelled on, working himself into a froth. He sat up straighter and clenched his hands into fists. "All these immigrants and they come in, take our jobs, and make people think they're happy with them. It's disgusting. People like that Matthew O'Brian, sleeping with a man old enough to be his father. Living like that, and messing with good hard-working people, for his own agenda."

"What did you do to Matthew O'Brian?" Jack said, quickly, her voice low to prompt rather than interrupt.

"Nothing." Kevin blinked, seeming to come back to himself. "Nothing at all. Just found out where they lived and what they were doing."

"And who did you tell?" Piper asked, in the same low tone Jack had used. "Who wanted that information?"

"I dunno." Kevin grinned and folded his arms, self-satisfied smirk stretching his face back out. "It's all anonymous."

CHAPTER 17

Emmaline looked at the day ahead of her, and felt energised, full of potential. She and Jack had agreed there was no need for her to go to the station on Thursday, so she went for a long walk. The area Jack's townhouse was in was picturesque, a blend of upper-class Epsom and hippie but also expensive Mt Eden... Neither and both at the same time, and it was within walking distance of Cornwall Park.

Cornwall Park had quickly become important to her since moving in with Jack. It was a naturally occurring magical space, which over a hundred years ago had been set aside as a reserve.

She had first discovered it on an aimless amble, but now she went there as often as she could to ground herself, tap into the mystical energy of the universe and relax. She'd found a plaque her first visit that said the park had been gifted to the people of Auckland by someone called Sir John Logan Campbell in 1901... It rankled Emmaline that he had owned what was the site of a former Māori settlement, surely it should have stayed with the local iwi, but such was the way in most English territories.

Cornwall Park was a sprawling ode to English countryside, stone walls, green pastures and tall imported trees scattered the landscape, built around One Tree Hill or Maungakiekie as it was properly called.

It wasn't just picturesque though. Cornwall Park was a working farm with flocks of sheep and herds of cows. Every so often she would see chickens or some guinea fowl in her wanderings. But the magical draw of the place was impressively large. It attracted all sorts of people. The park was busy at all times of day with dog walkers, parents with young children and joggers. Perhaps it was just because it was a nice park that it was busy, but she thought the energy source had a part in it too. Even if the man jogging past with the marathon winner tattoo couldn't feel it, the air in the park sparkled with power.

Emmaline made her way to the grove of olive trees, halfway up the small mountain, using the winding walkway that followed the road up to the bistro. She climbed over the stone fence and sat with her back to one of the olive trees, looking out over the broad view of Auckland city and the harbour beyond. It was a lovely day, bright and sunny, and the horizon had a haze over it.

She toed off her shoes, peeled off her socks and stuck her feet into the grass, feeling the coolness of the earth below.

The visit to the reserve the day before had got her wondering if there was more that she could be doing to serve her community... and that question had brought with it a revelation.

She didn't want to leave New Zealand any time soon.

Unlike her previous travels over the last five years. That travel had been business, in a way, finding places to study with a particular purpose, to stay at a monastery or with a particular teacher. She had come to New Zealand out of curiosity. But now that she was here, and had got to know Jack and Piper, she found herself quite comfortable.

It was an odd thought. She'd always imagined herself settling down in Paris, or perhaps somewhere close to her older brother in the United States... but now the idea of leaving Auckland, of leaving Jack, was abhorrent to her.

She sighed, tipped her head back until it rested on the bark of the tree and smiled to herself. Well, as long as she was useful in investigations there was no reason not to stay. It was still a strange feeling, but as she breathed in the clean air of the park and felt the gentle tingle of energy passing from the ground through her and up into the tree, she decided she could be comfortable with it.

She stayed like that for a while, meditating on the sounds—the wind through the leaves in the trees, the people walking past and chatting, the distant sound of traffic and the occasional plane passing overhead.

Letting her thoughts pass by without fixating on them. Losing herself in the sounds around her, and her awareness of the world.

Finally she felt totally at peace and made her slow way back to the townhouse she shared with Jack.

Something was wrong with the door. The charms and protective sigils she had cast were still there, mostly, but they had been disturbed. It was exactly the same vague corruption that she'd seen at the apartment downtown.

"Hunters..." Emmaline's heart sped up. She closed her eyes, focusing all her magical energy on the sigils. With enough concentration she could sense when the disturbance had happened. And hopefully, if the people who did it had left again.

It took a moment. She reached out invisibly with tendrils of her power, her mind forming one question 'when?' It had been two hours, and the sigils had been passed twice by two people. Entering and exiting.

She turned, pressed her back to the door and looked up and down the street. If they were still around, they could be watching her right that moment...

She could see nothing out of the ordinary. A woman was walking a small child in a pushchair on the other side of the quiet side street. The traffic on the busy road at the end of the street was as noisy as ever, buses and four-wheel drives and every now and then a cyclist. The door of the house beside Jack's opened and the elderly man who lived there came out, a limp shopping bag in his hand. That reassured her more than any of the other signs of apparent normality.

"Good afternoon, Mister Yee." She lifted a hand to wave at him. "How are you?"

"Very well, thank you Emmaline," Mr Yee said. He eyed the door behind her and shook his head slightly. "The men from the electric company came by and let themselves in. Jack didn't say to expect them, and you weren't home. Very odd."

"Very odd indeed." Her heart thumped. Mr Yee had spoken to them; he'd be able to identify them. That was good. "We weren't expecting anyone at all."

Mr Yee frowned. "They had a key so I thought it was alright. I'll keep an eye out for them coming back. I watched when they left but they didn't take anything. Maybe the landlord organised it and forgot to tell you?"

"Thank you, Mr Yee. But don't speak to them again. It's best if they don't know you're around. I don't think they're really from the electric company."

"Hmmm." Mr Yee walked a few steps and then turned back to look at her. "You be safe now."

"Thanks, Mr Yee, I will."

He walked up the road and to the shops. Emmaline pulled out her phone to call Jack. The call went right to voicemail and then the phone shut itself down. This happened sometimes with mages and technology. Magic energy messed with the way tech worked. Emmaline was quietly impressed the phone had lasted as long as it had. Her high state of agitation was affecting her magic and in turn it had fried the phone.

"Fuck fuck fuck." She let herself into the flat and looked around. There was little evidence anything untoward had happened, but Emmaline could smell something unfamiliar. Cheap men's cologne.

She tried to turn the phone on again but it remained steadfastly off.

She eyed the landline. Less technology to mess with there. She picked up the receiver and dialled the police station. It took a few minutes to get put through to Jack. With every second that passed, she got jumpier. At any moment the hunters could return, burst through the door and try to kill her.

She went into her room and packed a few essentials into her large duffel bag.

"This is Duarte," Jack said. Her voice was flat, all business.

"Jack, it's Emmaline. Hunters have been here, in the flat."

"What?"

"Yeah, I know. I tried to text but my phone died. I can't stay, if they're watching they could be here at any time and they messed with my sigils." Emmaline paused to take a breath, grabbing the book from beside her bed and then the boots from under it and shoving them into the bag. "I can't stay."

"I agree." Jack's voice had gone hard and tight. Emmaline knew she was angry. "Where will you... no, don't tell me. It's best if I don't know."

Emmaline shook her head, forgetting that Jack couldn't see her. "I'm going to Gerard's. They can't follow there."

Jack huffed into the phone at her end. "Good. Uh. How can I contact you? If something happens?"

"Uhhh..." Emmaline paused, trying to think. Jack, without magic powers, couldn't activate the mirror to get in touch with her. "Valerie. She can find me with the mirror." Her stomach dropped as she said it, feeling guilty and awkward that there wasn't an easier way to contact her. But there was nowhere safer. "And I'll check in on you when I can."

"Right," Jack said. "Be safe. I guess I'll stay somewhere else as well, or...set a trap or something."

"You be safe. Oh and Mr Yee from next door saw them, they said they had a key and were from an electric company. He can ID them."

"Which side does he live on?" Jack asked.

Emmaline tsked her tongue against her teeth. "How many years have you lived here?"

"Maybe four years."

"It took me moving in for you to get to know your neighbours. *C'est pathétique, Jacqueline.*"

A pause. Jack cleared her throat. "Yeah, I know. Pathetic." It could have been her imagination, or distortion over the line, but it sounded as if Jack was holding back some emotion.

Emmaline felt her fear turn into sadness. She blinked back sudden tears. This wasn't goodbye forever, or anything like that. No need to get dramatic.

"I'll see you soon," she said, her own voice husky. "Stay safe and look out for Piper."

"Yeah, get out of there." Jack sounded a bit more like herself again. "I'll handle it from here."

"*Au revoir.*"

Emmaline hung up the phone, swiped her sleeve over her eyes and shook her head. No need to get weepy. Just get in touch with Gerard and get out.

She turned to the small wall mirror and started the spell.

CHAPTER 18

Arranging some surveillance over Jack's house was short work. She awful. Her stomach clenched every time she thought of people sneaking in to find and hurt Emmaline. The violation of her private space almost didn't register because she was so sick at the thought of something happening to Emmaline. An unmarked van was deployed to park on the street with two plain clothes cops and strict instructions to apprehend anyone trying to gain access to the house.

"The fact is," Jack said to Piper. They were seated in the break room, drinking coffees. Piper had the rabbit on their lap, after being informed that they couldn't just leave it with people who had jobs to do. "The fact is, we need Emmaline on this case, and now we can't have her. We have no way of knowing if any of these guys have real magic or not."

Piper grimaced into their coffee mug. "Yeah. But all of the magic users are in danger right now. All of them, and we can't protect them, not really."

Jack's stomach wrapped itself in a tight knot. "Yeah."

"On the bright side, we've arrested a lot of the local people involved in the movement." Piper set their mug down and leaned in, resting a hand on Jack's arm. Comforting her. "And while you were dealing with the surveillance guys, Wellington came through with ten more arrests, including that one with the really big channel. So hey, we're getting closer."

"Yeah, we just need to..." Jack lifted her hand to push her hair back, dislodging Piper's hand. "We need to find the actual killers. These people who have the channels and stuff, they're a part of the problem, but it's awfully hard to connect them to any actual crime beyond hate speech."

"Yeah." Piper frowned and petted Lucifer.

Jack felt bad for ruining their bright side. But she felt clean out of bright sides. "And no one we've arrested has the brand, the tattoo thing that Amy had, which means that although they're involved, they're not proper Mage Hunters. They haven't been...inducted or whatever it is."

Piper tilted their head to one side. "Maybe it's like a pyramid scheme thing. You have to earn the right to the next level up."

Jack picked up her pen and noted down 'pyramid scheme.' "I think that's exactly what this is like. Or a terrorist organisation where you only know for sure who one or two people are, so you can never rat out the whole lot. Or the people who are in charge."

They stared at each other, Piper puzzled, Jack frustrated and a bit afraid.

After a moment, Jack sighed. "We really could use some outside help. Someone with actual insight." She didn't say magic, as another officer had just walked in to microwave their lunch. "Is Valerie staying around town?"

Piper nodded. "She said the shop was secure against all comers."

Was there any chance that Emmaline's brother, and his ex-hunter girlfriend could come and help? There was really no way to justify their appearance to Sargent Apanui and the paperwork would be a complete nightmare, but...it felt like they needed more firepower than they had. Amy, as an ex-Hunter, would know a lot more about the organisation and how it worked.

But she'd have to wait for Emmaline to contact her.

"What are you going to do tonight?" Piper asked.

"I have to go home, act normal," Jack said. "If whoever broke in notices that we're neither of us home all of a sudden, they might back off. I want to draw them to attack and then we have the arrests."

Piper pulled a face. "I want to come as well. I hate the thought of you alone, just waiting to be attacked."

Jack smiled, despite the roiling emotions and the pressure of the puzzle weighing on her. "That would be very sweet of you."

CHAPTER 19

Jack drove them both home, more comforted by Piper's quiet presence and the snuffling of Lucifer more than expected. Their rocky beginning as partners had blossomed into something like true friendship, and Jack was glad of it. After many years she had become accustomed to working alone, relying on no one. Having a trustworthy person by her side made things easier to bear.

She parked the car in her normal spot on the road and let Piper and Lucifer in.

"What do you feel like for dinner?" Jack asked. "I'll cook something."

"Oh, just whatever you have lying around is fine," Piper said. "I'm not fussy. But if you have some cabbage or carrots, Lucy would like them."

"Sure." Jack found some cabbage in the fridge and pulled leaves off, putting them on a saucer on the floor beside Piper.

Piper had their phone out. A soft smile played about their face as they replied to a text. Jack's curiosity got the better of her. "Who's that?"

"Ah, my brother," Piper said. Distracted, they typed a bit more then looked up at Jack. "My baby brother. His bakery's gone viral big time, and he's talking about moving up to Auckland to open a franchise."

"Up to Auckland? That's great news. I'd like to meet him. Might shed some light onto why you are...how you are." She smiled so Piper would know she was teasing.

Piper chuckled. "It might, although he's very different to me."

Jack went into the fridge, closed the door and picked up the landline. "Let's order in, I don't think my energy is right for cooking any of that."

Piper eyed her. "What's your energy right for, then?"

Jack shrugged. "Eating Indian food and trying to puzzle out how to solve a gigantic puzzle."

"Sounds good to me."

They ordered bhaji, tandoori chicken skewers, Rogan Josh curry and rice. While they waited for it to arrive, Jack got some beers out of the fridge. They cracked them open, sitting on the couch. Jack wasn't sure what to say. She wanted to work on the case, but at that moment all she could think about was how Emmaline wasn't there.

Her absence in the townhouse was like a presence itself, tangible. There was no soft humming of a song Jack didn't recognise. No gentle scent of vanilla from Emmaline's shampoo, no sense of movement.

"Are you okay?" Piper moved closer on the couch and put a hand down between them.

Jack realised she'd been staring into her beer as if it held the answers. "Um." Jack swallowed, pulled her eyebrows together and nodded. "Yeah, just. Emmaline leaving was...a bit of shock."

"Yeah," Piper nodded. "How about we put on some TV or something while we wait for dinner? We could just distract ourselves for a bit. Sometimes it helps me think better."

Jack picked up the remote and turned on a game show. It was a delightfully daft one in played on a giant video screen floor called Five Gold Rings. Watching this show and yelling at the contestants when they got the placement wrong was one of Jack's guilty pleasures.

"Oh, I've not seen this episode." Piper tucked their feet under them and took a swig of beer.

"You watch too? It's ridiculous," Jack said. "But so fun."

Piper was right. Forgetting about the case and about Emmaline being gone, even for a few minutes, was soothing. It allowed Jack's shoulder muscles to relax, and the tension headache from clenching her teeth eased.

By the time their dinner arrived, Jack felt refreshed in a way she hadn't expected to. Yelling at the TV had released some of the energy she'd been bottling up, and a little of the frustration as well.

When she opened the door to the delivery person from the Indian food shop, she saw the surveillance van had gone.

Jack's phone buzzed. She hurriedly thanked the delivery woman and closed and locked the door before answering. "Duarte here."

"Jack, it's Constable Lee." Suzan Lee was often on the phones at the station, she had a knack for it.

"Hey Suzan."

"Just calling because two men have been apprehended outside your house. There was minimal fuss. The officers on patrol caught them fiddling with your front door and arrested them. They're in the holding cell, waiting for processing. We'll get your neighbour tomorrow morning to identify if they were the same two. Just in case there are others involved we'll send another car in to watch overnight."

Jack's chest loosened and she even managed a smile. "That's great, thank you Suzan."

"No worries, you get a good rest tonight, okay?"

"Sure. Take care."

Jack hung up and made her way up the narrow stairs. "Good news, rookie! While we were yelling at the TV, they arrested two men trying to get in."

Now, maybe Emmaline can come back, Jack thought.

CHAPTER 20

Piper watched Jack as they both ate. The news that two men had been arrested had lightened the mood, but they sensed that there was more she hadn't expressed yet. Something still weighing on her mind that maybe Piper could help with.

The curry was delicious and soothing. Piper gave Jack time to be silent and think things through, but it was a careful balance. By now Piper knew that too much time inside her own head would lead Jack to brood, and then obsess and stop sleeping.

Lucifer hopped over to Piper's feet and looked up at them with big eyes, so Piper picked her up and settled her on their lap, petting her slowly.

Jack helped herself to seconds.

Piper cleared their throat. "So, uh, how are you feeling? Like, really feeling?"

Jack's eyes met theirs with a distinct deer-in-the-headlights expression.

"I know that was abrupt of me to ask. But a lot has been happening, and talking things through helps me so maybe it'll help you too?"

Jack sighed, tore a strip off her roti and nodded. "I miss Emmaline." She looked first surprised then then regretful. "Urgh, I sound pathetic."

Piper shook their head. "Not at all. I miss her too, and I don't have the same..." Piper hesitated from saying relationship. They knew it was a sticky subject between Jack and Emmaline. "Proximity," they said, finally. "I mean, you went from having a roommate to not, so."

"I had no one around before her," Jack said. "I should be used to it."

"Okay, but it's normal to miss someone." Piper said softly, inviting Jack to be a bit more vulnerable with them. To open up.

Jack didn't reply for a while. Piper finished off their dinner and dabbed at their mouth with a napkin, letting Jack have her time if she needed it.

"I was used to her," Jack said. "And this case is doing my head in. I don't know how we can ever finish it off. How we can get to the bottom of something so nebulous and strange? How do we find someone who's used to being invisible online and in the real world?" Jack sighed heavily.

"We'll get there," Piper said. "I know we will. I'm not sure exactly how, but we will. And Emmaline will be in touch, and we can tell her it's safe to come back."

Jack scrunched her face up. "It's not safe for her to come back, though."

"They arrested the guys, didn't they?"

"Those two," Jack said. "But someone obviously knows that she was here, that this place is, I dunno, a haven or something for magic users. They'll just send someone else."

Piper frowned, their stomach sinking. Lucifer shuffled in their lap and huffed a sigh, falling asleep. "I hadn't thought of that."

Jack rubbed her forehead. "We need to solve it. She can't come back until we can be sure that no one's going to come knocking."

Piper smiled softly and reached out to touch Jack's other hand where it rested on the table. "You want to protect her." Jack looked up, mouth opened, about to protest, so Piper barrelled on. "I do too, and I want to protect Kier and the reserve, and Valerie, all our friends who aren't exactly normal. We will. We'll solve this. You're brilliant, Jack. I asked to be partnered with you for a reason. I'll do some more digging online, try and find the anonymous person behind this, and we'll solve it."

Jack closed her mouth and managed a lop-sided smile. "Thanks Piper."

"I mean it." Piper squeezed Jack's hand and let go. "I don't just say this shit to sound good. I believe in you, and I believe in me. Together we can do anything."

Jack's mouth twisted to the side. She chuckled and shook her head. "Okay, okay. I'm gonna get mushy if you keep going, so that'll do."

"Okay." Piper grinned.

Something scratched at the window. They both looked over to see Jack's broad shouldered orange tomcat asking to be let in. Piper put a hand on Lucifer to keep her in place as Jack hopped up and opened the window.

"Hey sweetie," Jack said, her voice softer, higher. "You're a bit late for dinner tonight, mate."

Piper felt a wave of affection for the grumpy, messed up detective, pleased that they had in some way been able to get her smiling again.

CHAPTER 21

Jack dropped Piper home. They let themself into their apartment, humming. They set Lucifer down on the ground to run around while they changed her bedding for clean straw. They felt good, humming a song as Lucifer hopped around the living room, making herself at home.

Piper washed their hands and sat down on the couch and picked up their laptop. Lucifer hopped to them and sat on their haunches, looking up at them with bright eyes.

"Do you want to come up?" They leaned down and lifted the rabbit up onto the couch.

Lucifer sniffed around, investigated the cushions and then sat down beside their thigh, leaning against it.

"Awwww..." Piper grinned and took a photo from a high angle, framing themselves and the rabbit and sending the photo to Ben.

Piper: Lucifer says hi

Ben responded within a minute.

Ben: Hi Lucifer. By the way, you never told me how did you get a rabbit? And why?

Piper: Her owner was killed, so... I adopted her.

Ben: why is her name Lucifer?

Piper: you called your dog Captain Brick you don't get to judge me, Benny boy.

Ben responded with a rude emoji.

Piper laughed. "Well, Lucifer, I don't know if you've decided to be my familiar or what, but I appreciate the moral support."

Lucifer snuffled closer.

They opened their laptop and went into the research rabbit hole again. "Heh, rabbit hole." They scratched Lucifer gently between her floppy ears. "Maybe I need a better term for it, now."

The YouTube trail had largely gone cold. The same channels were still up but no new videos had been uploaded. Piper spent a little time on social media tracking the known suspects but their feeds had also gone cold.

They suspected it meant they had gone deeper into a private website, or possibly created new accounts. Maybe the online community had given all it would for the moment. They shut their laptop and pulled Lucifer onto their lap, petting her fur until she went to sleep.

On Friday morning Jack picked Piper and Lucifer up. Piper could hardly control their energy, and their leg bounced as Jack drove. Lucifer was safe in a sling bag they'd found in the back of their wardrobe. "The online stuff has kinda died out. I reckon we could go and talk to Val, see if there's anything she can do to track down the anonymous people."

"Sure," Jack said. "I don't have any better ideas, and besides, maybe she can get a message to Emmaline as well."

"Perfect."

Jack drove them to the Full Moon magic shop on Karangahape Road. Valerie was waiting in the doorway.

"It looks like we were expected," Jack said, dryly.

Piper couldn't help laughing. "Magic is so cool. I love this."

"I'm glad you're not as afraid of it any more, Piper," Jack said.

Valerie smiled as they got close. "Morning you two, wait—" Her eyes fell on the sling, "—you three. The kettle's just boiled." She waved them closer. "Chamomile? Or something for some energy?"

"Energy," Jack said immediately. "Please."

Valerie escorted them inside and shut the door behind. She peered into Piper's bag and cooed as Lucifer stuck her face out of the opening. "Hello sweetheart, how are you?"

Lucifer twitched her nose at Valerie and then curled back into the bag.

"She's very sweet, and rather powerful," Valerie said.

"Good to know. I guess you knew we were coming." They had to know more about the how of it, their own energy demanding answers where they might have been a bit too shy to ask on another day. "Did you uh, scry? Or see us coming in a crystal ball?"

"Not exactly." Valerie gave Piper a soft, indulgent look. "But I saw two familiar people in my card reading for the day. That and a message from Emmaline. I was going to call you today, Jack, just to check in on you for her."

Jack visibly perked up, her eyes widening. "You've heard from her?"

Valerie ushered them both into her back room where the comfy couches were. "She left a note, so to speak. I haven't talked to her directly."

"Oh." Jack sat down on the couch and sighed.

"But that's good, that means she's safe," Piper said, as brightly as they could manage.

"Indeed," Valerie said. "She said she's in the spare room at Gerard's house, and looking around for anything that can help from that end."

Piper noticed that Valerie didn't directly refer to the fae realm. Was that something to do with the nature of the magic Valerie did, or if it was more akin to a superstition?

Valerie had already got out some mugs and was looking through her glass jars of home blended tea. "Did you want the same as Jack, Piper?"

"Oh, uh, something more calming might be nice," Piper said. "Please."

"Of course."

There was a comfortable silence as Valerie made the tea. Piper moved around the room, not touching anything, but reading the spines of the books Valerie kept on the shelves and eyeing the jars of dried herbs and other specimens for spellcasting.

There was a small altar set up in one corner, a brightly coloured scarf covering a portion of the workbench. Piper stopped in front to examine it. There was a tall white candle, a small crystal bowl half full of water, some crystals arranged in front and a bundle of what looked like rosemary stems. There was also a jar of dried bay leaves and a small box of matches. In pride of place at the front was a deck of cards. Tarot cards, Piper guessed from their size and the pattern on their back.

Piper felt drawn to it. The altar emanated safety and welcome, as if inviting them in to learn more. Their chest warmed, and they found themself smiling at the cards, although they didn't touch them.

In the bag, Lucifer shifted, poking her face out of the opening again. She looked at the alter with interest.

Pinned to the wall behind the altar were some pictures of what looked like deities or magical beings from Celtic myth. Piper didn't want to ask about it and seem gauche, or risk prying into something private, so they moved back and sat with Jack on the couch, pulling Lucifer out of the bag to sit on their lap.

Valerie handed them their cups of tea and set one down for herself. Before she sat down, she collected her deck of cards from the altar. Valerie shuffled them as she got comfortable.

"I'm guessing that you two are here for information, for some kind of lead," Valerie said. "In my reading, the cards said there were questions and that I could probably help."

"Please," Jack said. "Anything at all would help. The hunters have been doing this for so long, and they're practiced at going unnoticed."

Valerie nodded and shuffled the cards ten seconds longer, before offering the pack to Jack. "Cut the deck and give it a bit of a shuffle, will you?"

Jack did as she was told.

Piper watched enviously. They'd always wanted a proper tarot deck for themself, but they were so expensive. Besides they'd read somewhere that you weren't supposed to buy your own deck, but have it gifted to you. Then they'd gotten busy with police training and their interest had fallen by the wayside.

Jack handed the cards back to Valerie, who laid her hand over the back of them and closed her eyes, taking a slow breath before smiling softly. "Perfect."

She leaned forward and started to deal onto the coffee table. Four cards in a sort of circle. Another card fell out of the pack while she was dealing them.

"The fool?" Valerie set the rogue card on her lap, put the rest of the deck aside and looked at Piper and Jack. She touched the card at the top of the spread and turned it over. "This one is the Moon. This represents the nature of the challenge, what you need to know about it and, well, maybe you know this already but maybe you don't. The Moon is intuitive, speaking to things hiding in the dark, the danger of losing your way, but also dreams and a certain amount of feminine power."

She turned the second card over, the one on the left-hand side. "This is your strength, what the two of you both bring to the challenge and your greatest asset for the trials to come. It's the King of Swords, he's good. He's powerful and ready for a fight. Sharply intellectual, cutting through deception with his blade."

Jack's knee started to jiggle. Piper could see she wanted to know more. But they felt like Valerie would tell them in her own time. In their lap, Lucifer moved around, snuffling and sniffing before lumbering over Piper's thigh and onto Jack's lap instead. Her knee went still.

"This card," Valerie continued, touching the card on the right-hand side of the spread. "This card is your weakness, it's what might get in the way, it might slow you down or cause you to self-sabotage while you fight..." Turning it over she revealed the Queen of Swords. "Oh, very interesting. She is a sharp mind, independent and analytical..." Valerie hummed for a moment and then touched the very last card. "This is the advice the cards and the universe have for you. How you can use your strength to counterbalance your weakness and face the challenge in the best way." She turned the card over and frowned slightly. "The Hierophant, pursuit of knowledge, and the weight of tradition. This is an interesting reading..."

"So, what does it all mean?" Jack blurted.

"Give me a moment," Valerie said. "I need to look at what all these cards mean, not just in their position in the spread, but in relation to each other. You have two... three..." she glanced at the card on her knee. "Three of the major arcana cards, and then the two royals from the swords suit."

"Did you say our strength was sharp intellect, but then it's our weakness as well?" Piper tilted their head to the side.

Jack glanced at Piper and then back at Valerie.

Valerie shrugged. "The card's meaning isn't always clear, let me think for just a moment... The Queen of Swords, when she turns up in the negative, can indicate that you are in danger of alienating others, people who may not understand the world as you do, or may not think in the same way as you do. She can be isolating."

Piper bit their lip. Jack certainly seemed to think a few steps ahead when she got her teeth into a good mystery. But then, the case was so wrapped up with people who thought differently to them, and who had become isolated from the world. If that was the weakness, then the solution would be understanding and compassion, wouldn't it? Slowing down to understand and to get others to understand...

"The King of Swords, he is authority. He can mean legal action, a determined man who makes decisions and has what it takes to get the job done. It sounds like you are in a very good position to use your resources to solve the case."

Jack stroked Lucifer's back slowly. "So, use our intellect and our position but don't alienate people, Okay." She smiled sadly. "My entire career has been about alienating people so, I'm very familiar with how it could be a weakness."

"It may mean inviting more help," Valerie said. "What's the opposite of isolation?"

"A community?" Jack pursed her lips. "Hmm. And the hierophant, what's he about again?"

"The universe's advice to you... The Hierophant can represent teachings, a mentor or teacher character, but it's also scholarship and philosophical intellect. Tradition and ritual are indicated, but that doesn't necessarily mean sticking to the same path you always have. It could be about learning new rituals or ceremonies." Valerie paused, straightened her back and took a sip of tea before continuing. "He is a deeply spiritual character, so it does indicate you need to connect more to how you understand magic, the world around you, and take inspiration from your own spirituality, however you understand it."

Piper sat back, making a 'hmm' noise. They hadn't been considering their own spirituality at all. Their notebook was about the things they'd learned and noticed, but less about how it had affected how they understood their place in the world.

"And what about the moon, you said it was sort of night-time stuff?" Jack asked.

"Right, a deeper reading of this card shows the link between the domestic and the wild. How are you following your instincts, how are you using your psychic energy?"

"I don't have any psychic energy," Jack said.

"Everyone has a touch." Valerie looked between them. "But I do feel more of something from Piper, I think. Maybe this card is trying to urge you, Piper, to listen to your dreams, and do some work on your creative practices, encouraging your own psychic gifts."

"My what?" Piper's hand went to their chest in surprise. They shook their head. "My psychic gifts? I don't...have any."

Valerie chuckled and tapped the Moon card. It showed two dogs, or maybe a dog and a wolf, baying at the moon. Then she looked significantly at Lucifer. "Inside you are two forces, well, more than that, but see the scorpion as well? The domestic, and the wild. You need to find some balance."

Piper swallowed, their mouth suddenly dry. Their stomach turned over, threatening to cough tea back up as their heart raced. They didn't want psychic powers. Being told you were a part of the thing which scared you the most... Was there some way to turn off whatever Valerie had sensed inside them?

"You okay, Piper?" Jack squeezed their shoulder.

Piper set their teacup down and leaned forward, trying to suck in some air. After a moment, it worked. They sat back up, their head spinning a little less. Lucifer hopped back into Piper's lap and put her front paws on their chest, clearly concerned.

"I guess I'm panicking a bit. I don't mind learning about magic, but the idea that it's inside me?" They shook their head and cupped a hand around Lucifer's back.

"Okay, you want to get some air? Head outside?" Jack asked.

Piper slipped their other hand onto their stomach and focused on breathing, so their belly pushed out. They exhaled as slowly as possible. "No, finish the reading, please."

Valerie handed Piper a glass of water. They hadn't even noticed her getting up. She took her seat again.

CHAPTER 22

Jack's gaze flicked between Valerie, Piper and the cards. She wanted to know more, but she was worried that Piper was in a panic state. The implication that Piper was more spiritual, or more in tune with the forces of magic didn't surprise Jack in the least, but she didn't like the effect it seemed to be having on them.

Valerie cleared her throat. Jack's gaze snapped back to her. She needed to focus, to learn as much as possible from this reading.

"The Fool." Valerie tapped the card with one finger. "It's the very first card in the deck, and despite its name it doesn't mean anything negative. The fool is someone filled with the joy of life, and the awakening of the spiritual inside them."

Jack looked back at Piper, still ashen around the cheeks and looking like they were concentrating too hard on breathing. Lucifer was a small ball of fluff in their lap, possibly responding to the panic?

Valerie was looking at Piper too.

"So," Jack said slowly. "It sounds like both the sword people, they're kind of... me. I use my intellect and I alienate people, I'm pretty isolated, or at least I was before Emmaline and Piper... Both of us have the position in the police to take action and make decisions and all that, but..."

"They do have a very Jack energy to them." Valerie nodded. "I do think the Moon and the Fool cards are more about Piper, though."

Piper sucked in another breath and then took a drink of water. "Yeah." Their voice was strained but louder than before. "I think so too. I don't know if I have any gifts or anything, but I have been fascinated by the world of magic and it's changed how I look at the world. I do want to tap into something more spiritual for sure." They swallowed hard.

Jack's hand was still on their shoulder. She squeezed it again. Part of her wanted to protect Piper from all this as well. To keep them somewhere safe, where they wouldn't panic about the unknown. But that was unfair. Piper loved it, even if it scared them. And they were too good a partner to give up on.

"So, the universe's advice. What did that mean again?" Jack started.

"We need to make a community." Piper drummed their fingers on Lucifer's back until she protested. "These men, the ones who were online, they were on their own. They wanted to reach out and make connections, and they did it with the hunters. But there are other options, right? Other places they could go."

Valerie sat back in her armchair and grinned at the both of them. "Of course there are. Look at history. People hate what they don't understand, and they work to dehumanise those people."

"But if we show them that magic users aren't about to hurt them, that they're just people," Piper continued. "Maybe they'll change their minds."

Jack imagined taking Joseph Larson out to the reserve to meet Kier. She, just for a moment, enjoyed the idea of Kier attacking Joseph and teaching him a real lesson. But then she imagined Joseph getting to know Kier and Richie and the others, seeing the magic for himself. Seeing how it was just like any other reserve with people and other beings just living out their lives in peace.

"It's risky," Jack said, finally. "But maybe there is a way. If we can offer these men something else, the hunters lose their source of information. We don't even know how many hunters are involved, but they're obviously leaning on these guys for surveillance and for local knowledge. Maybe if we can take away that strength, they'll reveal themselves more easily."

Valerie collected up the cards and shuffled the ones from the spread back into the pack. "I hope that helped. It seemed to, I think."

Piper nodded enthusiastically. "Definitely."

"It doesn't bring us closer to the anonymous killers, or the hunters themselves," Jack said. "But it's definitely more than we had before. Thank you, Valerie."

"It's my pleasure. Now don't forget your teas. Piper, do you need some more chamomile?"

"I think I'm all right," Piper said. "I feel like I'm sitting on a bouncy castle and I can't quite find my feet, but I'm all right. Heart's slowed down, I think."

Jack picked up her teacup again and drank. "This is delicious, by the way. Thank you, Val. Do we owe you anything, for the reading?" Jack had vague memories of seeing a movie where the card reader demanded a piece of silver. The last thing she wanted to do was take advantage of their friend.

But Valerie shook her head, reaching up to pull her thick red hair out of its braid. "No, this mission you're on, this path, it benefits me, it benefits all my friends and let's face it, my livelihood, even my life. It's my pleasure to be able to aid you in it. No payment. Take my blessing to do your best with the challenges before you."

Jack smiled, feeling responsibility settle on her shoulders. This case was a big one, and Valerie was right that it affected a lot of people. Her words sounded charged with something. Perhaps it was magic or perhaps it was just the truth. Either way, she felt the need to solve the case even quicker.

"We'll do the best we can. I just wish it was safe for someone a bit more magical to help us out." Jack couldn't keep the rue from her voice. Missing Emmaline, again.

"Maybe…" Valerie said. "Maybe Raphael's girlfriend could come through. She's nowhere near as vulnerable as Emmaline or me, after all."

"She…" Jack swallowed. "She seemed like she was still healing from her own trauma, though."

"That's possibly true, but time is different in the fae realm, and she might be a lot further along than the last time you saw her." Valerie shrugged. "At any rate, I'm sure Emmaline will contact you soon and you can discuss things with her."

"Thanks Val, we really appreciate all your help," Piper said.

Jack bit her lip. She'd been about to ask when Valerie thought Emmaline would be in touch, but that was probably too needy. And there was absolutely no evidence Valerie would know when Emmaline would be in touch anyway, especially with time passing differently between realms.

"Yeah, thanks Valerie." Jack managed a smile. "We'll be in touch as soon as we make headway. I want to keep you as informed as possible so you can be in touch with the community…"

Jack swallowed. Was the magic community the one the cards had been referring to? But they couldn't ask them to endanger themselves in a police investigation. It was unethical when the people they were hunting deliberately had it out for magic users.

Piper led the way out of the shop. Jack followed, puzzling to herself, thinking of the warning of the Queen of Swords. Once they were in the car, Jack in the driver's seat, she turned to Piper. "Do you think the magic community is part of what the cards were talking about?"

Piper grinned, as they settled Lucifer back in the bag with a carrot stick. "I was wondering something very similar. If we can draw out the men who were affected by the YouTubers, the online recruitment, and have the magic community around, and us, and show them that we're all just people. That our common purpose should be understanding and helping each other, rather than hate."

Jack smiled. "Okay, Detective Optimistic, I was just wondering if we could involve them more in the investigation." Piper ducked their head and their cheeks went pink. Jack felt guilty instantly and she put her hand on their shoulder. "But I like your idealism, let's see if we can get there, together, all right?"

"Sounds good to me," Piper said. "So, where are we going now?"

"We need to go and talk to the men who tried to break into my house," Jack said. "Find out what they know about the anonymous killers. Or well, anything."

"How do we know they weren't the anonymous killers?" Piper asked.

Jack turned the car on and started to drive to the station. "Well, they were caught, for one. If the beat cops had reported weird, accelerated speed and strangely strong people, I'd know we had the hunters, but they said the arrest was pretty straightforward."

"Mm." Piper tipped their head back on the headrest and sighed. "I really hope we can solve this soon."

"You and me both, partner."

CHAPTER 23

The interview with Tod Ryan was infuriating. Unlike Joseph Larson, he wasn't self-assured or confident at all. But he was convinced he was right in his beliefs. He had the fervour of a true believer or a religious zealot. Worse, he was too afraid to be quiet. They were in the smallest holding cell in the station, and the air was getting close. Warm, and stale with Tod's sweat. He wore a black track suit, and there were stains at the cuffs and down his front, as if he had perhaps been wearing it for quite a while.

"So." Piper sounded tired. The interview was wearing on them too. "You say that you were told to break into the house with a magic key, but you're also saying that magic is evil and those who use it are corrupt. Yeah?"

"I had a special dispensation to use it," Tod said. "From our leader."

"And your leader is who exactly?"

"I don't know his name, it's too important for people to know. I wouldn't give him up to you for anything, and I can't even if you use magic on me, because I don't know his name."

"You know something though." Jack stopped pacing. She leaned on the back of her chair and stared him down. He couldn't keep eye contact for more than half a second. "Where did you get the magic key?"

"I was trusted over that simp, Bingo." Pride seeped into his words. He reminded Jack of the weaselly guy from the second Lord of the Rings movie. Gríma Wormtongue. "I was trusted with the drop off location and the ..." He trailed off, probably realising he'd said too much already.

"And what location was that?" Jack let her voice go syrupy sweet.

Tod dithered. "I don't know any locations. I'd like to talk to my lawyer."

Piper scrunched their nose up. "You just said you were trusted with the drop off location, Tod." Piper leaned forward; their voice sweet but with more sincerity than Jack had managed to get into her delivery. "Jack will go and call your lawyer right now, but we need you to tell us this one thing. Just that location, and you'll talk to your lawyer, and I'll bring you a coffee and everything."

Jack moved towards the door. "What's the name of your lawyer?"

She prayed that Tod was just parroting things he'd heard on American TV. In New Zealand, he had the right to a private call with his lawyer. Jack had no intention of denying him that, but she wanted to hear the location before he spoke with his lawyer.

Tod bit his lip, looking between Piper and Jack. He was wavering, he just needed another motivator. Something that would incense him, perhaps, or outrage him enough to spill without thinking. He'd been proud that he'd been trusted over his partner, maybe that was a good place to try and leverage. Jack decided to try it.

"Your partner, Bingo, he gave us a location already. Now, I don't know if I believe him, he doesn't seem as uh, onto it, as you do," Jack kept her tone casual off-handed even. "He said the boss trusted him and didn't believe in you."

"That idiot, he'd say anything!" Tod leaned forward, his cheeks going red. "Did he tell you Stoneway business park?"

"Oooh," Piper said. "No, he said the drop off was at the wharf. That's interesting."

"I wonder who we should believe?" Jack said, idly, resting her hand on the door handle. "I'd like it to be you, Tod, but I just don't know. Bingo had some pretty interesting things to say…"

"If he told you he knows who the boss is, he's lying," Tod said. "None of us know, and that's for sure. But I did find out that his ISP is registered to Remuera. I got the street number and everything…"

"Hmmm…" Jack nodded. "Okay, I'll think about it. Be right back with a phone."

She left the room and retrieved a landline receiver for him to use to call his lawyer.

Piper made notes as Tod spoke rapidly. Jack saw an address written at the top of the page. "He's hiding it of course, with a VPN and everything, but when you know what you're looking for those things can be cracked. I'm really good at that kind of thing, ever since I was a teenager."

"I bet," Piper muttered. Their hand flew over the page as they wrote. Tod looked up at Jack and smiled, pleased with himself for some reason.

He had pushed the sleeves of his hoodie up to his elbows, revealing a mark on the inside of his wrist. It didn't look like the brand of the Mage Hunters, more like the start of a tattoo which had been inspired by that design.

Jack didn't need to ask what it meant, but the sight of it brought up goosebumps on her arms. "Thanks for your help," she said. "We'll be charging you with stalking, and breaking and entering. You can tell your lawyer that." She set the phone on the table. Piper gathered up the papers and pen, and the two of them left.

CHAPTER 24

Piper's heart raced with excitement rather than anxiety. "Two locations off him. Two locations leading to the big boss, hopefully."

"Hopefully." Jack didn't sound convinced. "If Tod's broken the case open, well, I'd be surprised. But it's more than we had going in."

Piper glanced into the holding cell where Tod's partner in crime was seated. He had refused to say a single word, and there was absolutely nothing they could do about that. But the bluff Jack had tried, saying he'd talked, it had worked beautifully. "How did you know he'd talk if you brought up Bingo?"

Jack shrugged a shoulder. "People like that, they're all so obsessed with their own intelligence. They all think they're secretly Iron Man or I dunno, Elon Musk. You appeal to their vanity and they want to show off, impress you with how clever they are. I've met dozens of them."

Piper nodded. "Funny, how you were able to use his intelligence against him. I wonder if that's part of what the King of Swords was about in the tarot reading."

"It could have been? I don't really know how any of it works. Do you think, if it did mean that, that was the only thing the King of Swords meant?" Jack pursed her lips. "Or could it mean multiple things?"

Piper sighed, shook their head. "Your guess is as good as mine. I have done some reading on tarot, but it was a few years ago. I think they are usually just a guideline rather than a solid clear answer... But I've never had an actual witch do a reading for me, so."

"Let's check out these locations, right now," Jack said. "I'll see if we can't get warrants for both."

Jack went to see Apanui about the warrants, and Piper spoke to Constable Wilson, explaining that both men were being charged but needed to speak with their lawyers.

"No worries, Piper," Wilson said. "And good work. From what I caught of the interrogation you two are a really good team."

"Aw." Piper felt their cheeks warm. "Thanks. It feels good to me, but it's nice to have it noticed from outside."

"It's also good to see Jack like, communicating with people and being a real person," Wilson said. "I think she was getting pretty lonely before you came up. The other detectives aren't exactly welcoming to her and her speciality."

"I get that," Piper said. The word lonely repeated in their head, reminding them of the tarot reading again. "Hey, thanks again. It's good to have nice feedback. Call us if there's any developments, yeah?"

"Of course."

Piper retrieved Lucifer from the nest she'd made out of Piper's wastepaper basket, settled her into the sling bag and headed out to the front of the station where Jack was waiting in the idling car. They got into the passenger seat to see Jack looking at them, incredulous.

"You're really bringing the rabbit?"

"She's in danger," Piper said. "I have to protect her."

"She's safe at the station, surely."

"Well. She maybe sort of had chewed through some cables," Piper said. "I got her out before anyone noticed, but maybe it's best she stays with me and away from dangerous cables."

Jack sighed significantly.

Piper opened up the maps app on their phone, ignoring the sigh. "So, which one first?"

"What do you think?" Jack asked.

Piper bit their lip. Jack sometimes asked questions like this, testing Piper's intuition perhaps? It always felt like a test. Piper thought it through quickly. "The drop off point is probably less important. If you're using it as a drop off, it's because you're not living there or running a business there or anything. I reckon the ISP address in Remuera, there's more likely to be someone there."

"I agree." Jack grinned.

Piper's shoulders relaxed. They'd passed another test.

Jack drove to Remuera, one of the older suburbs in Auckland and one of the most expensive to live in as well. Piper liked looking at the old houses, the weatherboard villas with verandas and finely landscaped gardens. The shops were noticeably richer as well, fashion boutiques and organic green grocers, as opposed to the grimier fish and chip shops or discount butchers in the more run-down neighbourhoods.

As with most of Auckland, there was an abundance of trees. Tall oaks and vibrantly coloured maples arched over the streets, their leaves carpeting the footpath. Frequent parks and reserves were downside streets or dotted between houses.

Jack pulled up to a house which looked much the same as all the others. It wasn't the richest part of the suburb—no mansions hidden behind lush trees on this street—but they were generously sized houses with immaculate paint all the same.

Jack parked two houses down from the location Piper had noted down and turned off the engine. Piper set the rabbit in the back seat with a piece of cardboard to shred, and wound the windows down just enough to let a little air in. It wasn't a very hot day, so they figured she'd be all right while they searched the house.

They made their way to the house. Piper trying their best to look inconspicuous in case someone was watching them approach. The neighbourhood was quiet, barely any traffic and no noise of children playing anywhere. When a dog barked from behind a fence Piper jumped less from fright as from the surprise of the sudden noise in the stillness.

The house with the dog was next to their target. The dog, barely visible behind the high fence, followed them around the boundary, barking and growling.

"Quiet." Jack's voice was serious and authoritative. The dog went quiet.

The house was large with a new looking set of stairs leading up to a mahogany door with an elaborate brass knocker on it. Although the stairs were fresh, the building had to be over a hundred years old. Nicely upkept though, no cracks in the paint or any sign of weathering on the woodwork.

Jack knocked on the heavy wooden door and the two of them waited on the front deck.

Piper looked down at the doormat, which said 'welcome'. There was no sound from inside. Jack pressed the doorbell button. Piper held their breath, trying to hear if it had chimed or not.

There was still no noise.

Jack turned to look into the driveway which ran up the left side of the house. "No car." She pulled out her phone and looked up at Piper. "We've got a warrant to search, so... If we can get in, anything we find will still be admissible."

What were the chances are of there being a spare key in one of the plants? It wasn't likely, but it also wasn't exactly impossible. In their experience rich folks like this either had a locked down electronic gate with security cameras or keys under the doormat.

On the third potted plant, a hanging spider fern, they found a key.

"Hey, Jack!" they called.

Jack had gone down the driveway, but she came back at a jog. "Yeah?"

"Found the spare." Piper held the grimy key aloft. "Shall we?"

She grinned. "Perfect."

Piper slipped the key into the lock and the door opened silently. Piper eyed the wood stain finish, wondering if there were any sigils or charms in it that they couldn't see.

Jack leaned into the house and called out. "Hello! Is anyone home?"

Nothing but silence.

Jack led the way inside. Piper followed, bracing themselves for a magic spell or some sort of curse. Nothing came. But then, this wasn't the house of a mage was it? It was the house of a Hunter if it was anything. The likelihood of their being magical traps was slim.

Inside the house looked immaculate, tidy and clean. Jack immediately went to the side table where there was an open book with creamy white pages. "A guest book."

Just as she said it, Piper noticed a piece of paper posted on the wall. Heart sinking, they read out loud. "Welcome to our AirBnB. Please make sure you follow the instructions..."

CHAPTER 25

Jack sighed, and went further into the house, resisting the urge to kick the wall. "If he was contacting people to arrange a drop off and illicit meeting from here, he could be anywhere by now." She couldn't keep the dejection from her voice.

"I wonder how long he had it booked for?" Piper mused. They closed the door behind them.

Jack eyed a house alarm box. It had been left disarmed. "Perhaps he's expecting to return here. Or maybe he left in a hurry..."

Piper ducked their head into the first room. "Living room."

Jack looked down the hallway. "Kitchen and dining down there..." She walked into the room. A dirty cereal bowl sat on the countertop. Jack sniffed it, and it smelled of nothing but fresh milk. "Looks like someone was here this morning. There might be fingerprints."

Piper appeared in the kitchen door. "The living room is immaculate, like it's just been cleaned, or like it hasn't been used ever. I guess the guest rooms are upstairs."

The two of them made their way upstairs without further discussion. Jack was relieved to see a room had been used. The bed was unmade, there was a drawer sitting open and a few things on the desk.

"This might be what we needed," Piper said. They made a beeline for the desk, pulled out a pair of latex gloves and put them on before looking through the papers. "Locations, a map... This has a mark on it."

"Oh yeah?" Jack had taken a photo of the bed and now joined Piper to take photos of the papers. The map showed downtown Auckland, near the waterfront... "That's Victoria Park."

"I don't know it," Piper said.

"It's just a couple of blocks from Queen St, a park with an elevated motorway flying over it. The park is mostly grass, but with trees all around, big trees. Old. There are people there all the time, working out or playing soccer or just picnicking. Why have they got a map? That's not good."

"They must be planning something for there," Piper said, frowning. "But what? A ritual? A rally of some kind? Trying to drum up interest in their cause, maybe?"

"Any dates listed?"

Piper turned each paper over but there was no date or time noted anywhere. "I guess we can just be on alert, maybe see if we can get surveillance on it as well?"

"We can try." Jack felt sick at the thought of asking Apanui for more assistance. There were only so many constables in Auckland, and they already had a few watching the reserve for intruders. They needed to solve this case faster, damn it.

Jack looked at the room, checking for anything they may have missed. The small wastepaper basket was stuffed to overflowing with discarded food wrappers. There was lots of fast food packaging, energy drink cans and protein bar wrappers. There was also an empty protein shake container and some bubble tea cups. "Guess whoever it was, they got pretty hungry. Or there was more than one of them."

Piper glanced over. "It's a really big place for just one person to rent. I'll take a look at the other rooms."

Jack eyed the bedclothes, wondering if it was worth pulling them back and deciding against it when Piper came back in. "Nothing, those beds are perfect, they look like something out of a magazine. And that's three bedrooms unused, plus en-suite bathrooms."

"So, whoever it was, they have money to burn, and they got very hungry. It was either one person or a couple who slept together." Jack noted that down in her notepad and underlined Victoria Park.

Piper checked in the open drawer and found nothing but a dusty old Gideon's bible. "No evidence here that anyone's coming back," Piper said. "No clothes, shoes or luggage."

"I'll call in forensics to dust for prints, see if they can find anything," Jack said.

"Do you think it's worth checking the drop off point as well?"

Jack pursed her lips and nodded. "Not really, but we should do it anyway. It'd be best if we had a mage with us but..." She had to stop bringing that up. She had worked for years without a mage, although, well. That wasn't technically true. She had thought she was hiring a psychic but Cameron had really been a mage. "We need to check there's nothing there, confirm it."

"Gotcha," Piper said. "Want me to drive?"

"Sure."

When they left the front door, they caught the sound of running feet pounding the pavement.

"Lucifer!" Piper rushed to the car. The back window was cracked, but not broken. They must have interrupted the attempted burglary. "Someone tried to get her." They opened the door and pulled the trembling rabbit into their arms. "I told you she's a target."

Jack surveyed the damage to her car. The lock had been tampered with but not damaged badly, and the rear left window was spiderwebbed with cracks. Good old reinforced police standard glass. She looked at Piper and the rabbit and sighed. "Okay, yeah, she really does seem to be in danger."

CHAPTER 26

J
ack felt frustrated at the end of the day. The drop off point had been clean of any evidence, which Jack had expected, but it was still disheartening. They had got access to the security camera that pointed at the lot, but there was nothing more than a blurred movement at the edge of it, which passed briefly. Clearly whoever it was had experience on avoiding security cameras.

She let herself into her empty flat, tired out but also on alert in case someone had somehow broken in. She checked each room and was about to start making dinner when a noise startled her.

Someone cleared their throat.

Jack spun to face the bathroom—the room the sound had come from. It was empty and the door stood open. But there was another sound from within.

"Jack? Are you home?"

Emmaline.

Her disembodied voice.

She must be in the mirror.

Emmaline!

Jack hurried into the bathroom. Yes, there was Emmaline's face. Looking into the mirror and seeing someone else there should have been unsettling, but Jack was so pleased to see Emmaline all she felt was relief, loosening her shoulders.

"It's so good to see you," she said. Instead of 'hello or how are you' or 'yes I'm home.' Emmaline's smile lit her eyes up. "It's great to see you too, Jack."

They smiled at each other, goofy as two teenagers. Jack realised what she was doing and coughed. "Uh, so you're good? You're well?"

"Yes, I'm fine," Emmaline said. "Raphael and Amy are here, so it's been nice catching up with them properly. And Gerard's good fun, of course."

"Of course." The mention of Amy reminded her she wanted to ask about the Hunters. "Listen, we're having a bit of trouble with the case. The Hunters seem to be one step ahead all the time and we've arrested some people but they're lackies rather than the people who were actually doing any killing." She swallowed, took a breath, and tried to slow down. "Do you think Amy would be willing to talk to me about some of this? It's not safe for you or Raphael or Gerard to come through, but if Amy could, even for an hour... Or just talk through the mirror, we might be able to find something that cracks it open."

Emmaline nodded, not looking surprised by Jack's suggestion at all. "I was actually thinking something similar. Amy has a lot of inside knowledge the rest of us don't. I'll ask her, okay. I just wanted to check in. How's Piper doing?"

"Good," Jack said. "They're really good. They miss you."

"Aw, I miss them, too." Emmaline smiled and started playing with her braid.

Jack found herself quite distracted, watching the blonde hair. "Yeah, Piper... Piper has missed your presence. On the case, I mean. You just kind of balance things out, more than ... more than we'd have with just the two of us. And we've both really been missing your magic." She swallowed, wondering why she was babbling.

Emmaline's expression softened. "You okay all alone in that flat?"

Jack nodded. "Yeah, it's quiet, of course, but I'm okay." Even as she said it her voice wavered, ready to break although there wasn't really anything to be sad or upset about. Yes, she missed Emmaline, and she wished that she could come through the mirror just then and into her arms and then they could hug and kiss and...

Jack shook her head. So that's what she was upset about. Her growing affection was stirring her emotions. Maybe absence really did make the heart grow fonder?

Emmaline watched her shrewdly, a soft smile playing about her fine features. "Good. I miss you and that cat. How's the rabbit doing?"

"Piper has been enjoying having her there," Jack said. "They were going to the pet shop for more supplies this evening."

"Good." Emmaline smiled wider. "Listen, how about I go and ask Amy now and then I'll call you back?'

Jack snorted out a laugh. 'Call you back' like it was a regular phone call and not a magical spell that used mirrors to transcend different worlds. "Yeah, that sounds fine. Just yell when you get back, I'll hear you."

It didn't take long before Emmaline was calling for her. Jack had gone to the kitchen to start preparing dinner. She set her knife down and hurried back to the bathroom. "I'm here!"

In the mirror was Emmaline as expected, and next to her, the familiar face of Amy. Amy the ex-hunter. Her ash blonde hair had been cut since the last time Jack had seen her, and now it hung neatly to her shoulders. She was wearing a black T-shirt and looked just as upright and military as ever. Her expression though, was soft and warm.

"Hi Jack." She raised a hand to wave.

"Amy's agreed to come through and stay with you for a bit," Emmaline said. "I don't know why I didn't think of it sooner. She's like a magical personal bodyguard."

Amy chuckled and nudged Emmaline in the arm. "Not too far off what I've been doing for Raph. But yeah, if it's okay with you Jack? I have a bag, and I can come through right now."

Jack felt another knot of tension release itself, this time from the centre of her stomach. "Yeah, I mean, if Raphael can spare you and you don't have other things you need to do?"

Amy shook her head. "Nope, Raph's a big boy, he can look after himself. I'm interested to see these recruits and see what the Order is up to at the bottom of the world."

"Well, yeah, great. Emmaline's bed is made up so all ready for you."

Amy gave Emmaline a quick hug and then moved towards the mirror, getting larger as she did. Jack stepped back out the room, waiting in the doorway to give Amy plenty of space. She came through quickly, graceful as a cat—or perhaps a mountain lion was a more appropriate comparison. There was a certain amount of menace about her.

She had put on weight since Jack had first seen her, which meant her muscles had grown as well. She was just a little shorter than Jack, but she looked like a club bouncer, or a top martial artist. Someone not to be messed with.

Amy landed soundlessly on the tiles and turned back to wave at Emmaline. "See you soon!"

"Bye, Em, and thank you," Jack said.

"Of course," Emmaline said. "Be safe, both of you." The mirror rippled and she vanished, leaving the glass an ordinary reflection.

"Great, well, welcome," Jack said. "Uh, let me show you to the room, I was just about to make dinner."

"Oh. Before I forget." Amy dug in her pocket and produced a thick roll of twenty and fifty dollar bills. "This is for food."

"What? It's fine, you can just eat what I'm eating." Jack wondered where the money had come from. Was it magicked up? Had Amy stolen it from someone?

"No, you don't get it." Amy held the money out again. "I eat a lot. *A lot.* Hunter metabolism. The thing they do to enhance us, it increases our metabolism so we're pretty much always hungry. Take it, you're a cop, you can't earn that much."

"Oh." Jack swallowed. "Where did the money come from?"

"It's Raphael's. He earned it selling magic widgets or something in Chicago, then he got it issued in New Zealand dollars. It's totally clean, nothing to worry about."

Jack took the roll of bills and pocketed it. "Uh, yeah, okay. How about we hit the supermarket after dinner then and make sure you have enough to eat?"

"I can't wait," Amy said. "I've never been to a New Zealand supermarket; I've never been to New Zealand!" She bounced on her toes.

For a moment Jack forgot she was anything but a normal woman excited to try something new. Her accent was definitely North American, and from her casual mention of Chicago, Jack expected that was where she was from. Jack shook her head and smiled. Hunter or not, monster or not, people were just people.

CHAPTER 27

The next day was Saturday. Piper's normal routine was thrown out the window. First of all, they had to clean up after Lucifer who had taken to pooping between the couch and the wall.

"If I get you a litter box do you know how to use it?" Piper demanded.

Lucifer stared back with a look so wise that Piper immediately took her to the nearest pet shop, bought a cat litter tray, a bag of cat litter, and a backpack with a clear dome back for carrying cats around in. Lucifer nosed at some bunny food packages so Piper bought those too.

Once the litter tray was set up, Lucifer cheerfully used it immediately and then hopped to her bowl for some water.

"This is what I've come to." Piper looked at themself in the mirror while adjusting the straps of the bunny carrier backpack. "I'm a police officer with a bunny I have to bodyguard." There was more they could say regarding the spirituality reading Valerie had done, the implications of it, but Piper looked away from their reflection and said nothing at all.

Piper's phone buzzed. Their blood ran cold.

Apanui had asked Jack and Piper to come in for a conference.

Piper waited outside for Jack to pick them up because they were antsy. Too antsy to wait up in their apartment. Wound up and afraid. Lucifer was in the backpack, and making annoyed sounds at the amount Piper was moving around.

It felt like they were being called into the principal's office, and on top of that, they hadn't had a day off all week. They were tired and worried, they missed Emmaline and they were worried about Jack stopping sleeping and obsessing over the case.

The car pulled up faster than Jack usually drove. Amy was driving, a wild smile on her face.

Jack undid her safety belt and got out of the car.

"Nope, no more. Sorry Amy, but we can't just drive like that. It's dangerous and some other police officer will pull us over. And they'd be right to!" Jack snapped.

Amy pouted but got out of the driver's seat. "Fine! But I think I should get credit for staying on the wrong side of the road."

"It's the right side of the road, here."

Piper hugged Amy. "Hi, it's so good to see you again."

Amy hugged Piper back. "You too. Even if Jack doesn't appreciate my driving."

"It's dangerous." Jack got behind the wheel.

"Awww, look at the bunny!" Amy peered over Piper's shoulder and then spun them around to poke a finger through one of the airholes for Lucifer to sniff.

"This is Lucifer. Lucy, meet Amy."

"Nice to meet you," Amy said, perfectly seriously. But she probably had a lot more experience with weird magical things than Piper did, after all.

Piper gestured to the passenger side door. "You take shotgun if you like, I don't mind riding in the back."

"Thanks, Piper."

Once they were all in the car silence descended. The quiet brought back all Piper's anxiety about the upcoming conversation with Apanui. "So, how is the fae realm, Amy?"

"It's all right," Amy said. "You know, weird, magical and dangerous, but it's been a good place to detox from all the Hunter bullshit."

"Yeah, how does that work?" Piper asked. "You still have the mark and the powers and stuff, right?"

"Mmhm." Amy lifted her arm, pushed up her sleeve and regarded the weird looking mark. "I don't know exactly. Most of it was brainwashing so it's hard to remember, lots of meditation, physical drills and hard work, but the magic stuff.... Raph redirected the source of power. The Order had it going to some weird thing, I didn't care to know too much about it, but now it's linked to the Heart in Faerie."

The mention of Raphael brought an image of his handsome face to Piper's mind and they allowed themself a small smile. "Interesting."

"It's... probably for the best if you don't come into the station," Jack said to Amy, when they pulled up.

Amy nodded. "Agreed. I'll keep an eye on the car from that coffee shop over the road."

"Wait," Piper suddenly didn't want to haul the rabbit into the station when it was probably going to be a serious meeting. They handed the backpack to Amy. "Take Lucifer, and be on guard. They're really trying to attack her."

"Poor little bun, of course." Amy carefully shouldered the backpack and gave them a little salute before crossing the road.

Jack and Piper made their way to Apanui's office, Piper's heart beating quicker with each second. There was so much at stake here. Was Apanui calling off the investigation? If that happened, so many innocent people would be at risk. Piper couldn't bear that.

Sergeant Apanui was at her desk, dressed in a pink floral dress Piper had never seen before. The pink was a sweet baby pink and the flowers were large and lush, gerberas maybe, splashed over the fabric. On the desk in front of her sat a white straw hat with flowers set on the brim. Was she was going to church after this? Piper imagined their intimidating and efficient Sergeant at the church that Reverend Zebedee ran and suppressed a smile.

"Good morning, you two," Apanui said. "I wanted to talk to you about this murder suicide case."

"Yes, Sergeant," Jack said. "What did you want to know?"

"You've made a number of arrests, I understand that, conspiracy online and so on. That's fine. I don't understand why we have such a number of constables on constant duty at the nature reserve up North. I feel like you're withholding information."

Jack cleared her throat. Piper glanced at her. They could see Jack was trying to come up with a plausible explanation. "The people who run that reserve, we believe they could be targets of the conspiracy."

"DOC workers? Why would that be?"

"You remember the Wiccans are being targeted, and we told you the DOC workers were also Wiccan?" Jack said.

Piper bit their lip, hoping that would be enough. Apanui was unmoved.

"A tenuous link, from what I've seen of the reports, the men you've arrested are obsessed with the idea of magic being real."

"Right, and the dead men found in town had Wiccan paraphernalia in their apartment."

"I don't see how the nature reserve factors in and you've given me a very weak reply." Apanui folded her arms.

"Because-" Jack started.

Piper moved forward, interrupting her. "The fact is magic is real. We've both seen it. These men, the hunters, they're like a terrorist cell who hunt down and kill people who can do magic. They're like, crazy racists and they think they're in the right."

Silence.

Piper opened their mouth to say more but Apanui held up a hand. "Detective Gage, do you really expect me to believe that?"

Piper's mouth remained open and their eyes widened in horror. Their entire body flushed cold. What would this mean for their career?

Jack sighed heavily and moved beside Piper. "Sargent, I know it sounds totally bizarre, but it's true. We can't prove it to you right now, but a month ago when we were dealing with the Armstrong case, we both saw some stuff. There are people who can do things that are totally unexplainable."

Apanui breathed out through her nose and shook her head. "What it sounds like is that I have two overworked Detectives who have let stress and pressure warp their perception of reality. Jack, it pains me to say this, but you need to take some time off."

Jack pushed her hair back from her forehead and jutted her jaw out. "No, Sargent. We can't afford to. More people are going to die if we don't do something. There have already been deaths. The people we've brought in are part of it, but they're not the ones doing the killing. Those people are still out there. It doesn't matter if you don't believe us on the magic, but please believe that we have some leads and hopefully a way to prevent more killings."

Jack had stepped forward, and was close to Apanui's desk now. Apanui stood up, her eyebrow arching. "Please, Sargent." Jack softened her voice. "Please just let me do this and then I'll take time off or whatever you want."

"I might have you put on disciplinary action..." Apanui said.

Piper's breath caught in their throat. No!

Apanui's expression softened. "But I get your point. These killers are dangerous, we're not closing the case. But we might... I might reassign it."

"You can't do that!" Jack cried out. "We have the thread. If you give this to someone else, they'll take days to catch up to where we are."

Apanui frowned. She took her time thinking, one hand tapping lightly on the desk.

Piper watched Apanui's hand. Was the Sargent about to fire both of them? Was that even a thing that happened outside of cop movies? They tried to catch Jack's eye, but Jack steadfastly watched Apanui, a bead of sweat glistening on Jack's forehead.

"Don't take that tone with me, Detective Duarte. But fine, you can have a few more days on this and then I'll review."

"Thank you, Sargent," Piper said, quickly, before either of them could blurt something else damaging out.

CHAPTER 28

J ack strode out of the station, forcing Piper to half jog to keep up with her.

"That didn't go too badly, really," Piper said. They could feel the rage and frustration coming off Jack and they wanted to smooth it over as fast as possible. Suppress their own fears and horrors by focusing on Jack.

Jack stepped out into the sunshine before turning back to Piper. "Not too badly? Were you in the room? Sargent's not just going to take us off the case, she's this close to putting us both on enforced relaxation leave." She held her finger and thumb a centimetre apart and jabbed her hand towards Piper. "Because of your bright idea to tell her that magic is real. She's probably going to have us go to psychological assessments, and who could blame her?"

Piper felt tears well and blinked furiously to keep them back. Now was not the time to cry. "I wanted her to understand. I didn't think you'd react this way."

"How did you think I'd react?" Jack's hand flicked out to the side, as if she were brushing Piper off, or dismissing their idea physically. "Gee, thanks Piper, tell our boss just what we're really up to, I'm sure it will sound totally rational."

Piper planted their hands on their hips and lifted their chin. "There's absolutely no need to be mean about this." They narrowed their eyes and fixed Jack with a gaze they hoped didn't betray how hurt they felt.

Jack heaved a sigh and raked both hands through her hair. "Right. I don't mean to be—I'm not attacking you personally. I'm just really frustrated with what you said and how it went down."

Her words didn't make Piper feel better. They looked away, catching sight of Amy over the street. She was stalking towards them. There wasn't a better way to describe how she was walking, it was definitely a stalk. She was frowning behind dark glasses. Dressed all in black she looked every inch the dangerous bodyguard or the lead character of an action movie.

Although Piper couldn't think of many action movies where the lead character carried a rabbit around in a backpack.

"I'm sorry." Piper turned back to Jack.

"Yeah, well." Jack sighed again. "We'll drop you home. Let's just process today and go over what we've already got. Maybe there's something we've missed. We'll touch base later tonight."

Jack wasn't meeting their eyes and that felt worse still. "Yeah, okay."

Amy looked between the two of them. "I guess it didn't go well."

"Not great, no."

The car ride home was quiet. The air around Jack vibrated with suppressed anger and they felt completely responsible for it. Amy seemed happy enough to sit in silence, and Piper didn't want to poke the bear any more than they already had.

It was a relief to say "see you later" and get out of the car. Piper took a breath of fresh air before heading into the building with Lucifer on their back. The lift had been repaired, so they pressed the button and waited.

The lift opened and out walked Beau Kaminsky. He looked like he hadn't slept in a while, and Piper was shocked to see the pallor of his skin.

"Hey Beau. Are you okay?"

He looked at them with wide eyes and swallowed. "None of your business, Piper."

"Well, okay but you look like you're coming down with something," Piper said. "You sure you feel okay?"

Beau hunched his shoulders forward and folded his arms. "Had some sleepless nights," he said. "Just back off."

He scuttled away and Piper went into the lift. It was totally likely that he had stayed up playing games or just... suffering from insomnia, but the interaction had bothered Piper. What was he up to? What did they even know about Beau?

Piper leaned their shoulder against the wall of the lift and sighed. "I might be being paranoid."

When they got to their floor, they looked briefly at the door to Beau's apartment. They could bust in or ask the building manager for access, and scope out his place. See if there was any magical paraphernalia, or worse, hunter stuff... But what would they be basing the search off? One weird interaction and a hunch?

Their gut was off this morning. They'd thought it was a good idea to come clean with Apanui and that had been a disaster. Busting into their neighbour's house to snoop around was a terrible idea.

They stared at his door for another moment and then let themselves into their apartment.

They set the bag down and let Lucifer out. She immediately hopped to her nest of straw and buried herself in in.

"Wish I could do the same." Piper locked the door behind them, kicked off their boots and tossing keys onto the table with their grandmother's ring.

"I don't know what to do, Lucifer." Piper said. Their voice sounded tired, defeated.

Whenever they felt like this, there were two clear options. One was to sit around and mope. The other was to call Ben and talk things through with him. Ben was sensible, kind and he loved them. Even better, he didn't open the bakery on Sundays so he'd be at home relaxing. Well, unless he was out with his dog. But if he was doing that he'd still have his phone on him.

They hit the video call button and he picked up on the third ring. "Hey Piper, what's up?"

"Hey Ben." Just hearing him say their name was a balm, as was seeing their brother's smile through the phone screen. They went to the kitchen and leaned against the bench. "I'm in a bit of a ... I dunno. It's a bit of trouble at work, and I've pissed off my partner, and I feel like absolute shit, and I don't know what to do next."

Ben chuckled. "Whatever this case is you're on, it's really put you in a spin, huh? I haven't heard from you this often since you left."

A wave of guilt accentuate the sadness and confusion Piper was already feeling. "I'm sorry."

"No need to be sorry," he said. "I'm here for you, I like that you call me. Come on, lay it all out."

"Wait, what are you doing right now?" Piper picked at their loose nails and sniffed. "I don't want to interrupt your running around with the dog time."

"You're not, we just got back." Ben laughed, soft and low. "He's sacked out in a sunbeam and I'm on the couch. Perfect timing."

"Okay." Piper took a deep breath. The temptation to explain about magic was there, and it was strong, but they resisted. Gut's wrong today. So they summarised the difficulty of the case, the pyramid scheme shape of the criminal organisation and how unsure they were about what to do next. Then how badly the meeting with the sergeant had gone.

"And I blurted out this detail about the case," Piper said. "I thought it might help, but it didn't, and Jack was pissed at me for saying it out loud." They sighed. "I've messed up, and I don't know how to make it right. Jack thinks there might be repercussions, like, professional consequences because of what I said and how the case is going, and that's terrifying." As they spoke a huge yawn broke in.

"How many days in a row have you been obsessing about this case?" Ben asked.

"Well, we usually take the weekend off, but yeah, it's been full on, some pretty long days and I guess... Six in a row by now."

"You need some down time," Ben said. "That's the first thing. Do something restorative, something that will allow you to disengage from the case, and then you can unwind enough to process all these emotions. Then you might find when you come back to it, you'll know exactly what to do. Your instincts are usually spot on, Pipes. You just gotta trust them."

"Sometimes, I think you have too much faith in me, Benny." Piper couldn't help smiling though. It was nice to have someone on their side no matter what.

"Nah," Ben said. "You just don't have enough faith in yourself. I have to make up the deficit."

"You're adorable," Piper said. "I miss you. How's the possible planned expansion of the best bakery on the South Island looking?"

Ben smiled, wider. "I'm looking at places to rent, I was gonna ask if you'll be around next weekend? I could maybe stay on your couch and we could look at some places together?"

Piper's heart thumped and all the sadness and annoyance vanished from their chest. Their brother, moving up, and before that coming to see them. Things seemed easier to deal with all of a sudden.

"Of course, I'll be around. If I'm really lucky this case will solved by then and I'll be able to spend time with you and everything."

"Cool." Ben nodded and suddenly moved sideways as his dog, a golden retriever knocked into his shoulder and filled the screen of the call.

Piper laughed. "Hi Captain Brick."

Ben's hand appeared, scratching the dog around the neck and easing him back over. "Okay, someone needs some more play time, I think. Call me back if you need to, Pipes. I'm free all day."

"I think I might be okay, but I'm gonna take your advice anyway," Piper said. "The whole self-care thing sounds pretty good about now."

"I'll let you know when I've booked some flights," Ben said. "Love you, bye!"

"Love you, bye!"

Piper checked on Lucifer. She had emerged from her bedding and was having a drink of water. Piper sat down to watch. She was a very good companion. Very clean now that they had the litter box, and she seemed very happy to spend time in Piper's company. Piper was quickly getting used to having her around to talk to.

"Well, Lucifer, I might make myself a big cup of chamomile and play a video game. That should distract me. But first maybe I'll just text Jack..."

They picked up their phone and fired off a text to their partner. Was there any point in saying sorry again? Well, it couldn't hurt.

Piper: Hey Jack, sorry again. Just remember, we need to trust our instincts. Yours are really good.

Then they put on their gaming console and loaded a fantasy game where they could fight monsters and forget about the monsters in the real world for just a moment.

CHAPTER 29

J ack and Amy had dropped Piper and the rabbit off. The obvious thing to do would be to head home and think things through. But for some reason that wasn't what Jack wanted to do at all.

She tapped the steering wheel and frowned, looking at Amy. "Feel like a drive? I don't want to just go home right now."

"Fine with me," Amy said. "I'm just here to follow you around and make sure you don't die. If you want to go for a drive, then so do I."

Jack nodded. "Fair enough."

She took a left and drove down towards the waterfront, taking the turning for the motorway which would take them over the Harbour Bridge and North. For whatever reason, Jack wanted to go and see Richie at the reserve. Maybe it was because it sounded like they were about to lose their Constable security guard. But maybe she wanted to show it to Amy. Show her the pretty scenery and the place where good work was being done.

Possibly the biggest reason was because Jack herself needed the calm of the countryside. She felt the need to walk under the tree canopy, to breathe the clean air. Maybe it would soothe the rattling emotions which were threatening another headache.

Amy was quiet on the drive out, maybe picking up on Jack's need for silence, or perhaps just distracted by the scenery as they drove out of town. She was also preoccupied with eating some of the energy bars they'd bought at the supermarket for her.

They reached the reserve quicker this time, although when they got to the side street Jack realised the flaw in her plan. She wanted to turn back. She didn't want to turn down the side road which would take them to the barrier arm.

But she gritted her teeth. It might be a magical compulsion, but she knew it was there, and she knew that she had a strong will. It had been remarked on before. She wasn't immune to magic, not by a long shot, but she had some ability to fight it off.

"Amy, there's a spell on the perimeter." Jack's voice was strained as she concentrated on turning the wheel to go into the side road. "It's trying to make me turn back."

"Oh, yeah, I feel it," Amy said. "I can feel it but it's not compelling me. Hey, do you want me to take over driving, Jack?" She looked a little too pleased at the idea of taking the wheel.

That put Jack off, but also she wasn't sure what the compulsion would do if she slowed the car down and stopped it. "No, I think, just tell me to turn down that side road and keep telling me to drive forward. That should do it."

"Uh-huh, well, turn down that road, Jack."

Jack hauled on the wheel and they were trundling down the side road approaching the reserve. "Good, this is good."

"That's it, just keep on driving," Amy said. "You're doing great, honey."

Jack fought a laugh. "No need to be sarcastic."

"I wasn't!" Amy chuckled. "I'm encouraging you."

"It sounded condescending."

Amy giggled, a light warm sound so out of keeping with her tough exterior that it gave Jack more strength to fight off the spell.

They pulled up in front of the barrier arm. It was a struggle to wind down the window and press the button on the intercom, but Jack managed it.

"Richie?" Jack said. "It's Detective Jack Duarte and a friend."

There was a slight pause and then the barrier arm started to raise. The intercom cracked. "Come on in, Jack. You should have called, we'd have eased the spell for you."

"No worries, we made it in," Jack said.

His voice sounded a little winded. "I'm just up a trail. Be down in ten minutes, wait at the hut. I think Kier's in there doing school stuff at the moment."

"Gotcha," Jack said.

The arm raised and with it the driving need to turn back. Jack drove through and pulled out, sparing a glance at Amy. She was looking around, her manner that of a sniper checking an area was secure, but her expression was of interested curiosity.

"Who's Kier?"

"A kelpie," Jack said. "He's trying to learn how to integrate into human society. Piper likes him."

"Please don't take this the wrong way," Amy said. "But Piper likes absolutely everybody. It's not that they're a bad judge of character, but they're a lot less picky than I'd be."

Jack felt that sentiment deep in her bones. "Yeah, that's very accurate."

Amy grinned as they pulled into the parking space in front of the hut. "Ugh, this place is pretty cute though. Like, something out of Little House on the Prairie, except in New Zealand."

Jack chuckled, liking Amy more and more by the moment. "Less prairie and more rainforest but, yeah."

They got out of the car and Amy stretched her arms high over her head, going to her toes before she shook her limbs out.

Jack knocked on the door to the hut.

Inside there was the sound of movement. "Yeah?"

"It's Detective Jack," Jack said. "That you Kier?"

The door opened and the young kelpie peeked out. He looked much the same as the last time Jack had seen him, except he was wearing an oversized navy coloured hoodie with a cartoon character horse on the front. "Hey Jack, good to see you again." He sniffed the air, eyes narrowing as he looked at Amy. "Who's your friend?"

"This is Amy," Jack said. "She's an ex-hunter."

Amy was giving Kier much the same suspicious look as he was giving her.

Jack felt protective of him, with his big moon eyes and his hopeful outlook. She moved slightly in between the two of them and tried to diffuse the tension. "Amy's never been to New Zealand before so I thought I'd show her around a bit."

"Mm." Kier looked past Jack and frowned slightly. "You didn't bring Piper?"

Jack's breath caught in her chest, waves of remorse threatening to choke her. "Uh, no, we're... having a day off. Sort of. Stuff to sort out."

"Look," Amy said, abruptly. "It's not that I dislike kelpies or anything, I just know what you're capable of so I'm ... wary."

"I get that." Kier shrugged. "I'm wary of Hunters too."

"And I," Jack added, "am wary of people. Any one of us is capable of all sorts of horrible evils."

"Well, yeah, uh, I mean I'm still human," Amy said.

Jack bit her lip. This wasn't exactly going as smoothly as she wanted.

Kier burst out into laughter. Jack startled, but Amy started to laugh as well. Soon they were all laughing, although Jack wasn't sure at what.

Finally, Amy wiped her eyes with the back of her hand. "You're all right, Kier." She patted his shoulder then whipped around to face the path which led into the bush.

There was a whistle from up the trail. Kier grinned. "Here's Richie."

Richie ambled down the trail, his eyes sparkling as he whistled. Jack wondered if the tune was some kind of spell. Emmaline used music frequently.

"Hey there." Richie waved with one hand.

Jack returned it. "Good to see you, Richie."

Jack moved forward as he got closer, and they shook hands, both of them smiling softly. It struck Jack as odd how quickly she had come to trust Richie, but sometimes people just gave you that aura. She introduced him to Amy, who shook his hand, her smile a little tight.

"Cup of tea?" he asked.

Jack shook her head. "I think I need a walk, blow the cobwebs out."

"Ugh, a walk won't do that." Amy eyed Kier, a flash of mischief in her smile. "How about you and I go for a run, Kier, really blow the cobwebs away?"

Kier's reply grin was bright and showed off his too-pointy teeth. He started pulling off his oversized hoodie and tossed it back inside the hut. "You're on."

"You're slow!" Amy took off, easily sprinting as if she'd been warming up for the last hour instead of sitting in a car. Kier chased after, laughing, and gaining speed just as quickly.

Richie chuckled and Jack glanced at him. "I still just want to walk."

"Thank the stars for that." He nodded at the trail Amy and Kier had just dashed up. "Shall we?"

They walked a few minutes in silence. The sounds of Amy and Kier running had faded within seconds, leaving just the gentle lap of the waves on the shore of the lake, the birdsong, and the wind in the trees. Jack sucked it in like a soothing balm. Finally, she sighed, feeling looseness in her legs from the walk up the gentle incline and her heart speeding up with the light exercise.

"So, what brings you out here?" Richie's tone was light, as if he didn't really care too much. "I'm glad to see you, don't get me wrong, but I don't think it was just so Amy could go for a run with the kelpie."

"No, although it looks like it could be a good side benefit," Jack said. "No, uh. The Sargent isn't sure we're on the level with this case. She wants results and more evidence for what's going on."

"Mmm. Can't imagine that will be easy for you." Richie stuck his hands in the pockets of his cargo shorts.

Jack tipped her head back and looked at the sunlight pushing through the leaves of the canopy above them. "No. Piper thought the best course of action was to come clean. You can imagine how badly that went down."

"Ah bless them," Richie said. "Honesty is a good policy, but despite what everyone says it's not always the best one."

"We had a fight," Jack said. "I was so angry with them. Like, what did they think would happen?"

"You had a fight with your partner and then you and the hunter drove all the way out here? I guess you really were annoyed."

Jack raised both hands to her forehead and raked her hair back, tugging on it, hoping it would somehow absolve some of her guilt. "I don't like being angry. I never know how to solve it."

"Well, I'm not exactly an expert," Richie said. "But uh, anger is an emotion, and you don't solve emotions, you feel them."

"What are you, a Buddhist zen master?" Jack cut her eyes at Richie, joking to mask the impact of his words. They struck like a sword slash to the chest. She felt exposed and raw.

"Far from it, but when you use magic, you learn a little about control. What should be controlled, what can be harnessed and what can be let to run its course."

"I know Raphael and Emmaline do a lot of meditation," Jack said, slowly.

"That's a part of it, for sure." Richie paused to tug a dead branch loose from where it had fallen from a tree. "But to me the bigger part is just knowing yourself. Understanding what it is that you're really angry about." He started walking again.

Jack followed, worrying at the thumbnail on her left hand. The anger she'd felt, what had it been about really? Frustration that Piper was too trusting? That they'd offered the truth when Jack had been too afraid to? So then, what Jack was feeling was actually a sort of envy, a wish to trust people the way Piper had. But then it was complicated by Apanui's response. She hadn't wanted to believe, hadn't given them anything useful, which meant that Jack had been right not to trust.

Jack shook her head. "It's pretty tangled, I don't know if there's just one answer."

"That's fine," Richie said. "Just means you need to think about it some more."

They lapsed into quiet. Jack listened to the noises of the forest, of their feet on the dirt path, and she thought. As she did, she started to see what she should do next.

CHAPTER 30

Piper lay flat on their back on the floor while Lucifer hopped around them. It seemed to be a game. Piper wasn't exactly sure what the rules were, but they were enjoying it all the same. Once Lucifer had done a circuit of Piper's body, she nosed in under Piper's ear for bunny kisses, which were ticklish but so adorable Piper wouldn't dream of stopping them.

They hadn't had a lot of experience with rabbits. Were they usually so playful and affectionate? Piper had no idea if Lucifer was just acting like a normal rabbit or if this was a familiar thing.

It didn't matter, really. Piper enjoyed the company, and Lucifer was eating and drinking well, toileting only in the designated spot and seemed happy. Nothing to worry about unless anything changed.

Piper laughed, stretched their hand out to the left so Lucifer had something to jump over when she came around on another circuit. Lucifer's nose twitched when she approached the arm and gamely hopped over it.

The intercom buzzed, startling them both. Lucifer hopped under the nearest chair and sat in a concerned bun shape, nose twitching. Piper got up and went to push the intercom button. They had sudden vision of Jack waiting below, chewing on her fingernails.

"Hello?"

"It's Jack," Jack said. "And Amy."

Piper frowned, unsure what would have brought Jack to them. Were they ready to talk to her again? Maybe it would be better to have some more time alone? Piper checked their watch and saw it was almost four in the afternoon. They'd had a lot of time to think.

Realistically, Piper wasn't going to ignore Jack. They couldn't just pretend they hadn't answered the intercom. They pressed the door release button. "Come on up."

They took the door off the latch, put Lucifer in her cage with the door open, and put the kettle on.

Whatever Jack had to say, Piper needed a coffee to hear it. Things always seemed easier with a cup of something hot between their hands.

The door opened. Jack walked in as Piper was setting cups on the counter. They'd picked the one which said "Elementary, my dear Watson", the panromantic flag mug and the Care Bears one. The collection felt right somehow.

Piper smiled automatically, seeing Jack. Jack looked... more relaxed than Piper had seen her look in a while. Although she winced, seeing Piper's expression. Perhaps the smile had been too automatic and had come off as forced or strained. Amy came in after her, closing and locking the door behind her.

"Hey Jack, Amy."

"Hey Piper," Amy said. "Got any snacks?"

"Oh, sure," Piper said. "Tea? Coffee?"

"Coffee," Amy said, quickly.

"Yeah, coffee sounds great, please," Jack said. She moved closer to Piper but didn't come into the open plan kitchen.

Piper bustled around, bringing out a packet of biscuits for Amy and pouring out coffees from the French press. "Milk and sugar are just here. Help yourself." Amy added an obscene amount of sugar to her coffee, and then some milk over the top. Jack took hers black.

Coffee in hand, Piper eyed Jack. "I'm sorry about earlier. I just don't like lying much, but I should have spoken to you first about what we would say and what we wouldn't."

Jack smiled, lopsided and slightly sad. "I'm sorry too. It wasn't fair of me to blame you for everything the way I did. I just want to solve this case."

"Come sit down," Piper gestured for them to sit on the couches in the lounge area. Amy sat at the table, working her way through the toffee pops with determination.

Jack sat sideways on the couch; one foot tucked under her to face Piper. "We drove out to the reserve."

Piper's eyebrows shot up and their mouth popped open. "Oh really?"

"Yeah, I wanted to... I don't know, I wanted to understand what I was angry at. And I wanted to show Amy the place as well."

"Kier and I raced," Amy said, around a mouthful of chocolate biscuit. "I trounced him."

Piper swallowed a giggle. This was a serious conversation and it appeared that Jack was really trying to make a connection. Piper focused on her face. "Did you get to understand it?"

"A little." Jack dropped her gaze and stared into the coffee cup. "I'm feeling less and less like this work is sustainable within the, well, the police force. It's certainly a nightmare in the judicial system, and I don't know what that means for me or for my future. I don't imagine Apanui will come around and just give us carte blanche to do what we like, and although the back up and the resources are important... When it comes to the magical world there are obviously workarounds."

At this she nodded at Amy, who was licking chocolate off her fingers. Piper grinned at her and she smiled back. "These are delicious. Are there any more?"

"I guess they aren't a thing in the US, right? That's where you're from, before... Faerie?" Jack asked

"Uh-uh, Chicago," Amy said. "It's all variations on Oreos or chocolate chip cookies."

"Look in the pantry," Piper said. The speed with which Amy jumped up scared them. Piper forced themself to think of what Jack had said and what it all meant.

Lucifer climbed into their lap and they felt instantly calmer. "Yeah, so, we can't just go around putting fae creatures in jail, and hunters, well, they're a whole international conglomerate of bad, and then mages... Like, they can probably magic their way out of prison, right?"

"Yup!" Amy shouted from the kitchen.

"So, the options are I try and ignore all the magic shit," Jack said. She held up a finger and frowned at it. Then put another up. "Or I quit the force and go freelance."

Piper's stomach sank and their chest tightened. It was true, those did seem to be the obvious choices, but they hadn't been prepared to hear it stated so bluntly. They took a deep breath in through their nose and let it out in a huff. "Right. Um, and you're uh, not exactly likely to want to give up the magic, are you? You love a mystery too much."

Jack smiled tightly and nodded. "Yeah, now that I know about it, I couldn't just give it up. Especially once Emmaline comes back. But I'm not asking you to do anything at all. I haven't made my decision and I wouldn't imagine I could suggest what you should do with your life. You're a fantastic partner, and I actually like working with you, which puts you miles ahead of any other partner I've ever had."

Piper blushed, feeling their chest loosen somewhat. "Thanks."

"But the police, this career, it's starting to feel like a prison to me," Jack twisted her fingers together and frowned at them.

"I get that." Piper sighed and set their coffee cup down. "Thanks for telling me all this. I guess it... can't have been easy for you."

Jack shook her head, looking up. Her face looked less relaxed now. "No, not really. My heart rate is way up, I can feel it."

Piper shifted closer, pressing their hand on Jack's knee. "Just breathe in and out as slowly as you can. Try and control it."

Jack nodded and did so, sighing on the out breath. "Okay. I'm okay."

Piper rubbed her shoulder. "So, uh, have you got a plan or is it too early for that?"

"I have to finish this case. It's too important, and the reach the force has is essential." Jack relaxed her hands and rested them on her knees. Piper thought they could detect them trembling. "But maybe after this I'll talk to Apanui about leaving and if they can pair you with someone else. If you choose to stay on that is, I mean, I know I've made no plans and I don't have a clear goal in mind, but if you'd like to freelance with me, I'd really appreciate the help. But don't decide anything now," Jack said, seemingly all in one breath, staring at their knees. "No pressure, take time and think things over."

Piper swallowed a lump in their throat, their own heart was starting to race. This was big stuff. *Big*. "I've only been with the station a few weeks, really," Piper said, their voice small. "But I know what you mean. This feels... so much bigger than the things I learned in training college."

Amy brought over a large bag of salt and vinegar chips and sat down in between them. "I think you should both quit. Hire a little place near the magic shop and be like, Private Eyes for all the mages and freaks and stuff. Just my two cents."

Piper exhaled slowly, trying to regain the calm they'd had earlier in the day, playing with Lucifer. Changing the topic of conversation would help. They could deal with their reaction later on. It would take some time and maybe some crying but that was fine.

"Do you two need to hug it out?" Amy asked. "It helps. I was sceptical of it to start with but it's actually really good."

"Maybe," Piper said, their voice soft. They set Lucifer down on the floor and she hopped towards Amy.

Jack got up without answering, so Piper got up too. Jack opened her arms. "Sorry, I know this is a lot. I kinda made this decision quickly, but I'm actually really scared."

Piper hugged her tight, rubbing a hand up and down the detective's back. "Yeah, I'm scared too, but I also think it's the right choice."

Jack slumped against Piper's shoulder and mumbled into their shirt. "Yeah, me too."

They sat back down, and Piper felt a brightening in the room. They looked around the room, but nothing had changed. Maybe it was just a clearing of emotions? "In the meantime," they said, "we need to be solving this case."

"Yeah." Jack took a couple of chips out of the packet Amy was eating from. "I need to talk to Emmaline, I think. Ask if there's any tracking spells she can do. Damn, I should have asked Richie to open up a mirror for me or something."

"No need." Amy stood up and looked around. "Do you have a mirror?"

Piper pointed towards the front door, where they had an ornamental mirror on the wall.

"Raph gave me a thingy. It should get us through to the cottage and Em will be around there somewhere. Okay to use this?"

"Just for talking, all right?" Piper said, standing up. "If people are gonna be climbing through we need to clear off the table."

"Magical Facetime only," Amy said. She was at the mirror and dug in her pocket for something. "If Emmaline's decided she wants to come through she can do it at Jack's place, saves on travel time."

"You know, Jack, Amy's a little like you," Piper said, as Jack joined them.

"Am not," Amy said.

"I don't see it," Jack said.

Amy pressed the thing from her hand against the glass of the mirror. Nothing happened. A crease appeared in Amy's forehead. "It should be doing ..."

Movement on the floor caught Piper's eye. They looked down to see Lucifer standing on her hind legs, pressing her front paws against Amy's leg. There was an intent look to her, and a sparkle in her little bunny eyes.

Then there was a ripple, and the soft sound of the wind through the trees.

Piper's skin prickled with the sound. For a moment they felt something... something in the air, tingling or... humming perhaps. Something not quite audible, which they'd never noticed around the mirror spell before. They looked down at Lucifer, who gazed directly at Piper. The feeling intensified for a second, and then passed. Just the magic token doing its thing?

The glass of the mirror distorted. Instead of Amy's reflection, they saw the cosy looking interior of the storybook cottage in Faerie. There was no one there, so far as Piper could tell. They moved closer, to look over Amy's shoulder.

Amy leaned into the mirror and shouted. "Hey! Anyone home? It's Amy!"

There was the sound of a muffled bang and then footsteps. Emmaline hurried into view, her hair in two braids, hanging over her shoulders. She was dressed in pyjamas and a huge grey knitted shawl. "Hey Amy, oh, you have Jack and Piper too! Hello. Raphael's out on a run, he'll be pissed he missed you."

"It's fine." Amy waved a hand and stepped to the side. "Jack wanted to talk to you, really." Amy nodded to Jack and then at the mirror.

Jack stepped forward, pushed her hair back from her forehead and smiled at Emmaline. "Hi."

Emmaline's eyes widened and she smiled brightly. "Hi Jack."

Piper suppressed a smile, sure now that Jack was into Emmaline and that in time the two of them would hook up. They were so clearly gone for each other.

"How are... how are things?"

"Oh, all right," Emmaline shrugged. "Pretty good? I'm okay. It's nice spending time with my brother."

"Yeah, yeah I bet it is."

Amy made a delicate sound that might have been a snort. Jack and Emmaline didn't seem to notice, but when Piper looked at Amy, she winked. Piper hid their grin by bending down and scooping Lucifer into their arms, cradling her like a baby.

"Emmaline, I've really..." Jack hesitated.

Piper couldn't stand it anymore, they poked her in the ribs.

"Ow."

"Just ask." Piper hissed. They felt a bit giddy, like they'd got some kind of contact high from seeing Jack be so goofy about Emmaline.

Jack shot Piper a quelling look, then returned to gazing at Emmaline. "I miss you!" she said louder than anyone had been talking.

Amy grabbed Piper by the upper arm and dragged them into the kitchen. It wasn't exactly the same as giving them privacy, since Piper's apartment was open plan, but it gave the appearance of it.

CHAPTER 31

J ack swallowed, a little, no... quite humiliated from blurting out that she missed
Emmaline. But the honest talk with Piper had gone well, and she couldn't take back
what had already been said. She shook her head and ploughed on.

"I miss you, and we need you on this case. We know there are some hunters out
there, we found a place where they had been, and we've found so many people who are
pretending to be them, or have been partially recruited, but the leads are dry." She paused
for a breath, realised she'd dropped her eyes from the mirror and looked at Emmaline
again. She looked radiant. Beautiful and cheerful and everything perfect.

"I miss you, too, Jack." She took a deep breath. "There are spells I can do. Did you pick
up anything from the place the hunters had been? Tracking is easiest with a token."

Jack's stomach sank. "There was nothing personal from them that we saw. Just packets
from fast food and stuff."

"Huh," Emmaline frowned. "And I guess that'd all be well disposed of by now."

"Yeah. If only there was something..."

"The map!" Piper called out from across the apartment.

"Oh, yes!" Jack brightened, lifting her chin a bit more. "That'll be in evidence at the
station, we can grab that. There was a map of the park, and it'd been marked and stuff.
They didn't find any fingerprints on it but most likely they'd have touched it."

"Some hunters don't have fingerprints," Amy interjected.

Jack considered that for a moment and then shuddered. She didn't want to know the
process for removing a hunter's fingerprints. Hopefully it was a simple magical procedure.

"That'll be *magnifique*. If you can get a hold of it, or bring me to it then I can try a
locator spell."

Jack nodded. Her heart thumped and her stomach filled with butterflies. "Bring you
to it? Like you'll come back through so we can solve the case together?"

"Well, it might be getting a bit crowded at your flat," Emmaline said.

"I only need a few hours of sleep each night," Amy called. "I'll take the couch."

"Unless—" Piper started to say and then broke into giggles.

Jack, cheeks flaring red, looked over at them to see Amy tickling their ribs. Lucifer bounced up and down in Piper's arms, looking nonplussed.

Jack shook her head. "I'd love to have you back." She moved closer to the mirror. "I'd really like to talk to you again. I miss you."

Emmaline beamed. "You've already said that twice."

"Did I?"

"I'll come through at your place," Emmaline said. "It doesn't look safe to come through here."

"Perfect." Jack nodded and then realised she was nodding too long and stopped again. "We'll see you at home."

Emmaline blew her a kiss, which made her heart beat extra fast as if she were the fan of some pop star who had just singled her out in the crowd. Ridiculous.

"I... thanks," she said.

Emmaline giggled and was gone from the mirror.

Jack took a moment to compose herself before turning and going to the kitchen where Amy and Piper were both suppressing smiles. "Well, that's good."

"Very good," Amy said. "You two should bone already."

Piper burst out laughing.

Jack felt her cheeks burn. "Okay, laugh it up. But I am happy she's coming to help us out."

"Guess we'd better get back to the house, then," Amy said. "Since she might already be there and my dirty clothes are on the floor of that room."

Jack pulled a face. "Have I not shown you where the washing machine is?"

"You did, I just haven't got around to using it," Amy said. "Jaunts out to the country and everything."

"Right, yeah, let's go." Jack turned to look at Piper, sure there was something else she should be saying to them but slightly at a loss for what it was. "Sorry for barging in like this."

Piper shrugged it off. "I'm used to it. You've been barging in since the second day we were partnered. I'd almost say it was part of your charm, but maybe I shouldn't go quite that far."

"Sorry," Jack said, breezily. She felt light, inclined to crack jokes. The news that Emmaline was returning had taken a weight off her back and she was relieved. "Maybe you should move in, too, then I'd have everyone important in one place."

Piper's eyes widened and they smiled as if Jack had given them a medal of honour. Then they laughed again. "Yeah, yeah, go home and see Emmaline. I'll see you in the morning. We can go to the station and get her to do the thing with the map."

Jack grinned. "Absolutely."

The challenge was to not speed on the drive home. Jack had almost been tempted to let Amy take the wheel.—they'd have certainly been home quicker—but had decided that getting a driving infringement wasn't worth it. Especially since Amy was technically an illegal immigrant and there were no records of her entering the country at all. Which was difficult when you lived on an island in the South Pacific.

Jack parked outside her house, impatiently unlocked the door and practically flew up the stairs. "Emmaline?"

Emmaline stood near the couch, rubbing her arm. Her hair was still in cute braids, but now she was wearing a rainbow striped sweater and black jeans. Her face lit up when she saw Jack.

Jack didn't hesitate. She strode across the room, threw her arms around Emmaline and kissed her on the mouth.

Emmaline kissed her back instantly, a soft noise coming from deep in her throat which scrambled all of Jack's thoughts until there was nothing but how good and warm Emmaline felt in her arms, and how sweet the taste of her lips.

Amy cleared her throat.

The sound jolted Jack back into the real world. She pulled back from Emmaline and searched her face, her hands on Emmaline's waist. "I'm so sorry, I didn't think, I didn't ask if it was okay..."

Emmaline shook her head, smiling. "It was okay. It is okay."

"I'm just gonna..." Amy sidled past. "Get my things from the room, but uh, if you two decide to start getting it on, I'm happy to take the room back."

Jack let go of Emmaline and took a step back. "No, uh, it's too soon for that of course."

Emmaline nodded and stuck her hands in her pockets. "Yeah, of course it is."

"Okay, so ground rules for you being back." Jack flicked her hair out of her eyes and turning away. "You don't go out anywhere without me or Amy, and you can't stay home alone."

"Yeah, Raphael said much the same thing," Emmaline gave Jack a look of knowing, a warm, secret smile that promised that she understood Jack's desire to take things slow. "I'm just happy to be back."

CHAPTER 32

Piper relaxed for the rest of the evening and went to bed early, reassured that Emmaline was back and that with magical help they could move forward with the case. Lucifer insisted on snuggling in beside them on the bed, which was a delightful comfort Piper hadn't expected.

They woke abruptly at five on Sunday morning with an idea. It was too important to ignore or to go back to sleep on. It couldn't be forgotten.

Sitting up, they switched on the bedside light and picked up a notebook and pen.

Lucifer blinked at them from where she was sprawled over Piper's legs, blinked and went back to sleep.

"The hunters operate on secrecy, and they're using fear and misinformation," they said as they wrote. The act of speaking out loud made what they wrote feel more important. "Therefore, if we bring the information we have into the light, if we expose the conspiracy to the public, explain that there are these YouTube videos targeting the lost and lonely, perhaps we can weaken them. We can remove some of that power they have..."

They stared at what they'd written. Their heart pounded, with the enormity of what it suggested. They wouldn't have to go public and say that magic was real—just that there was a dark internet thing happening and that parents should look out for kids, people should look out for their friends, and reach out to neighbours who were acting strangely or in danger of becoming isolated.

Piper's mind, which was used to anxiety and the worst possible outcomes, supplied some immediate holes in the plan. For it to work, it would require people to really care about each other, to build and maintain a sense of community, and for them to care enough about the possible dangers to take action at all.

They were valid concerns. Piper noted them as bullet points, but then they stopped thinking about them. The problem was people, of course it was, but Piper believed that people were generally good. Show them a way to help someone else, and they'd usually take it. Most people weren't just out for themselves and trying to get ahead. Some were, of course, but they were the minority.

They sighed and rested their head back against the pillow. For this to work, they'd need a few things... They started to write again. They'd need buy-in from Apanui, and some kind of outreach strategy. Budget for TV and YouTube advertising, running ads on popular social media would be essential as well.

Then there was person power. They'd want to go into schools perhaps, to talk to kids directly. The University campuses too. Posters, which would mean a graphic designer, and then someone clever with words who could come up with slogans and catchphrases that stuck.

Piper filled in another page of the notebook brainstorming it all out. It was a big ask, but it felt important to try. If they couldn't get backing from the Sargent, though, it was going to be very hard indeed, and she was already on their asses about results. But surely this was something the Sargent could see the benefit of, and the impact of alerting people to internet conspiracy theories and rabbit holes would have a knock-on effect. It wasn't like the ant-magic brigade was the only group doing this online. Far from it.

"For the greater good," Piper said to themselves, and smiled, thinking of that old Simon Pegg movie. They checked the time, almost six in the morning. No point in going back to sleep now. They opened up the chat app and messaged their brother, who would be up and prepping at the bakery already.

Piper: For the greater good!

It was random and out of nowhere, but Ben would get it, they were sure. They hopped out of bed and scooped up Lucifer balancing the butt and back legs on one forearm and hand and the other under her front paws. Lucifer snuggled in against Piper's chest and then looked up at them so their eyes met.

A peculiar sensation came over Piper then, the knowledge that Lucifer was connected to them. That she had perhaps, planted the idea of outreach into Piper's mind, or per- haps... had helped Piper to puzzle it out in some way.

Which, well, Piper would have dismissed it as impossible, except that Lucifer had previously been a mage's familiar and now that they were holding her in their arms. What did this mean? They'd meant to ask Emmaline, but then forgotten.

Was it possible that Lucifer was bonding with Piper in a ... magical familiar way? Would that mean that Piper had some magic in themself? Or had Lucifer somehow endowed magic upon them?

They thought back to Valerie's reading, seemingly urging Piper to learn about their own spiritual life, the seed of something... Maybe Lucifer had sensed it too and was now nurturing it?

It was too much for so early in the day. Piper carried Lucifer into the kitchen, set her down on the floor and gave her a medium sized spinach leaf to munch. "Just one for the week. I read online that it can make you sick if you have more than that, Lucy."

Piper made themself breakfast and sat at the table, watching Lucifer as they ate. Lucifer had eaten the spinach slowly, as if she knew she could make herself sick, and then hopped to her water bowl.

If Piper did have magical powers, it would change some things...but they'd have to find out first what kind of magical powers. Maybe they'd be some kind of forest witch like Richie seemed to be, or one with charms and things like Raphael was.

Much as they liked Emmaline, they didn't want to be a necromancer like she was. It still spooked them to think about. Some of the things Emmaline had summoned populated Piper's nightmares.

No, Piper hoped that if they did have powers, that they were something earthier—maybe the ability to heal or read minds. No, wait, not read minds. Piper shook their head vehemently. That would be the absolute worst power, seeing everyone's weird dirty secrets.

They mused on that for a while, until it was time to wash and get dressed for work. They picked out black jeans, a patterned button up shirt and a soft grey merino sweater to wear over the shirt. Not too dressed up, but not sloppy. Approachable but professional at the same time.

Someone knocked on their apartment door.

Frowning because they weren't expecting anyone, Piper got up to open it. Lucifer hopped behind, curious.

Standing on the other side of the door was Kier, the kelpie. He gave her a sheepish smile. "Hey Piper!"

"Kier, what the hell are you doing here?" Piper's stress levels spiked through the roof.

In the hallway, another door opened. Beau stepped out of his apartment.

Kier turned to look at him and gave him a wide smile, his teeth obviously sharp as a vampire's.

Beau went pale. "What the hell?"

"Kier!" Piper grabbed his arm and yanked him inside the apartment before he could do anything else.

"Well, I was getting bored of being cooped up, you know?"

The implications of him, a magical creature—a *murderous* magical creature—being here in Piper's flat sank their stomach and made their heart race. They had so many questions but the first one blurted out. "How did you get out?"

"You know what I am right?" He crouched down to greet Lucifer.

Piper's heart beat even faster. "Don't hurt her!"

Lucifer gamely hopped up to Kier's outstretched hand and sniffed it. He looked up at them, obviously hurt. "I'd never! She's a familiar, she's people."

"Oh." Piper breathed out. "But I thought you ate people."

"I eat humans," he said, carelessly.

"That's not comforting." They sighed as Lucifer hopped into Kier's arms and they rubbed noses together. Lucifer wasn't at all worried, so that eased some of their fear.

Kier stood up and looked around their apartment. "I used the water table. You know that big lake? It's fenced up on the surface but you can't keep it from connecting to all the other waterways. The lake monster didn't really like me going through but we came to an agreement."

"Lake monster..." Piper pressed a hand to their forehead. "Wait but how did you find me?"

"You're in the phone book thing online. Then once I was close, I followed my nose."

"You sniffed me out?"

"Everyone smells different, and I know your scent." Kier shrugged his thin shoulders again, looking confused. "What's with all the questions?"

"I can't deal with this today, I have to go talk to my boss."

Kier frowned. "It's all good, I can just walk around the neighborhood and get my bearings."

"No, no. You should stay here," Piper said. "I only...I only have one key anyway so. You stay here, make yourself comfortable and when I get back, I can show you around a bit. I don't want you to get into any trouble on your own. It's busy out there."

For a moment, Piper worried that he'd argue with them, but Lucifers snuffled under his chin and then Kier nodded. "Yeah, okay. Can I watch TV?"

"Knock yourself out."

They showed him the remote and how to access their streaming services, poured him a glass of juice and took Lucifer back.

"I'll take Lucy with me, because she's sort of a target and, although I'm sure you can defend yourself, I don't want to put you through that."

The kelpie nodded, already flicking through the movie selection on streaming.

Piper looked at him, doubtful. They should probably call Richie and let him know that Kier was safe, but they also didn't want to bring the magical DOC workers to their apartment and draw more attention. Whoever was looking for Lucifer might notice that.

They would show Kier around and then send him back, that's what they'd do. He'd be all right for a few hours watching TV.

That was when Jack texted to say they were on the way to pick them up

Piper shrugged a light jacket on over their plaid shirt and cuffed jeans, coaxed Lucifer into the backpack and made Kier promise to stay inside and not make any trouble. They headed out, locking the door behind them.

Jack's proposal from the day before popped into their mind. It'd certainly be easier for Piper to bring a rabbit along if they didn't have to go into the police station and explain themselves.

And they didn't want to give up working with Jack, but the security of the regular salary was important to Piper, and not something that could just be given up without thought.

Something to consider, but not today. Today would be eventful enough, Piper could feel it.

CHAPTER 33

Piper looked a little spooked when Jack pulled up alongside where they were waiting. Jack assumed the impending meeting with Apanui had them freaked out. They climbed in the back with a brief hello.

Jack's car was getting rather full. With her and Amy in the front seats (Amy refused to be put in the back), and Emmaline, Piper and Lucifer in the back it was very different to the work commute of six months ago.

Jack reflected on it as she navigated the morning traffic through town. It wasn't a bad thing to have all these people around her. Six months ago, she would have been wary of those people's intentions, and wearied by spending so much of her time in company. Instead, she was pleased and reassured by their presence.

Reassured for different reasons for each of them. Piper for being such a good partner, a foil to Jack's serious determination, and a welcome ray of sunshine.

Amy because Jack and Amy understood each other on a base level. Amy was to the point and tough as nails. Whatever happened, if it came to blows or some kind of magical fight, Amy would react swiftly and with a cool head.

And Emmaline, well, her presence was welcomed for a myriad of reasons. Her magic of course, would ensure the case was solved as quickly as it could be. But above that, she brought a warmth with her that Jack could never hope to understand or replicate. Being in her presence was soothing, and the townhouse, even the car, felt brighter for her being there. She caught herself gazing at Emmaline in the rear-view mirror and quickly forced her eyes back to the road.

There you go, good bunny," Emmaline cooed.

"Please don't let the rabbit out while the car is in motion," Jack said.

"She's fine," Piper said. "Emmaline's just feeding her treats."

"Please don't let her run around," Jack said. Thankfully, despite her concerns, Lucifer behaved herself.

The memory of Jack's kiss with Emmaline was fresh in her mind. It was warm as well, warm and soft, full of light and promise. But Jack knew she didn't want to rush into another one. Well, she did, she absolutely did, but she wouldn't. Whatever it was that Jack and Emmaline shared, it was worth taking slowly. Worth savouring and being cautious with. Emmaline deserved that.

Jack hardly noticed they'd got to the station until she put the car into park and switched off the ignition.

"Welcome back," Amy said, amused. "Nice dream, was it?"

Jack turned to her, startled. "What?"

"You haven't heard a word anyone's said for more than five minutes," Amy said.

Piper and Emmaline got out the back of the car, laughing about something. Jack's cheeks warmed, hoping it wasn't her they were laughing about.

"God, that was, way too obvious, isn't it?"

"You're fine." Amy patted Jack's arm. "I saw that kiss, I'd be dreaming about it too."

Jack made a sort of groaning grump noise without opening her mouth and got out of the car.

Amy hesitated, eyeing the door of the station.

"Maybe you ought to come in," Jack said. "You're part of this, and I want to be as honest as I can with the Sargent. You and Emmaline can help with that."

Amy shrugged and stuck her hands in the pockets of her black leather jacket. "Fine."

Inside, Jack dumped her bag on her desk, checked her hair was more or less tidy and nodded at Piper. "Come on, let's check in with Apanui again."

Piper and snapped their fingers. "Yes. Now, what are we saying today?"

"Full honesty," Jack said. "Like you tried yesterday. Em and Amy can come with and do some tricks if we need to really hammer home that we're not lying."

"I am not a show pony." Amy flipped her hair back to show her disdain for the idea.

"Okay, well, you can at least show the Sargent your brand," Jack said. "We have photos of the copy ones from some of the people we've arrested to compare it to."

"I don't mind doing tricks," Emmaline said. "Lucifer might be able to help too."

Jack led the way to the Sargent's office and knocked on the doorframe. Apanui was inside, intent on paperwork, but she looked up at the knock. "Jack, Piper...and friends. Come on in."

Amy came in after the others and closed the door behind her.

"Right, so Sargent Apanui, you know Emmaline Perrone, but this is our friend Amy..." Jack swallowed, realising she didn't know Amy's last name.

Amy raised a hand in a casual salute. "I wasn't here, and you certainly didn't see me."

"Excuse me?" Apanui's eyebrows shot up, almost all the way into her perfectly arranged headscarf.

Jack's stomach dropped.

Emmaline giggled and put a hand on Amy's shoulder. "Maybe don't say stuff like that."

"Amy is part, no she *was* part of the terrorist organisation that we're dealing with in this case," Jack said. "She's reformed, but she has inside information that no one else does. Between Emmaline's gifts and Amy's knowledge I feel absolutely confident that we can get this case wrapped up."

Apanui eyed the group of them with a healthy amount of scepticism. "And Emmaline, is she..." Apanui said the next word as if it were something particularly distasteful. "Magical? In your opinion?"

Piper stepped forward, pulling Lucifer out of the backpack. "Please, Sargent, I know it's a lot to get your head around, but Emmaline really can do things which can't be explained away."

"Why are you showing me a rabbit, Detective?"

"I could show you some magic..." Emmaline offered.

Apanui held up a hand and shook her head, just once. "No, I don't want to see anything. Jack, you're leaning on every ounce of trust and goodwill I've ever been able to offer you, so please. Make sure my faith in you isn't misplaced."

Jack sighed, feeling her stomach unknot. That was probably as good as it was getting from Apanui. "Of course. I won't make you regret it.

"There's just one more thing," Piper said, their voice softer than normal, betraying their nervousness. "We'd really like to talk to you about community outreach and if there's any budget there, because well, the reason these people have been able to recruit is they're exploiting vulnerable people."

"Mmhm." Apanui scooted her chair back and opened a desk drawer.

"We thought if we could raise awareness and kind of, bring them out of the darkness so to speak, we could save more people. Make sure that these people aren't getting their hooks into our young people, or the misunderstood."

Apanui produced a wordy looking form. "Here's the application for funding. I'm happy for you to do outreach as long as you run it past the PR department first. You might even get lucky and find you can tag along on some stuff already planned; I don't know."

Piper handed Lucifer to Emmaline, hurried forward and took the forms.

Jack watched. Wasn't this going all too easily? Was Apanui saying they could do what they wanted so that they'd make a mistake and she could fire them?

Or maybe this past week had just made Jack even more paranoid than she'd been before. If Apanui wanted to, she could order them to stop this investigation entirely, and she hadn't done that. Jack had to judge her based on her actions.

"Thank you, Sargent," Piper said.

Jack gave Piper a tight smile she didn't feel and cleared her throat. "Yeah, thanks. Now, we'll... We'll get out of your way."

"Thank you," Apanui said, dry as paper.

They filed out of her office and back to Jack's desk.

"Fuck, that woman has such a powerful vibe to her. As soon as I walked in the room I could feel it," Amy said, appreciatively, her voice low. "Respect."

"That actually went pretty well," Jack said. "So where do we start?"

"Funding application." Piper sat down with the form and started filling it in. "Then I guess we start with the families of the people who were arrested. Go from there? I need to get back home sooner rather than later, though."

Jack nodded. "I guess we need to come up with some kind of script or basic points to hit before we jump in, as well. Otherwise, I'm likely to panic and say something inappropriate."

"Maybe we'll go wait in the cafe," Amy said. "People are looking at me, here."

Jack paused halfway to sitting down. "Oh, yeah, you do that. I'll grab some addresses and names and stuff off the database, then when Piper's done with the application, we can come join you."

"Take Lucifer with you?" Piper asked. "She's safe with you two and I need to concentrate on this paperwork."

"Perfect." Emmaline leaned in and gave Jack a quick one-armed hug. "You did great," she murmured. For a moment Jack thought she might be about to kiss her and felt the urge to turn her head and kiss her as well, but Emmaline pulled back and the moment was gone.

Jack pressed the map into Emmaline's hand for her to use later on.

Amy and Emmaline left the station. Jack took a half minute to regather her focus.

CHAPTER 34

That afternoon, when they got home, Piper took Kier for a walk around their neighbourhood. Lucifer was along for the ride in her backpack. The kelpie wasn't nearly as hard to keep in line as they'd dreaded. He was genuinely interested in every little thing.

"What's that for?" Kier pointed at a piece of public art, a huge boy walking towards the playground.

"Uh, well, it's not really *for* anything, it's just like, fun to look at. Art. You've seen art in your studies surely?"

"Paintings of a guy who died a long time ago, mostly," Kier said. "Richie said it was something called religion."

"Mm. Well, art's progressed a bit since then," Piper said. "I should take you to the art gallery, maybe? When this case is done."

They were suddenly struck by the absurdity of their situation. They were playing bodyguard to a magical rabbit and a boy who could transform into a monster. They had no idea how close the hunters were and if they had any idea what Kier was. They were very exposed, walking down Dominion Road towards the Balmoral shops.

"This is the café that does the best dumplings," Piper said. "You hungry?"

"Always. I've heard a lot about cafes and restaurants. Do a lot of writers spend time in this one? I bet writers are very delicious."

"You can't eat anyone," Piper said. Lucifer moved impatiently in the backpack, wanting to be let out. "I'll buy you some pork and chives dumplings."

"Thanks!" Piper found them a table near the front window so Kier could people watch. They sat with their back to the wall, feeling less vulnerable. Kier sat. He looked like a young man who'd grown up someplace very rural, wonderstruck by everything he saw.

Piper ordered a dozen pork and chives dumplings, some chicken and corn soup and sodas for both of them.

"This is so much better than the food I get at the reserve." Initially sceptical of the steaming little pouches of food, Kier devoured the dumplings enthusiastically.

Piper's heart ached for Kier. He was so full of life, of curiosity and passion for learning. It seemed monstrous to keep him locked up. He was obviously in control of his hunger, he'd been mentioning eating people but it wasn't like he was having to be held back or anything.

He just wanted to learn.

Maybe Piper wouldn't call Richie. Or maybe, maybe they'd just let him know Kier was safe and that they had nothing to worry about. Then something occurred to Piper. "Kier, can they track you?"

Kier blinked at Piper, chewing a mouthful slowly, one cheek puffed out with food. Then he shook his head from side to side, swallowed. "I don't think so. Or... maybe? They might have a spell."

"I'd better call Richie then, let him know you're safe and he doesn't need to come and get you," Piper said.

Kier's smile widened. "You're not going to ask him to take me back?"

It felt like the worst possible addition to Piper's problems, but their heart ached for the young kelpie. They wanted to see him smile like that more often. "No, you can stay with me."

The first half of the week continued around Kier's presence. He was happy to stay at home and watch television during the day.

Piper had even left him with Lucifer. "Just don't eat her, all right?"

Kier pressed a hand to his chest. "I'd *never*. Lucifer is special, and she likes me. I only hunt humans."

Lucifer had taken to Kier, that much was true. She followed him from room to room, and liked to sit between Piper and Kier on the couch, with her back feet on Piper's thigh and her chin on Kier's.

Piper deemed him safe enough to babysit, and Jack was visibly relieved when Piper showed up without the rabbit in tow.

Jack had suggested splitting up to cover more ground, but Piper had pointed out that if they were to stumble across real hunters being alone would probably be a bad choice. Emmaline had tried a locator spell on the map but met with some kind of magical resistance, so that was a dead end.

So, as a pair, with Amy in the car, or waiting outside the house or apartment, they'd gone through the city, checking off the list Jack had compiled of arrests and releases of those involved with the conspiracy. Emmaline had Piper's new spare key, and checked in every day on Kier and Lucifer, ready to be called in if anything happened.

The interviews had mixed results. Jack was quick to discount any of the interviews where the family didn't wholeheartedly jump on board with their suggestions of ways to help. Piper believed that at least having the conversation in the first place was an important first step. Perseverance and calm, respectful laying out of facts that people couldn't dispute, that would come through.

"I don't exactly understand what you're suggesting," one father said. His daughter, Gale, had been found to be spreading misinformation.

"The situation is this. Gale is likely to get away with just a fine, as she didn't seem to be involved in sharing people's private information," Jack said. "But she was disseminating the videos which inspired others to go deeper and engage in invasions of privacy and more. What we're suggesting you do is find some more ways to connect with her, and for her to connect to wider communities. Perhaps do some volunteering at the local community centre?"

The man, Mr Maddox, sat back in this chair and folded his arms. Piper didn't like that body language at all. "Is this something the police are requiring?"

"No, Mr Maddox, we're not ordering you to do anything. We just want to offer some suggestions for ways to ensure something like this doesn't happen again."

He grimaced and his hand came up to rub the bridge of his nose. "Her mother was very upset about the arrest. She called me and screamed my ear off about it."

"The last thing we want," Piper leaned forward to make eye contact with him, "is for Gale to go deeper into this group of radicals. So, we're offering some help. Maybe volunteering like Detective Duarte said, would help, or maybe something more social. Does she have any hobbies that might have meetups?"

"She used to like drawing," Mr Maddox said. He sighed heavily, looked between the two of them, his expression dropping. "I know your hearts are in the right place, but I just don't know. She's a teenager, you know? She hates everything I suggest on principle."

Jack nodded. "But we still have to try."

He swallowed. "Yeah. Yeah, of course we do."

At the end of the second day, they'd spoken to the direct families of most of the list and Piper was utterly exhausted. Although they trusted Kier, they were low-key worried about leaving him alone all day. Emmaline was checking in around lunch time, but the last thing Piper wanted was for him to get bored and go wandering.

Jack shouted them dinner at the pizza place they liked in town. Amy was there too, and Emmaline arranged to meet them with Lucifer. Piper was relieved to have Lucifer back, they hadn't realised just how worried they'd been–a fizzing irritation at the back of their mind because they couldn't see the rabbit. It vanished as soon as they held Lucifer again.

"Kier didn't want to come out. He's deep in some true crime show and he wants to know how it ends," Emmaline said. "I thought it was probably for the best we didn't bring him right into the city so I left him to it."

"Good call," Jack said.

Settling the rabbit on their lap, Piper looked at the faces of the three women and felt warm. At least they knew they had a community. Even if Amy was on loan and would likely go back to Faerie when the case was done. Piper trusted all of them with their life, and that felt good in the moment.

Amy had ordered two large pizzas and a side of mozzarella rolls for herself. Emmaline and Jack shared a few slices of mushroom and cheese, and Piper had a large pepperoni slice. They passed Lucifer a piece of cut apple from a packet.

Jack had been describing how the conversations had gone to Amy and Emmaline.

"From what you've described," Emmaline said. "It's going well."

"I think so, too," Piper said. "But Jack's being grumpy about it."

"I'm being realistic," Jack said. "We can go and talk to people all we want, and they might agree, or they might just say they agree to get us to leave them alone. We won't know until we see people taking actions."

"People can change," Amy said. "But it takes time. Or like, one really big event to show them the truth. Or..." she paused, chewing a pizza crust and swallowing. "Someone to show you the colour of your soul."

Emmaline tilted her head to one side. "You want us to go around showing people the colour of their souls? That sounds kinda involved."

Amy giggled. "Well, it worked on me. Raphael showed me, that's how I first started doubting the Hunters and trusting him."

Jack shook her head. "We've made a start, but there's a lot of work ahead of us too. Hopefully we'll have posters and flyers and things by the end of the week."

Piper hadn't had a lot of time to check their work emails and inboxes, but they had seen that the funding had been approved and a team assigned to the work. "Yes. It'll be good to have those. And they were asking about getting an ad or two from the Government, since they've already got a series about keeping kids safe online."

"Oh," Jack said. "Yeah, I've seen those, with the old guy turning up at the door saying he's been chatting to the teenager online and the mother is like, 'We're calling the police.' They're really good."

"New Zealand is a weird place," Amy said, shaking her head. "But in a good way, I think."

"Well, I like it here," Emmaline said. "It's so quiet compared to other cities. And the parks are so beautiful." Her eyes slipped to gaze at Jack as she spoke.

Piper felt vicarious butterflies. The flirting between Jack and Emmaline had definitely ramped up recently. Piper wanted so badly for them to just get together and be happy. Even if they knew it wasn't that simple.

Jack didn't seem to notice.

"You should check out Christchurch, some time," Piper said. "It's beautiful down there. There's a river through town and a huge park. Lots of flowers in springtime."

"That's where you moved up from?" Emmaline asked, turning her big blue eyes on Piper.

"Yep, and my brother Ben is there at the moment, but he's looking at moving up too." They couldn't help but grin as they shared that news. "He's coming up next weekend to look at places to rent."

"Oh, that's great," Jack said. "I know you're pretty close with him."

"Yeah, his bakery's doing really well so he wants to expand up here." Piper finished off their piece of pizza. "He makes the most amazing cakes."

Lucifer moved in Piper's lap and a small paw touched their wrist, they pulled out another apple slice to give to her.

"Sounds like I'll definitely want to visit this bakery." Amy had finished both her pizzas and was chewing on her last mozzarella roll. Piper inhaled in awe. They had no idea how she was capable of eating so quickly. "I might get some dessert, anyone want anything?"

There were all mostly finished. "How about we all go for gelato?" Jack suggested. "There's a really good place down the road a bit."

Piper's phone buzzed. Kier asking if it was all right if he went to the nearest takeaway for some dinner.

Piper's heart sped up, imagining all the terrible ways that particular scenario could go. "You three go ahead, I have to get back to Kier," Piper said. "Before he locks himself out, or eats someone, or... worse."

CHAPTER 35

It was Wednesday that Jack's suspicions paid off, although she wished they hadn't.

They were visiting Kevin Jones' family, the one who had gone on about snowflakes in his interrogation. Jack assumed it was his mother who had answered the door. The woman wore a plain but expensive looking cotton dress and designer house slippers. She looked them both up and down with narrowed eyes.

"Mrs Jones? We're just here to talk to you," Piper had said. "A follow up for Kevin and for yourself." Jack was pleased she'd convinced Piper to leave Lucifer with Emmaline again.

"I don't recall the courts mentioning this visit."

"No, they wouldn't have." Jack pulled out her police ID and showed it to the woman. Piper did the same. "This is a new venture we're trying out this week. It's not standard practice."

"Don't want anything that's not normal," the woman said. "We've had enough drama as it is."

"Really, sorry to bother you but we would just like a conversation. We can come back at another time if that would suit you better?"

Mrs Jones sighed dramatically, rolled her eyes and opened the door wider. "Might as well get it over with right now, I suppose."

"Great." Jack glanced down the hallway to where Amy was lingering on the corner, reassuring herself that the ex-hunter was close, then she went into the apartment. Her back was up from Mrs Jones' behaviour, and her gut complained as soon as she stepped in.

Jack considered calling it off and getting Piper out of there, but the apartment was so normal inside. A bookshelf full of books in one corner. A television paused on a hospital drama, a pot bubbling on the stovetop.

"Is Kevin home?" Piper asked.

Mrs Jones shook her head. "No, he went to pick some things up for me at the supermarket. He's such a good boy."

"I'm sure he is," Jack said. She mustn't have been able to keep the dryness out of her voice.

Mrs Jones gave them a sharp look. "So, what did you want to talk to me about?"

Piper started in on the spiel, emphasising how they wanted to help, and wanted to avoid worse outcomes for Kevin.

This did little to move Mrs Jones, who had one hand planted on her hip. Her expression was stony. "It all sounds very nice," she said, when Piper had finished the introduction. "But what do you want me to do? Send him to summer camp to meet other children? He's twenty years old. It's ridiculous, he's a grown man and he can do what he likes, last time I checked."

"Of course," Jack said, quickly. "We're not expecting you to send him anywhere, just maybe talk a little more about what kind of thing he's been learning online and talk about some different walks of life and so on."

Mrs Jones chuckled and shook her head. Her perfectly coiffed mane barely moved when she did. "We already talk about the things he's learned. And honestly, I don't see what all the fuss is about. He's just asking questions about the world around him."

Jack's gut told her, in so uncertain terms, to get out of there. "Right," Jack said, distracted. She pulled her phone out and looked at the blank screen. "Piper, maybe we ought to..."

"Asking questions is healthy of course," Piper said. "But what I've found is a lot of people caught up in this movement aren't looking at a wide range of sources for their information. They're choosing just one or two and then accepting it all."

"Well, if that source is telling the truth, I don't see the problem with it."

There was a noise behind Jack, a key in a lock. She whirled around.

Kevin walked in, a paper bag of groceries in one arm. "Detectives? What the fuck are you doing here?" He pocketed his keys and set the groceries down as the door swung shut.

Jack became uncomfortably aware of how tall and broad-shouldered he was. And how she and Piper were not in the police station.

"I didn't hear about any call or check in from you two."

"No, we're just here to have a conversation," Piper said.

Jack's hand went to her nightstick where it hung on her belt, and she saw Kevin's eyes follow the movement.

A nasty smile spread over his face. "What kind of conversation involves you upsetting my mother and bringing your nightsticks?"

"They're saying that you're misguided, sweetie," Mrs Jones said. Her voice falsely sweet, barely disguising the acid underneath. "That we need to get you talking to more diverse groups of people."

Kevin shook his head slowly and sneered. "Snowflake cops, never thought I'd see the day. Coming into my house and telling me how to live. What happened to the freedom of speech?"

"It doesn't cover hate speech," Jack said.

Kevin closed the distance between them swiftly, using his extra height to loom over Jack and sneer some more. "I don't hate anyone. I'm just concerned for my own safety. Want to get the gun, mum?"

"Threatening a police offer is a crime," Piper said, although their voice sounded strained and cracked on the word crime.

"I'm not threatening anyone." Kevin took another step. Jack used every ounce of strength not to take a step back. Staying in her place left her uncomfortably close to Kevin, and she smelled the hot, sour scent of his breath as he huffed out a breath. "I have a licence for my gun, and there's no reason I shouldn't ask my mother to fetch it for me."

There was movement, and Jack assumed it was Mrs Jones going to another room. Jack's mind raced. Kevin knew what he was doing. He hadn't broken any laws, yet. He'd got into Jack's personal space, and he was acting like he was going to do something, but he hadn't. Not yet. Jack didn't particularly want to wait and see what he'd do.

"Detective Gage," Jack said, her voice level. "Why don't you see what Amy's up to?"

"Who's Amy?" Kevin asked, his eyes narrowing. "You forget my mother's name or something? I told you, she's getting my gun."

Piper moved towards the door and Kevin whirled, putting himself in between them and the way out.

There was a tense few seconds where no one moved, although there was a rustling noise from the other room, and the distinct clang of a metal door hitting a wall.

"Please get out of my way," Piper said. Jack could hear the waver in their voice, but she hoped Kevin couldn't.

"Mm, don't think I will," Kevin said. With a quick movement he took hold of Piper's bicep. "I don't think we're done talking. I know how much you two *love* to talk."

"Let go of me." Piper yanked against his grip.

Jack went to pull out her nightstick when there was the distinct snick of a gun being cocked behind her. Fuck.

"Don't move a muscle, cop," Mrs Jones said.

Piper's eyes went wide as Jack slowly raised her hands.

"That's it, nice and easy," Kevin said. He pulled Piper forward and into the centre of the room.

Then there was a loud slamming noise on the front door.

Jack winced, hoped Mrs Jones' trigger finger wasn't itchy, as the sound came again.

"What the fuck was that?" Mrs Jones said. "Cops travel in twos, don't they?"

"I didn't see anyone else." Kevin twisted Piper's arm up behind their back so they whimpered. Jack clenched her teeth together.

Then with a third kick, Amy busted the door down and was on Kevin. She chopped her stiff hand into the side of his neck. Piper staggered free as Kevin's knees gave out under him, and he crumpled, his eyes wide and his mouth opening and closing like a fish.

Jack ducked and twisted, trying to get hold of Mrs Jones's arm. The gun fired. Jack flinched back, her heart pounding in her ears. "Fuck! Piper, you okay?"

"Yeah?"

Amy crossed the room so fast Jack had trouble tracking her movements, it was like motion blur on a movie. She kicked Mrs Jones' feet out from under her. Within seconds, she was on the ground as well, her arm up in the air behind her back.

Mrs Jones whimpered as Amy handed Jack the gun. "Sorry I wasn't here sooner," she said. "I should've just followed the big guy, huh?"

Jack looked at Kevin, who was breathing shallowly. "You're all right. Since they both attacked and a gun was fired, we can arrest them. If you'd been earlier, we might've had some trouble."

"Well, glad to be of assistance." Amy smiled coldly and twisted Mrs Jones's wrist.

Jack cuffed Kevin with no small amount of satisfaction and Piper called the arrest in to the station.

While they waited for the constables to come in and take the Jones' away, Jack, Amy and Piper looked through the apartment.

"Here," Amy said. "There's a big cache of weapons. And this one..." She picked it up before Jack could remind her not to touch anything. "This one is a Hunter altered one. A special." She hefted a semi-automatic rifle that was black and shiny. It looked like something straight out of a Hollywood spy film with a laser sight and a few other attachments. Jack was infinitely glad it hadn't been the one Mrs Jones picked up.

"So, they didn't just dip their fingers into the conspiracy," Piper said. "They were signing up."

They checked Kevin's wrists but there was no brand there.

"I was earning my way in. Nearly made it before you hauled me in," Kevin said. "Now I'm back down two levels."

"Stop talking, you idiot!" Mrs Jones snapped at her son. "Just be quiet, until we have our lawyer."

He closed his mouth, shamefaced.

CHAPTER 36

Arresting Kevin and Joyce, his mother, had felt like a win. It really had. But Mrs Jones refused to say anything useful, and her lawyer was a bulldog who barely let them question the two of them. It was frustrating. Piper felt disappointed beyond what they'd expected to feel. Breakthroughs on this case were rare enough, and now it felt like they'd had one but it'd been taken away, or walled off somehow.

They'd picked up Lucifer from Emmaline and told her all about it, cuddling her in their arms as they let themself into the apartment building.

Beau just got into the lift and he held the door for them to get in as well.

He looked tired, and more than a little stressed out. He had a big sheaf of papers under his arm, wrapped in a bit of brown paper as if he'd just had them printed or something.

Piper glanced at them and then away. "Hey Beau."

"Hi Piper," Beau said. "That rabbit..." He trailed off, his eyes narrowing.

Something prickled at the back of Piper's mind. Beau had been acting differently lately. Said he'd had some new friends who did meetups. Now he had a whole lot of what? Flyers? And was looking at Lucifer as if he thought she was suspicious?

Piper turned back to him. "What are those?" They tried not to sound accusatory but wasn't sure they succeeded. It had been a long day.

"Oh just some stuff the club asked me to get printed." Beau shifted the papers to under his other arm, the one further away from Piper.

"What kind of club is it?" Piper tried to pour as much mild but friendly disinterest into the question as they could. The lift dinged as it stopped at their floor.

"Oh it's uh, it's kind of a political thing." Beau got out of the lift and Piper followed.

"Like, a political party or more like a movement?"

"I guess a movement." He eyed them, bit his lower lip and then shook his head. "Why don't you just take a look?" Carefully, he tore the brown paper and pulled the topmost flyer off the stack.

Piper's heart sped up as they skimmed the text, it was all very familiar. 'Want to find out the TRUTH? There are those living among us who aren't like us! What do you know about your neighbours?' At the bottom under a large paragraph of text in which Piper picked out the words 'magic' and 'Satanic', was an address and time for a meet up. The logo in the corner was identical to the inked version of the Hunter's brand that Tod had on his wrist.

A chill went through Piper and they looked up at Beau. "Beau, you're not... These people, they're conspiracy theorists and they're dangerous."

Beau's eyes widened and he paled. His eyes flicked past Piper to look over their shoulder, and then he turned to look behind himself as well. "It's... look, I know they don't sound super nice or anything, but I've made some friends there. And it's not as bad as it looks."

Piper took a steadying breath and shook their head. "Beau, do you... would you like to come into my place for a minute? I need to tell you some things and it's not going to be super easy or fun."

Beau slipped the top flyer back into the stack and bit his lip again. "Okay."

"Cool." Piper smiled at him, trying to make it as reassuring and friendly as they could.

The door to the apartment opened and Kier peered out. He'd stolen one of Piper's oversized purple hoodies and he looked particularly gaunt wearing that, but still radiantly pretty at the same time.

Beau's eyes widened. "I didn't know you had a boyfriend."

"I don't," Piper said. "Kier, you remember Beau? Kier is staying with me for a while longer."

They ushered Beau inside just as Kier stepped back and grinned, showing his pointy teeth. "I grew up in a river."

"You what?"

"In a river. I can shape shift, I guess Piper didn't tell you?" Kier's eyes widened and he looked at Piper, apologetic. "I thought your friends all knew about magic?"

"Magic?"

Piper ran a hand over their forehead and sighed, leaning back against the closed front door. "This isn't exactly how I wanted to go about this. But Kier, maybe you sit down and stop talking. Beau, please don't freak out."

"Magic is evil, though." Beau looked between Piper and Kier, a caged rat trying to decide between fight or flight.

"It's not, it's a tool." Piper shook their head and pushed off the door. "Look, of course you can go if you want to. But I'd like to explain things to you from my perspective, and I really hope you'll listen and maybe get to know me and Kier a bit better."

Beau took a long moment to decide. He eyed Kier, who was sitting on the couch now, and grinned again. Not helping his case, Piper thought.

Then Beau turned to Piper. Piper returned his gaze steadily, trying to will him to see that they meant no harm.

"Okay. Twenty minutes, I'll listen," Beau said. "I mean, I'm really curious about this whole shapeshifting thing and if you're delusional or what."

"Let's start with Lucy. You asked before, so I may as well tell you, I recently adopted this rabbit." They held up Lucifer so she could peer into Beau's face. "Her name's Lucifer, but I've been calling her Lucy." They set Lucifer on the floor and patted her, encouraging.

"Aw. Hello Lucy." Beau set his stack of flyers down on Piper's kitchen table and crouched beside them, keeping one eye on Kier as he did so. She sat up on her haunches and sniffed the air in his direction. He held his hand out to her and she came closer.

"I got her because of a case, the same case I'm still working on, actually," Piper said. "Did you see in the papers there was a murder-suicide in town?"

Beau looked at Piper briefly and nodded, then returned his attention to Lucifer. "Yeah, two guys right?"

"Yeah, Lucy belonged to one of them. They were both murdered, that's why I'm on this case." Piper scooped Lucifer into their arms and stood up. "Maybe we should sit down before I tell you more."

"Sure."

Piper sat on the couch beside Kier. Beau took the far end with Lucifer settled in between them, allowing Beau to stroke her back.

"Those two men, they were killed because of what they believed, what they were." Maybe they should have offered Beau a cup of tea but they didn't want to wait to have this conversation.

Beau raised his eyebrows and looked up at Piper. "Yeah?"

"Yeah, by people like your friends that you've printed out flyers for," Piper said. "These people, they really hate Wiccans and pagans, and people who are just a bit different from the norm."

Beau kept his gaze down, focusing on Lucifer and slowly, gently patting her back.

Maybe Piper shouldn't have let him in, maybe he was already in too deep. A deep, anxious voice in Piper's mind worried that he was about to attack, the way the Jones' had. That he was already too far gone in this world of Hunters and magic, and that they'd made a terrible mistake asking him in. At least Kier would have Piper's back if he did choose to lash out.

But Piper's gut didn't agree with the fear, and Ben's words echoed in their head. Your instincts are good, you gotta trust them. Piper didn't believe Beau would hurt them, they believed they could talk him round. It would just take some patience and the right words.

"A lot of people don't like me." Piper let their voice drop a little lower. "Not because I'm a witch or whatever, but because I'm non-binary. They want to put me into this box of woman, maybe because of my hair, or my chest, or maybe into a box of man because of how I dress, or my voice, whatever. My life would be easier if I let them, if I just let myself be squeezed into a box like that, but I don't. It's not who I am. Who I am is not man or woman, but kind of both, and kind of neither."

"That's not fair. Of them, I mean." Beau glanced at Kier, who was pulling his legs up to fold under himself.

"And people judge Kier too, because of what he is, but we can go into that more later."

Lucifer turned, hopped into Beau's lap and flattened herself happily. That was a good sign.

"I get it. It can be really hard to understand," Piper said. "But the people who care about me, they'll try and they'll change their behaviour and accept my pronouns are they/them, and maybe more people will if they see how it can be done."

Beau sighed and leaned back against the couch. One hand continued to stroke Lucifer but the other came up to his face. "I know what you're getting at."

Piper chuckled. "Of course you do, you're clever and you care about other people."

"Not that clever," Beau said. "But yeah, I do care about other people. I know that group, the uh, the anti-magic ones, they're not all on the up and up. But they're friendly and it was nice to have something to go to, someone who'd notice if I didn't turn up, you know?"

Piper sensed he needed some more space to talk, so stayed quiet but gave him a soft smile.

He met their gaze and took a quick breath. "They were really nice at the start, made me feel... part of something. And... now that I'm saying that out loud it kind of does sound like they're a cult and I got targeted. Argh." He curled forward over Lucifer.

"Nothing to be ashamed of. Everyone wants to feel wanted, to feel like a part of something. It's really normal." Piper got up to fill the kettle and set it going, listening as Beau talked.

"But I've felt weird about it lately. When I saw what the flyers were for..." He shook his head. "I was trying to plan how to just recycle them and say that I'd distributed them. I don't want to be part of something dark. I don't know, they have my name and my number and they know where I live. It doesn't feel like the kind of thing you can just stop turning up at without someone coming to check in, and if they check in they might convince me to go back. I don't know..."

"It's okay," Piper said. "Look, you have me now, and I want to help. I want to stop these people from drawing good people like you in to do weird and potentially dangerous stuff. If you can help us out, tell me and my partner what you know, maybe we can really do it." They brought over three cups of soothing spearmint tea and set one in front of Beau and handed the other to Kier. He had yet to be convinced about tea, but Piper was determined to convert him.

Beau looked uneasy. He looked at the rabbit, flat and snoozing in his lap, her ears flat against her neck and smiled softly. "Yeah, okay. That'd be a relief. To help out, and to get out properly."

"Great," Piper said. They reached for their notebook and pen and flipped to a blank page. "Let's start with names and go from there."

CHAPTER 37

Piper made them all dinner and they ate it together while Beau talked. He'd even retrieved his laptop from next door and brought up a private Discord server that the organisation used for new recruits. He showed Piper through the channels he had access to.

It was clear Beau had been in the organisation deeper than he'd initially made out. He'd been able to name most of the people they'd already arrested, but in addition, he had some insight into the 'higher ups' and what their immediate plan was.

Once he'd exhausted his information, he looked at Kier and smiled shyly. "So, you said you can shapeshift?"

Kier, for his part, had listened avidly to all of this. It was new information after all, something he was thirsty for always. "Yeah, you want to see it?"

"Is that a good idea?" Piper asked.

Kier and Lucifer both gave them the same sceptical look. "It's fine," Kier said. "Nothing to be concerned about."

"Okay but just don't get my carpet wet, this place is a rental and I want my bond back when I move out."

Kier stood up from the couch, unfolding himself like a spider, all elbows and limbs. He stepped a few feet from the couch and moved the coffee table out of the way. Lucifer hopped onto Piper's lap and they petted her softly.

Kier shrugged off Piper's purple hoodie and tossed it on the couch. "Ready?"

Beau and Piper nodded.

It happened instantly, no magic sparkles or werewolf-like transformation. One moment Kier stood there, looking like a gangly but handsome late-teens boy, and the next there was a stunningly beautiful horse standing in Piper's apartment. He was sleek, with a deep black coat, his mane long and flowing, although here and there Piper could see long strands of pond weed in amongst the hairs. It was the same with his tail, also threaded with pond weed.

He was such a beautiful specimen that Piper felt the urge to get up and pet his flanks.

Beau breathed out a sigh of wonder. "I've never seen a horse so perfect," he said in a reverent whisper.

Lucifer kicked Piper once and then climbed right onto Beau's lap. The desire to touch Kier in this form faded abruptly and Piper shook their head to clear the last of it. Enchantment, something like Gerard had when he went dark fae.

Beau's hands absently stroked Lucifer's fur and his eyes cleared as well.

Kier stomped his front left hoof once and then shifted back to human form. His clothes had changed with him. He rubbed one of his arms, looking at the floor. "Yeah so, that's what I can do. I have a couple of other forms though, one's only good for in water and the other one...might give you nightmares."

Beau leaned his head back on the cushion of the couch and stared at the ceiling. "Holy fuck."

"It's so impressive," Piper said. "I think you had an effect on us magically, too?"

"Yeah." Kier looked as proud as a cat that's caught a rat. He folded himself down to sit cross-legged on the rug beaming. "It's a predator thing. You're meant to want to come to me, touch me, climb on my back and then I can drag you down into the water."

Piper shivered lightly.

Kier caught himself and looked at Beau. "But I don't do that anymore. I'm reformed. I eat dumplings and burgers now."

Beau lowered his gaze from the ceiling and smiled shyly back at him. "That's really amazing, Kier. My mind is blown. Can we hang out some more?"

"Of course!"

"I don't know what your schedule is like, Beau, but Kier's been chilling at home while I work. I'd be fine with you knocking on the door and hanging with him, but please no outings."

Beau nodded. "I'm a student, I have loads of free time."

"I'm a student too!" Kier shuffled closer to Beau, his eyes sparkling. "I'm studying absolutely everything."

They told each other all about their various classes and interests in an animated way for the next half hour. Bemused, Piper watched, relieved not to be the one who answered all of Kier's questions for once.

Finally, Beau had yawned too many times. Piper had thanked him, they swapped numbers and they encouraged him to drop around again any time. For now he'd gone back to his apartment. Piper called Jack, heart racing, bouncing on the balls of their feet as Kier cleared up the dishes from dinner and tea.

"Piper? What's up?" Jack said.

"Big news," Piper said. "My neighbour, he'd gone into the thing. He was carrying these flyers and we got to talking."

"Oh shit, are you okay?" Jack's voice was tense. Piper imagined her signalling to Amy and Emmaline that they had to get out and rescue Piper.

Piper shook their head. "Yeah, I'm fine. I talked to him. He said he was already feeling weird about it but they were so nice, and he felt like they were keeping tabs on him. He was totally happy to cooperate, and he's given me a whole lot of information. He and Kier have bonded as well, they're going to hang out."

"No way," Jack breathed. "Information like what?"

"The biggest thing is a plan to demonstrate at Victoria Park," Piper said. "On Saturday. They reckon they'll get there at midday."

"That's not much time," Jack said. There was a pause. "And it's not illegal to gather, I mean, they can demonstrate if they want to."

"Right," Piper said. "But they're trying to keep it secret so that there's no police control... But their plans mean traffic will be affected so they'll get attention, and I dunno, I have a bad feeling about it."

"Yeah." Piper heard footsteps, imagined Jack padding over to Amy. There was a beep and then some background noise. "Piper, I've put you on speakerphone."

"Thanks," Piper said. There was a bit of a clatter and Piper guessed Jack had set the phone on the table.

Jack spoke again. "Amy, the Hunters and the people they're recruiting are gathering in a public park, Saturday morning. You know what that might be about?"

"Huh." Amy said. "Nope. It was always deadly secrecy when I was involved. I can't imagine what they're planning unless it's recruitment."

"Or some kind of mass ritual," Emmaline mused. "If they were... I mean, I know they pretend they hate magic, but they obviously already use magic."

"Well, yeah," Amy said. "The ritual where we get properly imbued with strength and stuff, it's all kinds of weird blood magic. I can't remember most of it but, yeah. The message is all magic is bad unless it's the magic we do."

Jack grunted her annoyance at that idea. "Hypocrites."

"What kind of thing could they be doing with a mass ritual?" Piper asked.

Emmaline hummed. "I mean, there's a lot you could try. If it were me, and I was an evil magic hating cult... I guess I'd try something to sound extra charismatic and convincing, to get people listening and then to sign up. And then I'd want to scare them with something, so they'd think they needed me in particular to help them. Like, make the people think there was nothing else to do but turn to me."

"Damn, Em, you'd make a pretty good cult leader," Amy sounded impressed. Jack laughed.

"Let's hope she never wants to start something," Piper said. "So, okay, that sounds... Horribly possible. And if you get a whole big group of people afraid and convinced you have the answers..." They trailed off, not liking any of the conclusions they'd thought up.

"It could get dangerous really fast," Jack finished.

"Okay, well, we know the date and the time. We can get a police escort as if it was a regular protest and try and contain it."

"Maybe we need more than just the police," Amy said. "I'd feel a lot more confident about this if there were more mages on our side."

"We can't ask people to put themselves in danger," Piper said. "We can't just suggest they turn up and face a whole hoard of people who hate them and want them dead."

"A lot would do it," Emmaline said, quickly. "Especially if there's some kind of plan."

"So, we have tomorrow to come up with the plan and recruit whoever we can," Jack said. "I'd love to get it sorted tonight but I am utterly wrecked, and I need sleep soon."

"I might call up Gerard and Raphael and see if they have any good ideas," Amy said. "If they can come through it might help."

"And I can prepare some protections, and bind some helpful spirits," Emmaline said.

"That's great work you've done, Piper," Jack said.

Her words took Piper by surprise, but it was a good sort of surprise. "That was an abrupt change of subject, but thanks." Piper grinned at their reflection. Since Jack had mentioned being tired Piper had become aware of their own weariness. "I think I have Lucifer to thank, at least in part. She was really friendly with Beau and she absolutely loves Kier."

"That's *intéressante*," Emmaline said. "You two are really getting on well, aren't you?"

"Yeah, really well," Piper said. "I actually wanted to talk to you about -" They yawned suddenly.

"Tomorrow," Emmaline said. "We'll talk all about it."

"Okay, cool," Piper said. "Night everyone!"

CHAPTER 38

They didn't have a lot of time to plan, but Emmaline was confident that it would all come together. In the morning she made a large pot of porridge. Amy had already got up and gone for a run. Her endless Hunter energy wouldn't let her rest for too long. She hoped the pot was enough for her. It probably wasn't, so she cut up pieces of banana and pear to add as toppings.

Amy bounced in, flushed with exercise and bright eyed, a startling contrast to Jack when she shuffled out of bed, hair dishevelled and yawning.

"Sleep okay?" Emmaline asked. The urge to give Jack a warm morning kiss on the cheek stirred inside her but she ignored it. Not yet. Just be patient.

Jack shook her head and pulled down a mug for her morning coffee. "Uh-uh, I was making lists of what we could be doing today and tomorrow, for Saturday. Only dropped off around three."

Emmaline grimaced and started serving the porridge into bowls. "Well, we have two days, we can make it all work, somehow." Emmaline handed a standard size bowl to Jack and started filling a larger one for Amy.

Jack's phone buzzed and she checked it blearily. "Piper's on their way here. Probably best we plan here rather than at the station, they said."

"So, we calling all the area witches up or what?" Amy took the bowl from Emmaline and started covering her breakfast with brown sugar and slices of banana.

"I guess so," Emmaline said. "Valerie has ways of getting in touch with the ones she knows, then we can call up Richie and stuff... he must know a few more as well."

Amy sat at the table with her almost overflowing bowl of porridge and started digging into it. "How many do you reckon that will be? Taking into account that not everyone will show?"

"Not more than a couple of dozen," Emmaline said. "The community here is so spread out."

"We don't need an army," Jack said.

Amy curled her lip. "They are trying to form an army, so kinda, yeah we do. It takes an army to fight an army after all."

Jack shook her head, carried her breakfast to the table and sat. "We need to protect the innocent, that's the main concern," Jack said. "And that's why I'm not sure if we should even call Richie, what if he insists on taking Kier back to the reserve, or brings some of the other creatures? It wouldn't be safe for them."

Emmaline added a few slices of nectarine to her bowl and joined Jack. "They have just as much right to fight as anyone."

"Sure, but we don't even know if it will be a fight, which makes it hard to plan. I made lists and lists and then I looked at the names and felt like shit. This shouldn't be something we need to bring in anyone for, but by the same token I can't just send in a thousand constables and hope nothing bad happens. If the hunters see all those cops they might just ditch and try again another time..."

The doorbell rang. "Piper," Emmaline said. "I'll go let them in."

The mood at the table had got murky, and Emmaline very much hoped that Piper's natural optimism would lighten things up. She opened the door to see Piper in a black hoodie, Lucifer the rabbit settled in their hood, peeking over their shoulder.

"Oh my stars." Emmaline reached out without hesitation. "Good morning, Lucy, can I have a cuddle?"

"For sure, just once we're inside if that's okay?" Piper said.

"Of course." Emmaline led them upstairs.

Piper kept talking. "I'm feeling more and more uncertain about leaving her behind. I mean, people have tried to get at her before, so I want to protect her, but it's more than that." Piper paused to put the way they felt into words. "I feel like she understands me, and that I'm better with her next to me."

"She's a familiar," Emmaline said. "They're often much more than they look. Are you hungry? I've made porridge, unless Amy's already finished it..."

"I already ate, but thanks."

As Emmaline and Piper walked into the apartment, Amy was scraping the bottom of her bowl with her spoon. "Is there more?"

"In the pan," Emmaline said. Amy got up immediately.

"Morning Piper," Jack said. She raised her mug of coffee in salute. "Kettle's boiled if you want a drink."

"Coffee," Piper blurted. "Sorry." Their cheeks flaming, they carefully lifted Lucifer out of their hood and handed her to Emmaline. "Kier and Beau are hanging out today and I'm like, unreasonably nervous. They were getting on so well last night I have no reason to be worried, but... I am."

"Understandable. But if Beau tries anything Kier can definitely defend himself," Amy said.

Piper considered this. "Maybe that's what I'm afraid of? But I found a cheap prepay phone for Kier, so he can get in touch if he needs to."

"They'll be all right." Emmaline rubbed Piper's arm in an effort to comfort them. Maybe a change of subject was the ticket. "As for us, we're struggling with who to include, or...ask to be involved." She sat back down at the table, setting the rabbit on her lap. She felt warm against her legs, even through her jeans, and she smiled, stroking its back and feeling the gentle sympathetic magic emanating off her.

"Oh, everyone." Piper poured a coffee from the plunger and sat next to Jack. "We invite absolutely everyone, and if they don't want to show up they won't. People are perfectly capable of making their own decisions."

Jack frowned and nodded slowly. "Good point." She pulled out her phone and pushed it towards Piper. "Those are the lists I made."

"Instead of sleeping," Emmaline said, unable to stop herself.

Amy leaned over Piper's shoulder to look at what she'd written. "Looks good to me."

"Wait, so the plan is to invite these people to have like a counter-protest?" Piper asked.

"To observe," Jack said. "And to contain any magic that the hunters try to do. The danger, as I see it, is to the general public. If they're made vulnerable in some way, or brainwashed to attack mages, then we want to be able to fight back with something other than our fists."

"What about dark mages, like Deacon?" Emmaline asked. "If someone like that turns up, they might try and use the situation to their own purposes."

"We don't want that." Jack tapped her fingers on the table. "So not absolutely everyone. Maybe we ask Valerie to invite people she trusts?"

Piper nodded. "And have the Faerie people we know on standby, unless they want to come through."

Amy stood up. "I'll go call the others now, see if they're around. Em, okay if I use the long mirror in the spare... in your room?"

"Yeah, of course." Emmaline gave her a bright smile. "Need any help with the incantation or anything?"

Amy shook her head. "Nah, Raph made it easy for me." She grinned and carried her refilled breakfast bowl into Emmaline's room.

Piper and Jack were huddled over the phone, both of them looked very serious.

"I'll call the station," Piper said. "I'll start the process for police escort for a protest, and you can call Richie."

"Great, and I'll call Valerie," Emmaline said. She brought a finger to her chin and tapped it twice. "And see if I can't tug on some strings..."

"Strings?" Piper asked.

"Old favours, I don't know if everyone will be able to get here, or help, but it's worth a try."

"That's the motto for this whole case, I think," Jack said.

Piper's phone buzzed with a message from Kier.

Kier: we're okay

Kier: but also something happened you probably want to know about

Piper, heart in their throat, hit the 'call' button and was relieved when Kier picked it up right away. "What happened? Are you okay?"

"Yeah, we're fine. We took care of it."

Piper's heart stopped briefly and they hit the button to put the call on speaker phone. "Please explain."

"Beau and I went out for lunch," Kier said. "And I know you said not to, but it was just to that same dumpling place, and I didn't think you'd mind that if it was somewhere I'd been before."

A piercing pain flared up behind Piper's left eye. "Go on."

"Well, we were walking there, and Beau saw these guys he knew. I dunno how but they instantly knew something was up with me. And he was just saying hi, but one of them kinda forced us into this space between two building and tried to attack me."

"Oh fucking hell," Piper breathed out.

"Yeah and Beau's arm and ribs are hurt, and they took a chunk of my hair out but I managed to fight them off."

"You said you were okay but Beau's ribs are hurt?"

"And..." Kier paused. "I mean they slashed me up a bit too but I can heal pretty quick."

"Oh my god."

"I can heal them both," Emmaline said. "Where are you now, Kier?"

"Back at Piper's apartment," Kier said.

True to her word, Emmaline healed Beau's wounds and helped Kier with the worst of the cuts.

Piper though, was beside themself. Amy rubbed their back with slightly too firm a hand. "I can't believe something like this would happen in broad daylight," they said. "The audacity of it."

"I guess it was just an opportunity thing," Beau said, glumly. "They happened upon us and took their chance. I didn't expect that at all. I thought those guys were my friends, but they just...turned on me the second they saw I wasn't going to betray Kier."

Emmaline rubbed Beau's back sympathetically. "We're your friends now."

Jack paced up and down the floor, barely containing her rage. "This is just... and we can't even report this in, because they'd want medical statements about the wounds, and we can't take Kier into the Accident and Emergency room. Besides it's better that it's all healed now. Magic is so much better than boring old life."

Piper bit their lip and hurried to make tea, hoping it would soothe everyone, themself included.

"This just emphasises the importance of what we're doing tomorrow," Amy said. "If they're feeling bold enough to just attack, they need to be knocked down a peg."

"I feel like I'm choking in this stupid system full of red tape." Jack stopped and looked at both Kier and Beau. "Sorry, this really isn't about me. I'm sorry this happened, but we'll need descriptions of the men."

CHAPTER 39

Anticipation was killing Jack. It was late on Friday night, and she had nothing to do except for go to bed. They had arranged to meet a number of people in the morning, on the waterfront, nice and close to Victoria Park so that they could head over together in a cohesive unit. Richie, and Colin were driving down for the event, and said they'd bring a couple of others who worked at the reserve.

No one had mentioned whether Kier should come or not, and Jack hadn't been able to suggest it. The guilt she'd feel if he got hurt *again*, or if he lost control and hurt someone was more than she could bear even to think about.

Emmaline had a good response from the local magic users. Amy had disappeared for an hour or so, and returned through the mirror with promises from Gerard and Raphael to join them on Saturday.

With all of those allies, and the police force confirmed to provide protest escort, Jack knew they were probably as well prepared as it was possible to be.

Especially since for all they knew, it was just going to be a protest. They didn't have strong evidence to indicate a fight or anything dark at all would happen, aside from the nature of the people who had organised it.

But Jack's gut said it was more monumental than a protest. And Piper had repeated a few times the day before the importance of trusting one's gut.

Trusting her gut. It was something that Jack felt she was good at in general, but in this case, in this situation it wasn't just her gut. She was trusting others, and leading those who trusted her into an unknown situation. Her gut didn't like that at all.

She tossed and turned, her mind awhirl with various possible scenarios, unable to switch her mind off or trust that things would be all right. A part of her was tempted to leave her bed and see if Emmaline was still awake, but once again she quieted it. Best one of them slept, if possible.

Jack woke early, pleased she'd managed to sleep even a little. She felt grimy, her jaw aching where she'd been clenching it all night, imagining terrible outcomes to the confrontation in the park.

She had a quick breakfast with Amy and Emmaline. Piper came around a bit after eight, Lucifer the rabbit was riding in her domed backpack, looking nervous. Piper set the bag down and transferred Lucifer into their arms. They didn't appear to have brought Kier, and Jack was somewhat relieved.

They gathered in Emmaline's room, where she'd pulled the large mirror out into the clear space at the end of the bed. Plenty of room for people to step through comfortably.

Amy shifted her weight from foot to foot, utterly unable to keep still. "They should be coming through, now. Where are they?" Her hands formed fists and then relaxed over and over.

"They'll be through soon." Emmaline squeeze Amy's shoulder. "Try not to worry."

"I'm not worried."

"You've really missed Raphael, huh?" Piper smiled, watching Amy who was still bouncing.

"Ugh, you have no idea." Amy shook her head, then fussed with the two tendrils of hair that hung down either side of her face, left out from her ponytail. "It's like an ache. I can't stop thinking about him, and just, missing his arms around me and his lips, and... well." She spared a glance to Emmaline. "Other stuff."

Jack got it, although she hadn't exactly expected to. She'd been in love before, felt that first flash of lust where you couldn't stop thinking about the other person.

She wasn't being fair on Amy. This wasn't the first blush of love and longing. Raphael and Amy had been together more than a few months. With the way time passed in Faerie maybe it was years. Jack wasn't entirely sure of when they'd actually met in the first place...Maybe it was some kind of fated thing?

She looked at Emmaline. Recently she'd felt the ache of missing Emmaline when she was over in Faerie. Emmaline seemed to sense her gaze on her, because she half turned, gave Jack a shy little smile and reached for her hand.

For a second, Jack didn't think she'd let her take it. It wasn't the time. They were about to go into something unpredictable and probably dangerous. Jack's nerves were on edge, she'd barely slept, and her stomach was in knots.

But... Emmaline's hand was warm and soft in hers. It sent a wash of calm through her and Emmaline's hand squeezed hers, promising... promising what? Stability? An anchor in a world that Jack could barely rationalise?

Maybe this was exactly the right time to hold hands, after all. Jack thought again of her gut. She wanted to trust Emmaline and herself. Maybe she should just stop flinching back because of what her mind was saying?

She took a deep breath and squeezed Emmaline's hand back.

"There!" Piper exclaimed.

Jack nearly dropped Emmaline's hand again, startled, but Emmaline held on tight.

The surface of the mirror was rippling, and their reflections vanished. The others were coming through.

In a moment, Raphael stepped through into the spare room. With the same blond hair as his sister and even brighter blue eyes, defined cheekbones and a kind expression, Jack could see objectively he was a handsome man, even if he wasn't the sibling she preferred. Amy was on him in a second, her hands in his hair and her mouth on his before he could even say hello.

He chuckled into the kiss and lifted her up by the waist, holding her close as he moved further into the room, clearly mindful of who was behind him.

After a moment, Gerard stepped through in his human form, eyes brown and bespectacled, dressed in a plain black T-shirt and jeans. Emmaline dropped Jack's hand and went to give him a rather more platonic hug than Raphael had received from Amy.

He returned it and then turned to Jack. "Hello. It's good to see you again, Jack."

"You too." Jack was highly aware of how the last time she'd seen him in person he'd been fae and in leather straps mostly. But she still felt a warm kinship to him. He understood her. She opened her arms, and he closed the distance for a slightly stiff hug.

"I really don't know what we'll be facing, so we really appreciate you coming over to help," Jack said, letting him go.

"It's no problem, really," he said. "I just hope that there's something I can do to help."

Jack eyed him, reminded again of how different he looked now compared to his incubus form. The skin on the back of her neck warmed, remembering. He was a little like Jekyll and Hyde, with two vastly different sides of his personality. She imagined it must be the same for all humans who were part fae, or who had crossed over and eaten fae food—struggling to balance the two sides of themselves.

"Okay, calm down now, Ames," Raphael said, his voice slightly muffled. "We're not alone and—"

Jack glanced over to see Amy kissing him again. She'd pushed him across the room, shoved him against the wall and half climbed him.

Piper cleared their throat.

Amy got the message then, letting go of Raphael and stepping back. "Sorry, sorry everyone," she said. Her eyes were shiny. "Just, uh, Hunter metabolism and it uh, affects libido. I smelled him and it kinda got... I'm all right now."

Raphael took her hand and shrugged. "We'll be alone later, once everything is sorted, love."

Amy grinned and seemed to come back to herself more fully. "Anyone else coming through?"

Gerard shook his head. "Just us, although Alina said I could get in touch if things went really bad."

Lucifer squirmed in Piper's arms, leaning and reaching toward Gerard. He stepped closer and scratched between her ears. "Hello little one."

"She must really like you," Piper said.

"Sometimes familiars are like that," Gerard said.

"Right." Jack checked her phone for the time and saw it was nearly time to rendezvous with the others. "Guess we'd better head into town."

CHAPTER 40

Valerie and the others were gathered at a waterfront café in the Viaduct, drinking coffee and looking out at the boats on the water. It was a beautifully sunny morning, and the walkways which wound between apartment buildings were busy with joggers and cyclists and people walking their dogs. The café had opened up their glass panel doors and put tables and chairs out in the sunshine. The chairs were full of people, some of whom Jack recognised.

Jack made a beeline for Valerie. She waved. "Hello there, Detective."

"Morning, Valerie," Jack said.

Valerie grinned up at her from behind oversized round sunglasses. Her long curly auburn hair was pulled back under a floral headscarf, and she was wearing a loose T-shirt that said 'Hexes, 2 gold pieces.'

"Thanks so much for coming. Love your shirt."

"Of course," she said. "I wasn't able to get quite the turnout I was hoping for, but we have about a dozen."

Jack looked around, saw Richie sitting with two others in khaki walk shorts and sensible shoes. She waved and Richie nodded at her, raising a cup of coffee in salute.

"We didn't really want a huge crowd. It might agitate the hunters. We really just wanted back up." Jack gestured behind herself. "Do you know Raphael and Gerard? I have no idea how anyone's connected."

"I've heard of Raphael of course," Valerie said. She looked up at him with a more sober expression and nodded, showing respect.

Raphael, for his part, looked a little embarrassed. "Nice to meet you, Valerie, Emmaline's told me all about your shop."

Piper nudged Jack's elbow. Lucifer was back in her backpack, but she was moving around a lot more than normal, probably because of all the magic-wielders in the vicinity. "We should probably start walking to the park."

"You're right. We'll lead the way. Val are you ready?"

"Born ready, sweetheart," Valerie said, her voice steely. "Let's do this."

It felt like leading a very cheerful parade, Jack thought. The assembled mages, magic users and witches—Jack didn't really know the distinction between who called themselves what and why—were all in a bright mood it seemed. Perhaps happy to have an excuse to catch up with each other and do something social. It did seem from Emmaline's example that magic made for a solitary life.

They walked up the long stretch of Fanshawe Street and waited at the busy lights to cross the road. Hope welled in Jack's chest. Was it because although there were only a dozen of them, the magic users were making enough noise for fifty—or because there would finally be some action?

Or maybe it was the effect of the assembled mages, their energy somehow encouraging Jack, or making her feel she had a community behind her.

Whatever it was, Jack was pleased about it. She smiled at Piper, who beamed back.

"This feels good, right?" Piper said. "The energy of this group is really uplifting."

Almost exactly what Jack had been thinking. She nodded. "Yeah, I can feel it. Think that's magic?"

Piper shrugged happily. "Could just be the people have good intentions."

The lights changed and they crossed the road, entering Victoria Park from the Northeast corner. Two constables stood there, and Jack said hello to them.

Enid and Teulia, the two who had found the bodies that began this entire case. Jack thought it was fitting there were here now, as Jack tried to close it down.

"Morning, detectives," Enid said. "And...friends?"

"Oh yes," Piper said. "Good friends and good people."

"Looks rather like a counter protest." Enid eyed them both with suspicion.

Jack felt her throat tighten. There was a chance this could go very badly, especially for Jack and Piper's careers. "Not a counter protest. Just some concerned citizens. We're off duty, right now," Jack added, pointing between Piper and herself. "Just to clarify."

Enid nodded and waved them off.

Victoria Park was busy. It was used for cricket in summer and soccer in winter, but it was also a place for dogs to run around in, for people to do laps of, either jogging or walking, and the gyms in the area held boot camp style sessions there as well. All times of day it was a busy place. Several arterial roads circled it, including the ones linking the main city to the harbour bridge.

A gym was holding a session close to where they entered the park. A trainer stood with a portable stereo, playing something upbeat and shouting encouragement as ten or so people in workout gear jogged with heavy looking weights held in their hands.

But beyond the gym group, Jack saw a mob of people with signs.

"Looks like we're right on time," Piper said.

They used the paved path around the outside of the park to approach the group protesting, although it wasn't clear if they had started protesting or not. The group looked to be about thirty people strong, from Jack's estimation, although more people were arriving all the time.

They were a disorganised knot but as they got closer, one person got up onto some kind of box or platform and started talking through a megaphone. "Are you here with me?"

The crowd responded half-heartedly.

"Oh look, there's Beau!" Piper said. "I wasn't sure if he'd turn up." They pointed to the crowd, but Jack couldn't see him. "In the green plaid shirt." Piper lowered their hand again.

Jack followed the direction of their pointing figure and saw Beau not in the main group but a bit to the side, looking relaxed and at ease as he chatted to another person a bit removed from the group. "Is that safe for him, given what happened yesterday?"

"Probably not very," Piper said. "Maybe he's spun a story, or maybe...maybe we should just keep an eye on him?"

"Signs up!" Valerie shouted behind them, making Piper and Jack both startle.

Jack looked behind. She hadn't noticed anyone carrying placards, but they certainly had them now. Their signs read things like 'Peace, hope and acceptance', 'Love is love' and 'Just let me read tea leaves in peace.'

Jack's heart thudded and she felt control of the situation slipping away irreversibly. "I didn't say to bring signs."

Valerie deliberately didn't meet her eye. She must have planned to do a counter protest, ignoring what Jack had said.

The sinking feeling in Jack's stomach started to feel less 'dinghy taking on water in a lake' and more 'Titanic hit an iceberg'.

The constables had set up a perimeter around the park, standing at the entrances and looking vigilant. Being present but not invasive.

The man with the microphone had organised the anti-magic protesters into a loose ring, and they started to march slowly in a circle with him in the centre. Their signs had slogans like 'They're everywhere!', 'Question everything, do your research!' and 'Real truth now: expose the witches!'

Jack's jaw tensed and the last shred of the hope she'd felt earlier evaporated.

The group was almost entirely white and almost all male, which wasn't surprising but was chilling all the same. These were the kinds of people society listened to. They weren't chanting, but the man with the microphone was speaking loudly into it.

"The truth! That the government doesn't want you to know, that the police don't want you to find out, is that all around us there are people who want to hurt you! They want to control your minds and break reality! Doesn't that scare you?"

Valerie strode ahead, leading the other local magic users to stand facing the man with the megaphone. "You can't tell us how to live!" she shouted.

The men protesting shot glares and rude words at the magic users, but it looked like it would just be trading shouts for the moment.

Jack frantically tried to think of some way to regain control. She had to, before something exploded.

CHAPTER 41

Piper wasn't sure at all what to do now they were at the park, and there was a group of protesters and a group of magic users all yelling. Lucifer was moving so much in the backpack the straps were digging into Piper's shoulders. They were very concerned about Beau standing over by the protesters. At any moment they might decide he had been consorting with the enemy and attack him.

Or maybe it was all a complicated double bluff, and Beau had been hanging out with Kier to learn more so he could give information to the anti-magic crowd?

The man yelling into the megaphone was making it hard to think. They wished he'd shut up.

They couldn't just stride over there and confiscate the man's megaphone, could they? The right to protest was protected by law. But if he was spouting hate speech, it wasn't covered. Had he crossed the line into hate speech or not? He hadn't incited anyone to violence just yet, had he?

They chewed their lip, then directed their attention to Lucifer. The rabbit had somehow got out of the backpack and was climbing over their shoulder. They brought their hands up to catch her, and she settled in their arms, her nose up in the air, quivering.

"Who's this?" Raphael's voice was very close. Piper turned to see him peering over their shoulder.

Jack moved away, talking to Amy seriously as they approached the group of magic users.

Piper looked at Lucifer and then half turned to face Raphael. "Lucy, or uh, Lucifer. She was the familiar of the mage who died, the first two we found at the start of this case. I've taken her in."

"May I?" Raphael reached his hand out, but didn't touch the rabbit until Piper nodded, although Lucy was stretching up towards his fingers eagerly, clearly enraptured.

He gently rubbed the rabbit between her ears, and she closed her eyes in pleasure.

"You said was. She's still a familiar," Raphael said. "I can feel the magic sparking off her and into..." He looked up.

Piper's breath caught as they met his eyes. He was *so damn* handsome. "Into?"

"Into you." Piper's heart sped up but because of his words not his proximity. His voice was low, cutting under the racket of the protesters, and his words caried frightening weight. "She's your familiar now. You've awakened."

"Awakened to what?" Piper knew though, on some level. They knew but couldn't get their head around it. Needed to hear it spoken out loud. Their heart was pounding now, and they swallowed, trying to get rid of the sudden lump in their throat. They needed to hear it, but they were frightened of it as well.

Before Raphael could elaborate, there was a scream.

They both whipped around, Piper folding the rabbit protectively against their chest, to see the two groups were facing off. The loose circle of the anti-magic users had formed into a clump and were shouting at the magic users.

The scream had come from a young-looking woman, who was pointing at Valerie. "She touched me! She put something on my skin, she tried to read my mind! I felt it! I felt her trying to get inside my mind!"

This had to have got the attention of more of the park users. Piper looked around to see that yes, joggers had slowed to a stop, and a picnicking family was watching intently, tension written all over them. All over the park, people were watching, and some of them drawing closer.

Valerie scoffed. "That's ridiculous, she brushed against me on purpose! I didn't do anything."

Amy moved to the front, standing beside Valerie, looking like the bodyguard from Hell, angry and practically vibrating with physical strength.

"These people have come to shut us down!" The man with the megaphone said. His words echoed off the buildings that ringed the park and bounced back. "They don't want you to know the truth like we do! But we believe that EVERYONE should know what's really going on in this very city!"

Another person in the crowd pointed Piper's way. "There's that demon rabbit!"

"Demon rabbit..." Piper breathed. "Fuck."

Valerie and Amy leaned their heads together, spoke quickly and when Valerie spoke again her voice was as loud as the man with the megaphone had been.

"This man, and this whole organisation is preaching hate and fear! Don't listen to his poison!"

Beside Piper, Raphael inhaled sharply. "Not sure using magic so obviously will help our case, here."

"Do you hear that?! She speaks so loudly with no microphone, no amplifier! She's unnatural! A witch!"

Raphael mumbled something Piper didn't catch. They turned to him, and he was lighting a cigarette.

"What are you doing? What is it?" Piper asked.

"Just noticed, just caught whiff, the megaphone has a charm on it," Raphael said, through teeth clenched around the cigarette. He lit it and took a deep inhale. "It's convincing people who'd usually ignore it. I'm gonna try and diffuse it."

"Ugh, okay." Piper tried to draw all their courage up before they spoke. They were quivering with fear but Lucifer pressed against their chest, lending them confidence enough to speak. "Can I help?"

Raphael shook his head and raised his hands. Piper felt the wind whipping their hair back. It hadn't been windy before, had it?

Emmaline seemed to notice this, because she looked at Raphael, narrowed her eyes and then leaned in to whisper to Jack. Piper looked to Gerard, but he was watching it all unfold with an inscrutable expression. Piper didn't even know what magic he could do, aside from sex magic which didn't seem like it would be helpful then. They didn't know what magic they had inside them either. Hopefully Raphael would be able to help with that...

Emmaline raised her hand and brought it down forcefully and a spirit emerged from the ground under her hand. In the sunlight it was hard to see, but it was still there. A tall, eerie, humanoid looking shimmer of white light, stalking towards the anti-magic protesters.

"Emmaline, wait," Jack said. Her mouth kept moving but Piper couldn't hear anything now but the wind.

"See! That one has summoned a demon!" Megaphone man said. There were gasps from all around the park, and the anti-magic protesters started to scream, it sounded like they were more play-acting than not, but Piper could see Beau and he looked terrified. His eyes wide as he looked left and right, trying to find somewhere to flee too. "And over there, that person is holding a demon! That rabbit is unnatural, black like the souls of all witches!" To Piper's true horror, Megaphone man pointed right at them and Lucifer.

Desperate, Piper looked to Raphael. He was still murmuring, something in another language.

In their arms, Lucifer burrowed closer, pressed her face to Piper's neck and trembled, sensing Piper's fear.

"I don't know what to do," Piper breathed. They wondered why they'd said it out loud. Had they been hoping for an answer from the universe? From Lucifer? They breathed out slowly, feeling it shake in their chest.

Gerard stepped forward, pulling a mirror out of his pocket. He was going to summon some more people; he was going to bring fae through. That would only escalate things in the wrong direction.

As they watched, a delicately limbed woman with long dark hair and a similar look to Gerard stepped out of the pocket mirror, large pink wings folding out of her back.

Piper startled as someone tapped them on their shoulder. They spun to see Kier, grinning and breathless. "Sorry I'm late, Beau tried to leave me behind."

"Oh God, did you run the whole way here?" Piper had to raise their voice to be heard over the wind.

"Yeah. Why does Beau look so freaked? I'm gonna go get him." Kier took off at heightened speed, making a beeline for Beau, and panicking the anti-magic protesters who took his sprinting as a threat, some kind of battle charge.

The anti-magic users were screaming. "What is that wind?! Brace yourselves, they're attacking! Watch for that boy!" They surged towards the magic users and Kier, the signs they held wielded like weapons now.

This was about to get very ugly. The mages weren't backing down from the advance, in fact many of them were raising their hands as if to summon spells and curses.

Piper whirled around, trying to take in the whole scene. More and more innocent bystanders were coming closer, filming with their cell phones. The police escort was closing in, forming a safety ring around the two groups and in the centre, the man with the megaphone, who had pushed his way to the front and was nose to nose with Valerie. He screamed into the megaphone.

"Look at the freaks! They're causing this unholy wind! They're making the world more dangerous for all of us! What will they do next? Strike us down with lightning?!"

One of the witches let out a shriek and sent a blast of green sparkles towards the man with the megaphone.

That was the spark the protestors had needed to fan the flame.

Violence erupted.

CHAPTER 42

Jack's worst possible scenarios all seemed to be happening. The mages and the mage hunters were clashing physically now. Amy pushed forward and started punching the anti-magic mob, spurring off a fist fight. The strange, sudden wind made everything harder to hear. Jack's hair whipped in her face. She'd tied it back that morning but somehow it had come loose.

This is exactly what we didn't want, Jack thought. But it's why we brought the magic users after all, to protect the innocent.

Were the innocent being protected? She'd lost sight of Beau and thought she'd seen Kier tear past, but they were lost in the crowd now.

Raising her voice as loud as she could, she shouted over the sound of the wind. "Mages! Protect the bystanders! Protect yourselves but try and keep the peace if you can!"

Jack turned to see the police pressing closer to the two warring groups. "Stay back!" she shouted at the nearest constable. "This isn't what it looks like!"

Valerie tore the megaphone off the man who had been screaming into it and tossed it aside. The wind died down abruptly. Jack made a dash to grab it for herself. She was blindsided by a punch to the temple and staggered, rounding on the person who had punched her.

He was a blond young man, couldn't be older than twenty-one, with a pale blue button-down shirt tucked into tan chinos. He looked like he should be studying for an MBA, not punching people in the park.

Jack backhanded him and glared. "Stand the fuck down, you idiot. This isn't helping anything!"

He looked stunned, perhaps the anger she felt had poured some authority into her tone, and he stepped back.

Her head spun from the impact of his punch, but she pushed through it, focusing on the megaphone. She picked it up and backed away from the throng of people fighting.

One of the witches had brought up some kind of purple sparkling shield, which was holding some of the mage hunters back on the Western side of the fray.

Emmaline's spirit thing was moving through the shield, not attacking but looming over the protesters. They all seemed to be keeping half an eye on it. As Jack watched, it lunged forward and snatched a placard out of one of the protester's hands.

It was, probably, meant to be keeping the peace, removing a weapon from the hand of one who was about to use it as a cudgel, but the spectre was too frightening to be seen as anything but a threat. Its hand stretched out into thin tendrils of shiny light. The man whose sign it was went utterly pale, and his eyes flickered open and shut. Jack recognised that he was about to pass out. The spirit, sign in hand, turned its weirdly hollow eyes to the next person, who fell to his knees and started to pray, hands clutched together in front of him so hard his knuckles went white.

Raphael waded into the fray behind Amy, possibly to pull her back. He appeared to be shooting lightning from his hands like a Sith Lord, hitting people and stunning them briefly, so it wasn't a very comforting sight.

Several of the witches and magic users were chanting in unison. Jack had no idea of what they were trying to achieve, but from an outside perspective it was easy to look at them and see the evil coven from a horror movie.

She had the megaphone in her hands. She had to do something. Jack brought it to her mouth and pressed the button. "Everyone stop fighting!"

Her words echoed and there was a hush in the noise. Not a total cessation of sound, but a pause, as if most of the people assembled had stopped to listen.

Jack swallowed, unsure what to do next. "Please just, take a step back and a deep breath. The police are here, and they're going to..." Jack trailed off, mortified to realise she had no idea who the police should be arresting. Sure, the anti-magic protesters had been preaching hate, but the magic users had been punching and getting in there as well. It wasn't cut and dry, not by a long shot, and she didn't want them to just arrest everyone. There was no way that would go well.

Jack's mind went blank. But she had the people's attention and she had to keep going. Piper's idea had been about community, hadn't it?

"Maybe we should all just try and get along?" She had no faith in what she was saying, and it came out in her delivery. The rising intonation at the end, making it a question, the weak phrasing, as if she were a character on a children's cartoon, trying to deliver a moral.

A few of the anti-magic protesters laughed outright. The mages started up their chanting again. The purple-pink shield seemed to grow larger, stretch further across the field, separating the two groups. That didn't seem right.

Jack looked around, at a loss again.

Piper appeared beside her, Lucifer the rabbit tucked down the front of their shirt, her fuzzy little face peeking out and blinking at Jack.

"How about I have a go with it?" Piper said, smiling. "I'm a little better with the getting on with people, after all."

The relief Jack felt at handing over the megaphone was so great her knees threatened to buckle.

CHAPTER 43

Piper had never felt more confident in their life. They had a familiar in their shirt, warming them and magical power flowing into them. Well, theoretically, they had no idea what it would feel like if they did, but Raphael had seemed sure about it.

Jack had just given them the megaphone, which had the charm of persuasion or something on it. Jack hadn't said much of substance, but she had startled the crowd into something like quiet and drawn their attention, so there had to be useful magic on the thing.

Piper's heart thumped, but with certainty now. They knew what had to be said, something that would draw the crowd together in a way neither side had expected.

The words of Dr Martin Luther King Jr reverberated in their head *Hate cannot drive out hate, only love can do that.* They had to address the crowd with pure love.

But first, they had to address the bystanders. The random passers-by who were no doubt confused and alarmed.

"Good morning everyone," Piper said. Because even in a magical battle in the middle of an inner-city park, one should always be polite. They enunciated each word clearly. "I'm sure this is all very strange and confusing. But I am here to help. My name is Piper Gage, and I recently found out a weird truth about the world. That magic is real."

They paused. There were, predictably, some heckles from the crowd.

"You're on drugs!"

"Tell the truth!"

"Is this for a TV show or something?"

Piper smiled. As if there were any special effects in the world that could make Emmaline's spectre look as real as it did before them.

"What you are seeing before you is real. The people who first assembled here this morning are trying to tell you that magic is something to be afraid of. And it is, honestly." Piper shook their head and kept going. They had to be truly honest about their experience to get through to people. "I've had anxiety attacks over it. It's terrifying to realise that what you thought you knew about the world isn't right. But the thing is, we're finding things out that change how we think all the time. Every time we hear about a new scientific breakthrough, or someone breaks a world record, or a new thing is discovered in space, our idea of what the world could be expands."

Piper paused, looking around to see how their words were going down. They had people's attention, in fact there were dozens of phones pointed at them, recording what they were saying. There were still scuffles, knots of people fighting.

As they looked, Piper saw that a group of the anti-magic mob had surrounded Kier, and he was trying to protect Beau.

Piper swallowed, but Lucifer moved against their chest and Piper's heart swelled with love and confidence again.

"You lot over there, with the young guys you're trying to attack, let them go. Kier is much more dangerous than he looks, and Beau is just trying to get away. Come on."

One or two of the other anti-magic people tugged on the shoulders of the attackers.

"Come on, he's just a kid," one of them said, his voice carrying over the quietened crowd.

The scuffle stopped, and slowly, slowly, the men parted to let Kier and Beau move out, they came towards Piper. Beau looking utterly terrified, Kier looking like he was just waiting for his moment to start eating people.

That was good, a good sign of progress. Maybe it was just the magic in the megaphone but it was working.

Jack was beside them. She gave them an encouraging nod, putting her hand on Piper's shoulder. It felt like she was lending strength as well.

Not just strength, something else as well.

Love. There was so much love between Piper and Jack and their allies.

They could harness those feelings.

They could do this.

"The thing you really need to understand," Piper continued. "Is that we're all just people. People want to belong, and they want to be loved and respected. The people who can use magic are just people and the people who are afraid, the ones who are so afraid that it's turned to anger and hate, they're just people too. If we can do a little work to understand each other, then there's no reason to fight."

"Here, here!" Piper recognised Emmaline's voice. They smiled, not seeing her, but looking out over all the people who were watching.

"Please, I'm asking you all, but especially the people who were just wandering past, who were just using the park today for recreation, to look at the people around you and offer a smile. It's the first step to getting to know someone." No one seemed to move, so Piper dug deeper. "Did you know that the first step in trusting someone is finding common ground?"

The love Piper had felt before swelled in their chest. They had to keep going, to make this as convincing as they could, by speaking directly from their heart.

"If you can find common ground, even something as simple as liking the same movie, or having visited the same country, you have built the start of a trust relationship. My partner, here, Jack." Piper lifted Jack's hand in their own, as if she'd won a running race. Jack put up with it. "Jack didn't want a partner, especially someone who didn't have the experience she did. But we bonded over our curiosity. We wanted to solve mysteries and get to the truth of things. Together we have built something real and solid, even if it was based on her having no choice but to take me as partner."

Piper swallowed, their mouth was getting dry. But they needed to keep going. They could see Beau and Kier getting closer.

"These two men you see here," Piper dropped Jack's hand and gestured to Beau and to Kier. "They should be enemies according to some of you, but they're both just looking for companionship, for a friend. What do they have in common? They're looking for connection, and in the end, isn't that true of all of us?"

Piper felt they were rambling, they had to call for action, before they lost everyone's attention again, although it didn't feel like they were in danger of that immediately, it couldn't be far off.

"Kier, Beau, is it true? Are you friends, even though Kier is magical and Beau's so-called friends tried to hurt the both of you?"

Kier nodded and held his hand out to Beau.

Beau took it without hesitation.

Piper felt tears wetting their cheeks. Could this actually work? Beau was an easy example because he had already more or less given up on the anti-magic way of thinking, but maybe it would inspire others. "Please, everyone, turn to the person beside you, or opposite you, please drop the weapons and the shields, and look at the people around you. You're all beautiful, you're all strange in your own way, and we are, all of us, just looking for connection. Reach out to each other now."

In front of them, Beau started teaching Kier a complicated fist-bump and high-five routine.

Piper lowered the megaphone and wiped their eyes with the back of their hand. They hoped their words had been enough, because they didn't know what else to say.

"That was incredible," Jack said. "Do you think it'll work?"

"I hope so," Piper said. "The megaphone has a charm that should have helped it all along, anyway."

Beau and Kier were laughing together as they perfected the routine.

"I can't believe Piper just outed me as lonely," Beau said, but he was smiling.

"Oh, I'm definitely lonely," Kier said. "I'm not even technically meant to be out of the reserve, but here I am. Piper took me in."

Some of the random people who had stopped to watch were turning to each other, some were approaching the gathered magic users. After a moment, Emmaline's summoned spirit vanished, and the magical shield dissipated as well.

"That's a really strong bit of magic you just did." Raphael jogged up to Piper. He eyed the megaphone. "It was already pretty potent when that guy was using it but your magic really enhanced it, Piper."

Piper felt the charm tingle, flowing down the handle of the megaphone and into their fingers. Their own energy flowing back down their arm and into the handle. They nodded. "Yeah, I think I can sense that. I didn't notice when I was talking but I can feel it now. Honestly, I don't really like having that power."

"As long as you keep on using it for good," Raphael said. They both looked out over the assembled people.

The magic users mingled with the general public, and slowly, they reached out to the protesters as well.

It wasn't a perfect moment of unity, but Piper hadn't expected that. Instead, it was an awkward overture. But in their heart, that felt exactly right.

Piper didn't hesitate, they walked past the magic users and went to say hi to one of the anti-magic protesters. "I'm Piper," they said. "Would you like to meet my rabbit, Lucifer?"

CHAPTER 44

J ack signalled for a group of constables to accompany her as she followed Piper towards the anti-magic protestors. The man who had brought the megaphone, and three people who held themselves with the same military bearing Amy had weren't calming down, and were trying to incite the others to more violence.

There was a flash of movement and Amy was there, fighting one of them in complex hand to hand, trading punches and kicks at lightning-fast speed.

One of what must be true hunters engaged and was restrained by a few officers, and the other made a break for it, only to be frozen by a magic spell from Gerard.

"This isn't over." Megaphone man spat on the ground at Jack's feet. "These freaks may have won people over for the moment, but I will not be stopped!" He pulled his arm back as if he were about to punch her. Jack brought an arm up to defend herself if needed.

Someone in jogging gear stood beside Jack. "What the hell is your problem, dude? We've got a really good vibe here, and that guy's making little floaty lights with his magic. It's cool as fuck. No one's hurting anyone."

Megaphone man let out a cry of anger and lunged at Jack, his fist swinging through the air. The constable intercepted him, and he was led away under arrest.

Jack turned to the jogger. "Thanks for that, I'm Jack."

"Yeah, Piper's partner, right? I'm Kelly." They shook hands.

Jack turned back to look at the assembled people. Within minutes the battle, such as it was, had become something more like a community picnic.

The anti-magic protesters weren't one big group anymore. Instead, they were people, sitting here and there on the grass, talking to new friends. The magic users, and those who had happened upon them, were similarly scattered, lots of little groups of disparate people, but all in the same space together.

Even some of the constables had joined in, although most had gone on to other duties after Piper's speech had chilled everyone out.

The vibe continued. Jack relaxed, getting to know some people.

At some point someone went to the supermarket over the road and brought back large packets of chips, snacks and big bottles of soda and juice. Recycled paper cups were being passed around and filled with drink. People were laughing and sharing the chips.

Jack stopped in by Gerard, who was in a sort of half-fae form with his horns poking out from his hair, but otherwise looked normal.

"Jack, this is my sister, Alina." He pointed to a long-haired girl with large pink wings sticking out the back of her white T-shirt. She was making wildflowers of all colours grow out of the park's turf while kids watched and giggled with her.

She looked over her shoulder. "Hello Jack, Emmaline's told me all about you." Her eyes were larger than a normal human's, and faintly lilac. Her voice was soft, shy and musical.

"Oh God," Jack said.

"No, she told me all good things. She's really into you," Alina said.

Jack's cheeks flushed. "Uh, well, nice to meet you," Jack said. "I'd better...go now."

Alina laughed, a soft tinkling giggle that sounded like particularly pleasant wind-chimes.

Turning away, Jack sought out Piper, who was sitting with Raphael, Kier and Beau, Lucifer the rabbit hopping on the grass between them.

"Say that again?" Piper asked.

"Empathy," Raphael said. "I think your powers are all in your emotions."

"Oh?" Piper sat back on their hands and looked up at the sky. "This is wild."

"Powers?" Jack asked. She sat down next to Beau and plucked a dandelion to offer to the rabbit. "What are you talking about?"

"Piper's magic has woken up,\ because of proximity to a practised familiar." Raphael smiled at the rabbit as she ate the dandelion. "If you hadn't been able to project your love and hope the way you did, I'm not sure your speech would have had quite such an effect as it did."

"Ah, that's..." Jack shook her head. "Incredible. Piper has magical love powers, that makes so much sense."

"Does it though?" Piper asked, still facing the sky. "It feels to me like I'm about to fall off the world."

"Then look back at us," Jack said. "Take your own advice and connect with the people around you. You have magic? Cool. Emmaline can teach you, so can Valerie and Richie and Raphael and Gerard and all the others. And in the meantime, you have me, too."

"And me!" Kier added. He patted Jack's knee.

Piper dropped their chin and met Jack's eyes. "Okay, I really do have love magic, because there's no way the old Jack would have said something so soppy to me."

Jack laughed and handed the remaining stalk of the flower to Lucifer. "Maybe, or maybe I'm just feeling like it's time for some changes."

She looked around, and spotted Emmaline, over the other side of the picnickers, talking seriously with a little girl.

"I think we're all here for the changes," Beau said. He stood up and looked around. "I want to talk to some more people. Come on Kier,."

Kier stood up too and dusted off his pants.

"Stay close," Piper said.

"Don't let him offer pony rides," Jack called after Beau. "We're not that far from the ocean."

CHAPTER 45

O n Sunday, Jack slept and rested, watching cartoons on the TV with Amy and Emmaline. Emmaline cooked a huge lasagne which they shared, and Jack went to bed early.

On Monday morning, she walked straight into Apanui's office.

"The reports I have from Victoria Park are strange to say the least," Apanui said, apparently not at all surprised that Jack had come in. "Most of this can't be filed. And I don't know what to do about what any of it." She sighed and looked at Jack, one eyebrow raised.

"Is there... will you press charges on me or Piper? We more or less ignored your orders and brought an opposing faction to the protest. I didn't act much like a police officer that day. I'm aware."

Apanui fixed her stare on Jack, but it didn't have the usual intimidating effect. Jack felt too free, too loose in her heart, and sure of herself. Depending of course, on the answer to this question.

"No. There's nothing to press charges over. A cursory search of the places several of your arrests were staying has revealed massed weaponry and print outs with the names and addresses of people we assume they were targeting." Apanui sat back in her chair and steepled her fingers. "One of them has no records, no apparent entry record to New Zealand or ID, and his fingertips are smooth. I have no idea what to do with him except put him to trial, which... Well, we're calling him John Doe for paperwork reasons. Heaven knows he's not telling us anything."

Jack felt her chest loosen further and a smile tug at her lips. "He was the real Mage Hunter then. Or one of them. He came here from another country to start shit."

"It appears so. As for all this magic..." Apanui picked up a piece of paper, crumpled it into a ball and tossed it into the bin. "None of it happened. People can film what they like and put it online, they can believe whatever they want, but I can't have my paperwork made up of fairy tales. You know that."

"I do." Jack took a deep breath and straightened her back. "That's why I'm resigning, Sargent. For better or worse, my life is entangled with those fairy tales now. And I don't see any way I can keep doing cases like this within the framework of the police, not without having to falsify my paperwork, try and talk around the truth or find things to convict people for when there's no evidence. We can incarcerate a hunter, but for how long? He almost certainly has enhanced strength, how long before he decides to bust out of prison? Mages are even more slippery, and then there's creatures and..." She caught herself babbling. Jack handed over the piece of paper she'd written her resignation on. "My path is different, is what I'm saying."

Apanui eyed the paper then took it, sighing heavily. "I'm sad to lose you. You're a great cop, and we need more of those. But I understand."

"Thank you, Sargent. You've been an incredible boss."

Apanui gave her a brief smile and then started pulling forms out of her desk drawer.

"Since everything we do here is confidential," Apanui said. "You'll need to wrap everything up and be escorted out of the station. These forms are for return of police equipment, including the car you've been using, and these forms are to keep what you know secret."

Well, no standing on nostalgia or slow goodbyes around here. Jack took the forms and gave Apanui a slight bow. "It's been an honour, thank you Sargent."

Once the forms had been signed and everything returned including car keys, Jack was escorted out of the station and then taken for a celebratory farewell coffee by those in the station she considered friends. Enid, Suzan and a few of the others. Piper hadn't come in; they'd texted Jack to say they were taking the week off. But Jack knew she'd still see Piper frequently, so she wasn't too worried by their absence.

"You'll have to stay in touch," Suzan said.

"Who's going to take the weird cases now?" Teuila pouted, pouring more sugar into her cappuccino.

"I'm thinking I'm still going to take cases," Jack said. "But as a Private investigator. Maybe if there's something really weird, you could farm it out to me?"

"Maybe..." Suzan frowned, thinking it over. "I'll have to talk to Sarge about it, or maybe...just never talk to her about it. But yeah. I can't really see any of the others picking it up happily."

"No," Jack agreed. "You're right about that."

Enid bought Jack a slice of chocolate cake, and they sat and chatted for a half hour. Finally, someone's radio went, and they had to get back to the station. Jack said her goodbyes and walked out of the cafe.

No car to get home with, but there was a bus that went by which would get her close enough. She stuck her hands in her pockets and walked to the bus stop, whistling a tune she thought she'd heard Emmaline humming.

CHAPTER 46

Piper woke to the smell of fresh baking, grinned and rolled around in bed with sheer delight. Having Ben in the house was the best thing ever.

Beau had volunteered to have Kier stay while Ben was in town, and Kier was happy to do so, although Piper understood he'd been chatting to Richie about going back to the reserve to help out on a part-time basis.

Lucifer grumbled from the nest she'd made in Piper's bedclothes.

Piper got up, careful to not disturb the pile which held Lucifer, pulled on some worn in jeans and a baggy T-shirt and went out into the main part of the apartment to see their brother stirring a pot on the stovetop.

Even though Ben wasn't working, he had an early morning habit, and apparently that extended to making bread and scones and small cakes as well.

"What are you doing?" Piper hurried over to peer into the pot. It was full of something delicious smelling and red.

"Making jam to go with the scones," Ben said. "You didn't have any in the house."

"But I had masses of berries and sugar?" Piper hip checked him.

He laughed. "Well, no, I had to go out and buy a lot of supplies, actually. Your pantry is kinda bare. I had to get flour, berries, sugar, baking soda, yeast..."

"Yeah well, work's been a lot." Piper put the kettle on. "But if you went out for supplies and bought all this stuff, why didn't you just buy jam?"

"Where's the fun in that?" He flashed her a toothy smile and peered into the pot, stirring a little quicker.

"You need help, it's supposed to be your day off."

"Sure, but we need to go and look at lots of places today, and I am not going to let you be hangry about it."

It was Monday morning. Piper had taken the week off work to relax and recuperate, and see their brother. Jack had texted to let them know they'd officially left the police force. Piper needed to make a decision, although they were already pretty sure they knew which way they'd fall. They didn't have to decide immediately.

Right now it was time to stuff their face, feed the rabbit and then go and look at flats and shops for lease. They checked on Lucifer, who nuzzled them good morning, and allowed Piper to carry her out into the main room so she could look significantly at her food bowl. Piper filled it with seeds and fresh fruit.

Piper set the table and made tea , choosing the 'world's okayest grandad' mug for Ben and the Care Bears one for themselves. Ben laid the table with all the delicious food he'd made. Scones, little yellow cakes, cheese muffins and chocolate chip cookies.

"Well, no danger of me getting hangry." Piper helped themselves to one of everything and then a second cake as well.

"That was kinda the idea, I mean you're putting me up for nothing so, think of it as rent."

"You're my family, doofus, you don't pay rent." Piper bit into a scone with fresh jam on it and groaned. It was light and flaky, and the jam was the perfect level of sweet without being overpowering. Ben really did have a gift for making delicious food. They knew his bakery would make a lot of money up here, once word got out.

"You have the whole week off?" Ben asked. Piper nodded and kept chewing. "That's good, you look tired."

"The weekend was pretty full on," Piper said. "And then I had to rent a car and come out to get you at the airport. I hate doing that drive." They pulled a face.

"Well, I appreciate it."

Piper kept eating, slowly becoming aware that Ben was watching them, a calculating look in his eyes. "Okay, why are you staring at me like that?"

"There's something different about you," Ben said. "I mean, I knew you'd look different, because I think you're actually happy up here, but there's something else."

"I haven't had my hair cut in ages." Piper dropped their eyes to their plate and cut the cake into small pieces.

"No, I don't mean like, how you look you look different... fundamentally. Something's changed."

Piper's heart skipped. He couldn't know, could he? He couldn't know that they'd had a magical awakening, there was no way. Unless he had magic himself. Would he tell them if he did?

Piper hadn't told him, so there was no reason to believe he'd tell them if he'd discovered magic. They wanted to be open with Ben, but it was all so new and so strange. His visit had meant they hadn't had time to catch up with Emmaline or anyone about what having magical emotions would mean going forward. There were so many unknowns. They'd tell him when they knew more, probably later when he'd actually moved up.

Besides, they were well aware they'd made a lot of less than great decisions lately, and they needed to think things through before they blabbed.

Lucifer hopped over to tap Piper's foot and they flushed as they picked her up and put her on their lap. It was like she knew that Piper was holding back from Ben.

"I've made new friends, maybe?" Piper said. It wasn't untrue exactly. "Real good people who accept me for who I am. It's a relief, you know?"

Ben grinned and reached to pat Piper's arm. "I'm glad to hear it. Yeah, you look more yourself."

"And..." Piper took a breath. "I think I'm quitting the police force. Like, I haven't for sure decided to, but Jack has and she's going to start a private practise thing. I'd like to keep working with her."

"Bit risky," Ben said. "No regular salary."

"No, I know." Piper sighed and picked up another scone, smearing it with butter and then jam. "But I have this really good feeling about it. I think she's got enough contacts that there'll be work, and besides, I have some cash saved up. I'm just... not deciding immediately. I'm going to think it through slowly."

"Good call." Ben finished up his tea and grinned. "I'm proud of you, you know that?"

Piper grinned, hearing that from Ben always set warmth through their chest. "Yeah, I know. Now finish your breakfast so we can start hitting these home and office viewings, okay?"

"Yeah, yeah," Ben said.

Piper felt hope for the future. Not just the idea of quitting and following Jack, but the idea that Ben would be close by, and they'd have family as well as friends to lean on when they needed it.

Jack needed that too, Piper thought. They hoped she and Emmaline were getting some things sorted out.

As they headed out, they dropped the leftovers from breakfast next door for Kier and Beau, who Ben had met the night before and liked immediately. Piper reflected that Ben had their same gift for getting to know people quickly. Did Ben perhaps have a little magic of his own?

CHAPTER 47

The bus ride gave Jack time to think. Mostly she thought about how good and liberated she felt. Her head was free of paperwork and no one breathed down her neck to wrap things up. Soon, she'd have to do sensible things like buy a second-hand car and find an office to work out of and see about advertising, but for today, she was free to do what she liked.

She relished it.

Piper had said they understood about Jack quitting, and that they'd think about their future. Jack hoped that they'd decide to follow her, and to be a partner in the new firm, but she didn't want to push anything. She wanted Piper to do whatever they wanted, whether it was beside Jack or not. They'd still be friends; Jack knew that for sure.

She got off the bus on Manukau Road and walked the short distance down to her house. She let herself in. "I'm home!"

Emmaline's voice came from the far side of the lounge, as Jack climbed the stairs. "Welcome back! How did quitting go?"

Jack walked into the lounge and found Emmaline stretched out on the couch in a sunbeam under the window, which sat open. The orange cat was asleep on his side on the windowsill, enjoying the sunbeam as much as Emmaline seemed to be.

It was a lovely thing to come home to. Jack shrugged off her jacket and slung it over the back of a dining chair before sitting at the end of the couch, next to Emmaline's feet.

"Quitting went wonderfully. Sargent Apanui basically said they couldn't write up any of the magic, and they didn't know how to process the Hunter they arrested. She understood why I'm leaving. It was kind of cool." Jack stretched her arms over her head and let one rest on the back of the couch. The cat lifted his head and bunted his forehead against her wrist.

"Good work," Emmaline said. She closed the book she'd been reading and set it aside. "So, what now?"

"I need a car, a PI licence, an office, and like a bunch of stuff," Jack said. "But for right now I'm just going to relax."

"*Magnifique*," Emmaline said.

Jack let herself stare at Emmaline. The soft shape of her lips, the brightness of her eyes and those long eyelashes. The gentle peach blush of her cheeks, and her blonde hair, pulled back in a messy bun.

"What?" Emmaline grinned self-consciously.

"I guess we do need to talk about something else as well," Jack said. "When you were gone, over in Faerie, I really, really missed you."

Emmaline's cheeks warmed and her eyes crinkled as she smiled still wider. "Aw, Jack, I missed you too."

"Like, the house was really empty and cold without you here," Jack said. "And I missed your laugh, and how you balance me and Piper, kinda. It was nice having Amy here, but it wasn't the same."

"And why do you think that might be?" Emmaline rubbed her toe against Jack's thigh, gentle and encouraging.

Jack felt nervous, far more nervous than she had that morning, talking to Apanui. Her stomach knotted suddenly, and she took a deep breath, trying to get the right words out.

"I really like you, Emmaline." She dropped her hand down, letting it rest on Emmaline's shin. She dropped her eyes to gaze at her hand, and Emmaline's legs as she said the next bit. "And I want you to stay here with me. I was so worried for you, thinking what might have happened if those hunters had caught you. I hate the thought of you in danger."

"That's sweet of you. I feel the same way, honestly."

Jack's breath caught and she swallowed hard. "I know."

"We did kiss, you know," Emmaline said. Jack saw a sly smile and a sparkle in the young mage's eyes. "I haven't forgotten."

"No, I haven't either," Jack said. "I know I've been a pain, wanting things to go slowly. But I really liked that kiss, and I've been thinking about it. Wanting to do it again..." She sighed.

"I sense a but, again." Emmaline frowned.

Jack shook her head. "No, not a but. I want us to try dating. I just want you to know that with all this change, with Piper learning magic and me quitting the job I've had for years and starting something new... I might not be very good."

"Be... good?" Emmaline tilted her head to the side. "Explain."

"I might forget to spend time with you, or I might be callous, or forget our anniversaries or... I don't even know." Jack huffed out a laugh at herself. "I'm pre-warning you that I'm possibly going to be crap at dating you. But I still want to if you're okay with my possible crapness."

"I'm okay with it." Emmaline said it so fast Jack worried that she hadn't properly heard her.

"No but like, when I get a case, I get obsessive, I forget to sleep. I know I get into a weird place, and then people, relationships, they fall away."

"Doesn't matter." Emmaline tilted her head to the side, cute as a button. "Well, it does matter, but we'll be here, living together. I can make sure you eat and that you get some sleep and I'll remind you if I need attention. It doesn't have to all be on you. Besides, I might be spending a whole lot of time doing magic lessons with Piper, so I won't necessarily have all the time in the world for you either."

Those words were a relief, more than Jack had expected them to be. Emmaline was sensible and practical, and that was what Jack needed in a partner. She needed someone to pull her back to Earth when she was spiralling. But more than that, she needed someone to take care of her, that she could take care of in response.

"So, what are we saying?" she asked, feeling shy all over again.

"I think we're saying and correct me if I've got the wrong end of the stick." Emmaline sat back, watching Jack. "I think we're agreeing to try and date."

"Good," Jack said. She suppressed a giggle. "Should we shake on that agreement?"

"I have a better idea," Emmaline said. She beckoned to Jack with one hand. "Come here and kiss me, detective."

That was a command Jack wanted to follow very much. She shifted onto her knees, leaned one hand on the back of the couch and climbed up to kiss Emmaline. But she paused before their lips touched.

"I'm not a detective anymore, technically."

"Yes, you are," Emmaline said. "It's your magic gift, it's written in your veins. Even if you were working at sea drilling for oil, you'd be a detective."

Jack giggled then, couldn't help it, and kissed Emmaline on the mouth. Soft and warm, it felt like home, and better—it felt like a promise for a bright and amazing future. She hoped it was a promise they could make come true, together.

Emmaline pulled back. "You have to name this cat, though."

"Right," Jack said. "Cat..." She turned her head to look the cat in the eyes and try and divine a name for it. Nothing happened. She remembered the name Emmaline had suggested. "Bartholomew." She nodded. "Bart for short."

Emmaline pulled her in for another kiss. "I love it."

CHAPTER 48

J ack was baking in the afternoon sun as it beat through the windscreen.

Piper and Emmaline were talking magic in the back seat. It was something Jack wasn't used to yet, just as she wasn't used to the way her new car handled (second hand, hybrid, terrible mileage). But this drive out to the reserve was a good way to get used to things.

It was Thursday. Piper had resigned from the police after they'd dropped their brother off at the airport the day before.

Jack had spent Wednesday touring offices with a real estate agent, then Piper had called to say Ben had secured a place on Karangahape Road, which had office space upstairs they could rent off him. A bakery downstairs, a Private Eye upstairs... It was like fate had brought them all together at just the right time. Plus, they'd be close to Valerie's shop.

Jack needed to do some paperwork, set herself up as a PI and Piper too, but today they'd decided to road trip. Jack tuned out the back seat discussion, listened to music and let all her worries melt away.

They were welcomed to the reserve, with no trace of a charm turning Jack away and barely any wait at the barrier arm.

"Richie must have changed the locks," Jack said as they trundled down the dirt path to the hut.

"He should, after all you two have done for the community," Emmaline said.

Richie was waiting out the front, waving as they pulled up. "Welcome, welcome," he said. "It's actually working out even better than we hoped."

"Yeah?" Piper bounced out of the car. "Show us!"

"This way," Richie said.

Emmaline caught Jack around the waist for a hug as soon as she was out of the car. Jack laughed out loud. She still wasn't used to the joy of casual touching from her...well, they hadn't defined the relationship specifically, but there was no better word. Emmaline was her girlfriend.

"Can you feel it, Piper?" Emmaline asked, turning away. "The magic in the air? It's humming. It feels incredible."

"Doesn't it?" Richie grinned over his shoulder. "Come on, up here."

Jack watched as Piper concentrated and shrugged. "I don't know. Maybe? Is it sort of like a tingle?"

"Something like that." Emmaline grinned and followed Richie, with Piper next and Jack bringing up the rear.

Richie led them to the edge of the lake, where Kier and Beau were standing, talking to three more people. Jack recognised them from the gathering at Victoria Park. Two who looked like students who'd been on the anti-magic side of the protest, and one who Jack thought might have been one of the random passers-by.

Kier was standing thigh deep in the lake, holding some sort of pond weed and talking about its properties.

The three gathered on the shore were making notes in notebooks and nodding along. Beau seemed to be in the role of assistant teacher, as he fielded questions and asked Kier to expand on one point or another.

Kier noticed Jack and broke off, shoving the pond weed into Beau's hand as he waded to shore. "Hi Piper, hi Jack, hi Em!"

Piper didn't hesitate, they gave him a warm hug. Jack was still wary, but when he turned to her she couldn't say no. They had a quick hug, and then he was off to hug Emmaline too.

"You're a teacher, now?" Jack asked.

"Oh yeah," Kier said. "I teach them what I know about the plants and stuff underwater, the uh, magical stuff about them, and then they tell me about what humans are like. It's awesome."

"He's certainly got his own style of teaching," Richie said, his voice dry.

"Sounds like a great system," Emmaline said.

Piper looked at the 'students' and smiled. "Looks very productive."

"We'll let you get back to it, Kier," Richie said.

"See you Wednesday!" Kier bounded back into the water, splashing his students, who groaned.

"Not again!"

"Be more careful!"

Richie led them away and up the path into the bush. "Some of it is sessions like that," he said. "But some of it is one on one, like buddying. Especially with the ones who were pretty deep into the conspiracy. We figured it was safer that way for everyone."

He gestured into the clearing where the strange fairy birds had their tree. Colin was there, with a muscular man in workout gear. "All right Colin?"

Colin looked over and gave them the thumbs up. The two men looked to be planting something in the ground around the tree.

"Wildflowers?" Emmaline asked. "We should get Alina down here, she'd have a ball."

"Native plants and species only," Richie said. "But yes, we did extend the invite to her and Gerard. I think they're planning on coming by next week."

"Have you had a lot of take up from the ones in the conspiracy?" Jack asked.

"About seventy percent have said they're keen," Richie said. "Which is huge, really. I hope it makes a difference."

"It is making a difference," Piper said. They all turned to look at them and their cheeks pinked. "I could feel it, just now with Colin and that man, and back at the lake. Everyone's feeling warm, happy and friendly. People are learning."

Jack smiled, wide, pride swelling in her chest even though she couldn't take any credit for what Piper could do. "That's incredible."

"And we get more done around the reserve." Richie started walking again and they fell into line behind him. "It's a real win-win. The fences are getting full repairs, and some of the hunters, or, the ones who'd fallen in with them, they've been working on upgrading our tech as well."

"Good," Jack said. She'd worried about a lot of potentially terrible outcomes for the case, but she let herself be reassured now.

The evidence was all there. People volunteering, learning about each other, and forming friendships. Working together to maintain an important magical nature reserve. Her own decision to strike out on her own, but Piper choosing to follow and partner with her, and of course, Emmaline by her side in life and love.

There was no denying it. The future looked bright.

-End

ABOUT THE AUTHOR

Jamie is a non-binary kiwi who's always been wondering 'what if'? A number one best-seller on Amazon, they write optimistic urban fantasy and romance highlighting queer characters. Jamie grew up in Wellington but now lives in Auckland with his wonderful spouse and two formally-stray cats.

ALSO BY